Alison Davies

The Stories Behind Astrology

DISCOVER THE MYTHOLOGY OF THE ZODIAC & STARS

ILLUSTRATIONS BY
JENNIFER PARKS

FOREWORD BY
THE WITCH OF THE FOREST

Leaping Hare Press

CONTENTS

4 Foreword
6 Introduction

12 PART I: THE ASTROLOGICAL SIGNS

16 ARIES
The Golden Ram

22 TAURUS
The Princess and the Bull

28 GEMINI
The Dioscuri

34 CANCER
Gate of Men

40 LEO
The King of the World

46 VIRGO
The Goddess of the Grain

52 LIBRA
Lady of Good Counsel

58 SCORPIO
The Hunter and the Hunted

64 SAGITTARIUS
The Starry Steed

70 CAPRICORN
Father of Souls

76 AQUARIUS
The Cup Bearer

82 PISCES
A Fish Tale

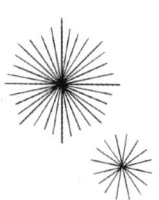

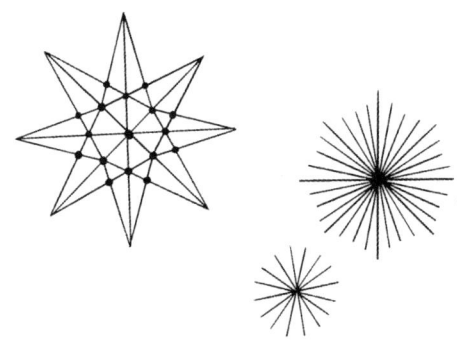

88 PART II: THE PLANETS

92 MERCURY
Gods, Humans, and Tricksters

98 VENUS
The Morning Star

104 MARS
War and Peace

110 JUPITER
The Twelve Shields

116 SATURN
The Golden One

122 URANUS
The Rainmaker

128 NEPTUNE
Behold the Sea

134 PLUTO
The Wealthy One

140 THE SUN
The Unconquered

146 THE MOON
The Light Within

154 A Final Word
156 Affirmations
159 Your Big Three
160 Creating Your Own Ritual
164 Glossary of Gods and Goddesses
168 Index
174 Acknowledgments
175 About the Author and Illustrator

FOREWORD

By Lindsay Squire, The Witch of the Forest

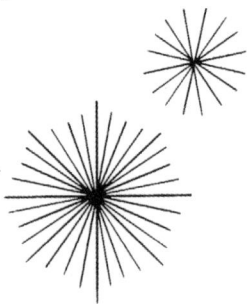

Astrology has been used for thousands of years in both political and cultural circles. Ancient Roman, Greek, and Egyptian civilizations tracked the movement of celestial bodies in the sky to avoid undesirable events and predict the individual destinies of kings, commoners, and all in between. Astrology is still important today. We read our Sun signs and our Star signs to look for guidance in our lives, to help us solve problems, and for self-care advice. We also study our birth charts to understand ourselves better, to find out what makes us tick, and to look more closely at why we do the things we do.

Astrology is like its own language and can often be indecipherable to those who have only just begun to read about it. I know when I first started learning about astrology, reading about terms like conjunction, ascendant, and aspects, I was utterly confused. The great thing about this book is it makes astrology accessible to everyone. By immersing yourself in the Greek and Roman legends found in the following pages, you'll gain a deeper understanding and knowledge of astrology. Alison beautifully tells the folkloric stories connected with the twelve signs of the Zodiac, so you can learn more about the origins of each sign and the traits associated with them, as well as the tales of the planets and their governing forces. Words are truly Alison's magick as she weaves the fundamental meaning of the planets and signs with each story she tells, and uses these meanings to help you harness the powers of the stars and these celestial bodies to bring meaningful change in your own life.

As part of each section, Alison includes a ritual and affirmation to help you to connect with the energies of the twelve signs and ten planets. A ritual is where a series of activities or actions is performed in the same way and in the same order each time. There is a magic to the actions of a ritual, and the rituals found in the following pages enable you to fully immerse yourself with the specific energies and powers of each Zodiac sign or planet. My favorite ritual is the one for Taurus, which is my Sun sign. I completely embody most of the characteristics of this sign—I am stubborn, down-to-earth, and loyal, but there is one characteristic I don't feel aligned with—patience. Taureans are said to have endless patience, but I have very little at all!

Since this book contains rituals for all the signs and planets, I thought I would include an astrological ritual I use a lot in my own witchcraft practice, with the hope you find it as helpful as I have always done. Using the energies of the Zodiac sign Leo, this ritual will help you manifest more confidence in your life.

You will need: an orange candle, three pieces of citrine, a knife, paper, a pen, a lighter, and a cauldron or heatproof dish.

- Use a knife to carve the Leo symbol on an orange candle.
- Light the candle.
- Take three pieces of citrine (for confidence) and place them near the candle.
- On one side of a piece of paper, write the words, "I am confident. I have confidence in myself," and the Leo symbol on the other.
- Read the phrase aloud nine times before using the flame of the candle to burn the paper in your cauldron or heatproof dish.
- Sit comfortably and focus on the flame of the candle until it burns out. Imagine yourself to be a highly confident person and how your life will change because you have this confidence. Feel the warmth of the flame and imagine that warmth being the confidence you seek coming into your life.
- When the flame burns out, repeat the words you wrote on the paper another three times, followed by the words, "So mote it be."
- After the ritual, carry the citrine with you to help you continually attract the confidence you seek into your life. When you need a boost, repeat the words you wrote on the paper.

For those new to astrology and those who have practiced astrology for years, I can't recommend *The Stories Behind Astrology* enough. Sit back and get ready to immerse yourself in the world of Greek and Roman astrological folklore, and bring empowerment to your own life through the magickal rituals associated with them.

INTRODUCTION

BEGINNINGS

Astrology, which is described as the study of celestial objects such as the planets and the constellations, has been a source of fascination for centuries. Wise men and women throughout the globe consulted the stars and looked to the heavens for signs and omens. They read the skies, just as we might read the news on our phones. They charted the path of each planet and the changes each one went through, to make sense of events and to predict the future. To them, it seemed that the sky was a reflection of the Earth, being directly above us, and yet it was also more exciting as it was the realm of the gods. It was easy for them to let their imaginations run riot and create wondrous tales filled with over-the-top characters, to explain such phenomena as a beautiful sunrise, or the shifting shape of the Moon. With little else to go on, the sky was their "go to" place for information and insights, and in contrast with today's Internet, it was unlikely to freeze or offer fake news. What you saw when you gazed at the stars was what you got: a vast expanse filled with potential. As humans we love to fill in the spaces, to connect the dots and create narratives, which in turn build a common landscape we can all understand. And so the stars and the various constellations started to take shape and we identified with each one.

The Ancients were a superstitious bunch. They were so used to taking their lead from the landscape and reading deeper layers of meaning into natural occurrences, that they began to attribute significance to the Star signs they had created. They acknowledged the power of the planets, and the importance of their position at birth, and soon everyone was using astrology as a way of divining their destiny.

MODERN ASTROLOGY

Fast forward to today. In a world so technologically driven, we are continually urged to follow the science, to be logical, to check and assess the facts and read the small print, and yet we are still searching for other ways to make sense of our lives. Spiritually we have evolved, and we want to believe in something more. Like those learned folks of old, we are beginning to see the benefit of connecting with our environment, of getting up close and personal with nature, and looking beyond the superficial. There are things we don't fully understand, but we are driven by intuition as much as logic and for that reason astrology has become a major influence and a way for us to tap in to our innate primal power and follow in the footsteps of our ancestors. We read our Star signs now for guidance, for tips on self-care, for problem solving, and to understand what makes us tick. We have come a long way since the very first horoscope column in Britain appeared in the *Sunday Express* in 1930, and our interest in all things astral continues to grow.

HOW THIS BOOK CAN HELP YOU

This book allows you to explore the world of the Star signs, and the planets that rule them, from a different perspective. By immersing yourself in their myths and legends, you will get a deeper understanding of the strengths and traits that define each sign, and the governing influences of each planet. You will also understand where each sign came from, and how the stars that form the solar system were shaped and named. While the stories therein are representations of the folklore associated with these celestial objects, they are not classical retellings. Based on myth and magic, and sprinkled with a little creativity, they have been crafted to give you an insight into astral wisdom, and how you can tap in to the energy of the Zodiac to discover your own latent talents and gifts. By reading each tale and using the associated ritual, you will be able to harness the magic of each sign and planet, and work with it for positive change. In effect, you are following in the path of those who have gone before, and learning to connect with the world around you, including the vast Universe above your head.

USING THIS BOOK

How you read this book is up to you. You may choose to dip in, to let the pages fall and reveal a tale for daily inspiration. You may prefer to go straight to your personal sign, and once you have read that story, move on to the associated planet, or you may want to read each section from start to finish, in the order it is laid out. There is no preferred way of navigating the narratives. It is more important that you suspend reality and let the Ancient Greek and Roman myths that the tales are based upon consume your imagination.

To make things easier for you, the Zodiac entries are organized as they fall in the Zodiac year, and their timing is highlighted at the beginning of each story. For example, Aries runs from late March to late April (the exact dates vary slightly from year to year). The planets, too, are organized by their geographical order, followed by the Sun and Moon. Each section gives some background on where the stories come from and how the signs and planets came into being. There is also a summary and a reading list, should you wish to explore a little further. All of the planets have been covered, except Earth, being the home planet.

This book takes you on a voyage through time and space, and offers some suggestions to help you make the most of your narrative journey. So relax, read on, and let the celestial landscape enchant heart and mind, and bathe you in starlight.

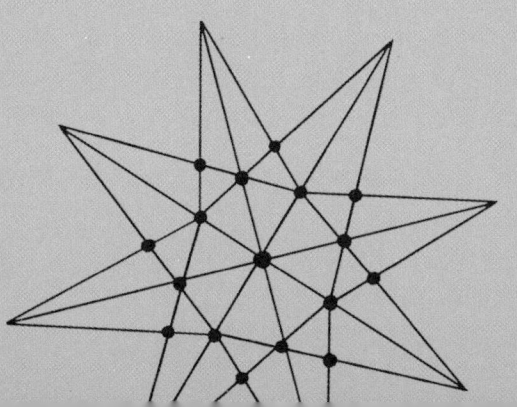

THE ASTROLOGICAL SIGNS

Your Star sign, also known as your Sun sign, is determined by the position of the Sun at the time of your birth, and the placement of all the other planets, which also have a bearing on your personality and the way you approach things. This mapping of the stars is unique. It's a heavenly blueprint of your character and a projection of how you might behave when faced with different scenarios. It can also reveal much about your destiny. A reflection of your inner and outer world, your birth chart, and the Star sign assigned to you, is a gift that can help to unlock your strengths and talents. It's also a tool you can use to navigate the highs and lows of everyday life, and that is why it's important to understand more about its origins, and how it was created.

While it is generally thought that the Babylonians first divided the sky into twelve zones, after observing and recording the movements of the planets, the signs as we know them today were named and shaped by the Ancient Greeks. Having caught on to the astral knowledge that the Babylonians so carefully charted, they went one step further, modifying the original signs to match the constellations and adding their own unique spin to them.

The Ancient Greeks spent much of their time perusing the skies in an attempt to predict the future, from divining the shapes of clouds and the flights of birds, to studying the path of the stars and what this meant for them. While this might sound like a precarious way to make key decisions,

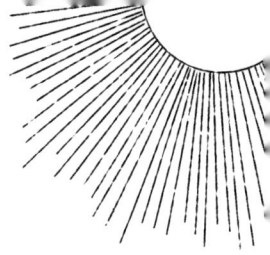

to the philosophers and astronomers of old it was a complex science and highly esteemed. Their mathematical minds applied logic to the star-scape and created order and sequence to the delicate patterns, which led them to attribute deeper layers of meaning to them. Taking their inspiration from the natural world, and the myths and legends that were a part of daily life, they worked these narratives into the stars and came up with the twelve Zodiac signs we now recognize. The stories they drew from reflected some of the key aspects and qualities of each sign, and just like that, astrology was born.

The narratives in this section of the book are based on the Ancient Greek myths and legends associated with each Zodiac sign, taking their inspiration from each one's original tale to create a story, which goes some way to explain the key traits of the astrological sign. Each one features variations, as is often the case in folklore. The narratives, having been retold in many different forms and formats, have deviated over the years, but the essence of the tale remains true.

Let the gods, goddesses, heroes, and mythical beasts therein take you on a journey of self-discovery. Let their exploits and adventures provide a deeper insight into your birth sign, and the signs of your friends and family. Enjoy the epic sagas for what they are, and delight in the fact that they came from the imaginations of astrologers, astronomers, and storytellers who lived thousands of years ago.

THE ASTROLOGICAL SIGNS   15

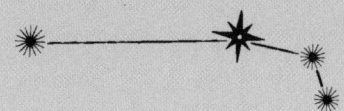

ARIES
The Golden Ram

DATES Late March to late April

CHARACTERISTICS Bold, driven, determined, dynamic, innovative, forceful, competitive, motivated.

ELEMENT Fire

PLANET Mars

A long time ago in the region of Boeotia, in ancient Greece, there lived a king called Athamas, and like many kings before him he was easily swayed by a pretty face, and a few choice compliments. For the most part he was a responsible leader and tried to do his best for the people of the land, but there were times when his behavior lapsed, and he craved the excitement of youth. When he first came into power, Athamas had adored the attention of the people. It made him feel special, which in turn made him feel more confident and helped to keep his insecurities at bay.

Athamas had two grown children from his first marriage to the goddess of the clouds, Nephele. These twins were the apple of his eye, or so it seemed. Phrixus was strong and athletic and a credit to his father, while Helle was a rare beauty and a devoted daughter and, for a time, Athamas was content with his lot. Nephele was a bountiful deity and had always

put her husband's needs before her own, but as time passed the king grew weary and longed for the thrill of something new. Fate seemed on his side when he met Ino. Being younger, she seemed exotic to the king, and he was instantly smitten because of this. He professed his undying love and claimed he would do anything to make her his wife.

And so it was that Nephele was cast aside for the king's new bride Ino, and the children had a stepmother, who seemed pleasant upon the surface. The problem was that Ino deeply resented Phrixus and Helle, for they stole the attention away from her. So she hatched a plan to destroy them, which began when she secretly stole and roasted all of the crop seed in the area so that it wouldn't grow.

As the crops began to fail, the people grew anxious and began to rebel. With no food to replenish their empty stores and the winter almost at their door, they blamed the king for this lack of abundance, which was exactly as Ino had hoped. She knew that Athamas needed the reassurance of his people's adoration to feel important, just as he needed her to fill his head with pretty words.

"You must do something." Ino leaned in to the king's ear. "It is up to you, my love, as the king, to make this right, and I know you will, for you are indeed a good leader."

The king sighed. "But what am I to do? I can control neither the weather nor the ways of the land."

"Maybe not, but you can consult the Oracle, and find out what must be done to appease the gods and help the crops to grow." She brushed his arm tenderly with her slender fingers. "The gods will listen to such a wonderful king, and they will tell you what you need to do, and how to make this right."

The king nodded. "You are right, my dear. You are always right."

Ino smiled. She knew just what to say to make him bend to her will. That night, Ino paid a visit to the men who the king would send to quiz the Oracle and, with a little persuasion and the promise of great riches, made a bargain that would secure her future forever. The following day the gullible king ordered his servants to consult the Oracle and report their findings to him, but while the men left the palace on their quest, they did not visit the Oracle, for they already knew what they had to say. On their return they told him that the only way to save the failing crops and his people, was to sacrifice his son and daughter.

"This cannot be!" he said. "Are you sure that is what the Oracle meant?"

The men nodded. "It is the only way to ensure an abundant crop."

The King rubbed his brow. "I do not know what to do."

"You must do what is right, husband," whispered Ino. "You are the king and that means you have to make difficult choices."

"But my children?"

Ino clasped his hands in hers. "I know, but it has been decreed by the gods through the Oracle. You cannot go against their wishes."

The king finally nodded. There was nothing he could do. He wouldn't stand against the gods, and at least he still had his beautiful wife by his side.

That night, as Phrixus and Helle lay sleeping one last time in their beds, Ino walked through the olive groves, her face turned to the Moon, and with a wide grin she squealed with joy.

"What a clever queen I am! I have at last got rid of my stepchildren. Tomorrow they will be sentenced to death by their own father!" And she chuckled with glee at the thought of their demise.

What Ino failed to realize was that beneath the veil of night, the clouds had gathered and were listening to her every word and, being the domain of the goddess Nephele, they recounted what they heard in the starlight. Nephele was filled with rage that this vile creature had usurped her, and knew that she had to save her children. Stretching herself across the sky so as not to be ignored, she summoned Zeus and petitioned him for help, and together they called upon the Golden Ram, known as Krios Khrysomallos, for assistance. Magnificent and magical, the enormous creature shimmered like a fiery ball of light. Charged with the Sun's rays, and the energy of one inspired and ready for action, the ram took flight. Its golden fleece burned a path through the darkness, cutting through the remaining clouds as it soared to new heights. Nothing would stop it from coming to the aid of Phrixus and Helle.

On and on through the night it flew, until eventually it arrived at its destination. The twins instantly understood the danger they were in, and mounted the creature's back. Up into the air the Golden Ram climbed, traveling with the speed of the gods at its heels. It carried the children away from Boeotia and their father's palace, taking them across great swathes of dusty land. Swooping over the tips of mountains, it carried the children with grace and gentleness, despite the urgency of its mission. Being a beast of the Earth and the sky, it was able to navigate each twist and turn with ease until they reached the sea.

Taking a breath, Helle leant over to peep at the tumbling waves below, and in that one moment lost her balance. Phrixus did his best to steady her, grasping at her with his free hand, but it was no use—gravity had taken hold and poor Helle fell to her doom in the ocean.

Beside himself with grief, Phrixus almost jumped in after her, for what was left for him now? But the ram's golden fleece exuded warmth and held him in place.

"Stay strong, sweet Phrixus," the ram seemed to say. "You are almost there, don't let go now."

And Khrysomallos's assurances calmed his troubled spirit, for he could sense the strength of the creature and it soothed his woes.

Soon they reached Colchis, where King Aeetes was waiting for them, having been forewarned of their arrival by Nephele. He welcomed Phrixus into his home with open arms.

"You are among friends. You will be safe here," he said, and Phrixus knew in his heart that he would.

"I am thankful to you, to the gods, and to my mother, too, for helping me this far, and for doing your best to help my beloved sister." He paused. "Most of all, I am thankful to this generous creature, which has carried me to safety, risking its life, never once giving up on me or the quest." He turned to the enormous ram and bowed his head. "I am honored," he said, to which Khrysomallos the ram responded with a graceful nod before communicating telepathically with the young man.

"The greatest honor you can do me would be to sacrifice me to the father of all, Zeus, for then I will be among the gods."

The young man knew this to be true, but he did not wish to harm the ram, after it had saved his life.

Still, Khrysomallos urged him. "Do not fear, I will not die. I will remain forever in the heavens. You must lay my golden fleece in the Grove of Ares, where it will be a sacred reminder of my exploits. There it will be guarded by a dragon that never sleeps."

Phrixus stared into the eyes of the ram, and for a moment was mesmerized by the creature's steely gaze. Then, nodding once more, he spoke. "I will do as you have asked, and I will lay your fleece in the Grove of Ares for all to see and be reminded of your immense strength and bravery. This will be my way of thanking you for all you have done."

And so it was that Krios Khrysomallos, the Golden Ram of Aries, was sacrificed to the king of the gods Zeus, and its infamous golden fleece, prized for its magical properties, was hung in the Grove of Ares, at Colchis, and guarded by a gigantic dragon. Zeus, being father of all and eternally grateful to the creature for its final sacrifice, decided to place it into the sky. Pinning its outline with a string of the brightest stars, he created the constellation Aries the Ram.

As for King Athamas and his cunning wife Ino, the superficial desires that had thrown them together would eventually tear them apart, and destroy any happiness they had, but this was of little consequence to Phrixus who went on to live a long and happy life, marrying the daughter of King Aeetes, and ruling the kingdom with her.

Nephele, the beautiful cloud goddess, looked on from her seat in the heavens with pride. Synonymous with good grace, her godly status meant she aged little, and radiated timeless beauty as she traversed the skies. And when, during her travels, she came upon the dynamic Aries, she would gather her clouds around the ram, blocking out the rest of the solar system so that all on Earth could see its dazzling vibrancy.

ARIES RITUAL TO PROMOTE ACTION AND MOTIVATION TO REACH A GOAL

You will need: A lighter or matches, a red candle, a piece of paper, a pen with red or gold ink, and a fireproof dish.

This ritual taps into the fiery proactive energy of this Star sign, by using the colors associated with it, and embracing the element of fire. It will help you generate positive energy and take action.

- To begin, light the candle and spend a few minutes gazing into the flame. Notice how it flickers and grows with time. Watch it extend upward, casting light and growing in strength.
- Imagine there's a flame within your chest that also extends each time you take a breath. Feel it growing inside and imbuing you with strength and positivity.
- Now focus on a goal or target that you'd like to reach. Bring it to mind and imagine what it would feel like to achieve your dream.
- If you can, see yourself doing this. Imagine you're watching a movie of you reaching the goal, and engage your emotions at the same time. Feel the elation as you attain your aim.
- Take the paper and pen and sum this up with a positive statement such as, "I've passed my exam and I feel fantastic!" or, "I am acing the presentation and I feel amazing."
- Try not to put your goal in the future, so avoid using "I will," and instead use "I am," or "I have."
- Take the written statement and read it out loud, then pass the paper through the flame and let it burn down in the fireproof dish.
- Continue to imagine how you'll feel when you achieve your dream, and let the candle burn down.

✷ **AFFIRMATION**

"I reach for the stars every day."

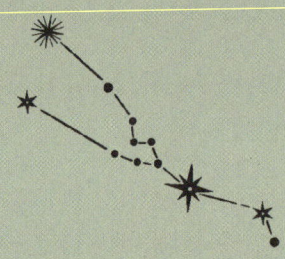

TAURUS
The Princess and the Bull

DATES Late April to late May

CHARACTERISTICS Steadfast, tenacious, loving, creative, loyal, sensual.

ELEMENT Earth

PLANET Venus

At the dawn of time when the fate of gods and mortals were intertwined, and humankind looked to the stars for inspiration, there lived a beautiful Phoenician princess named Europa. With smooth, honeyed skin that shone in the light of the Sun, and eyes that glistened like the brightest sapphires, she was the most stunning human.

Being such a beauty, she caught the attention of many, including the great god Zeus, but unlike others of her kind, she did not care much for his interest. To her, the gods were selfish and conceited and, while she paid them homage, she did not seek their attention. Europa was a simple girl with a kind heart and perhaps that was what Zeus loved the most. It's true, he'd had countless dalliances with humans, and was known for his passionate trysts, but this was more than just desire. He had a need to consume her, to win her heart completely, for it was only in doing so that he would be satisfied and experience the true value of love.

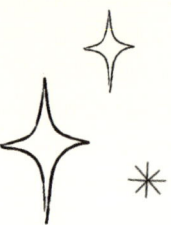

Being the most powerful god in the Greek pantheon, Zeus could have any mortal. A simple click of the fingers was enough to put them under his spell. Just being in his presence and feeling the aura of his greatness would make them swoon. But Europa was different. He could see that, and he wanted more. He needed to feel the flow of emotion between them, and to know that she, too, held him in high regard.

Every day he would watch her play upon the beach with her sisters. He'd smile at her joyful antics, at the way she ran along the shoreline, dipping her toes into the warm waters of the ocean. Her laughter fell like raindrops upon his skin, and only served to increase his ardor. He longed to feel close to her, to sense that she felt the same, but he knew that she would never respond to the advances of a god. And so, in a fit of desperation, Zeus transformed into a creature that she would love with all her heart. He became a bull with glowing fur that shone like the Moon, with beautiful horns that curled from his brow and sparkled. His eyes were deep and dark, and the words that he longed to say could be seen in their inky depths.

He was Taurus the bull: strong and steadfast, a determined creature that could not be distracted from achieving its goal. Like the god at the heart of the beast, Taurus was tenacious. But while the bull was mighty and magnetic, and somewhat unstoppable, it was also gentle at heart, and a symbol of abundance and love, with the kindest of souls. This was surely what Europa would want in a partner.

Zeus, being happy with his disguise, fell to Earth there and then, eager to present himself to the princess, and as expected she was instantly enamored. How could she not be? The bull that stood before her was magnificent. She reached out toward it and let her hand smooth its fur, gently.

"How soft you are," she whispered. "What a glorious creature." And she pressed her face against its skin and closed her eyes.

"I am Taurus," the bull seemed to whisper, wrapping her up in layers of comfort. "I am yours, sweet princess."

"And I, yours," she replied, and in that moment her heart quickened, and it felt like she was floating, carried by the clouds into the sky.

"I have watched you from afar for many days, and I have longed to be at your side," the bull continued.

"And I am glad that you are, beautiful creature," she whispered.

Her head was swimming, lost in the sensual daydream of a dance. It felt like her soul had left her body, and she was soaring through the heavens, and in reality she was. For while her eyes were tightly closed, her arms had wrapped around the sturdy neck of the bull, and they were flying, gliding through the air at speed.

Up, up, and far away, Taurus carried the princess, stealing her from the beach and the home that she knew, taking her to the island of Crete, where olive trees grew in abundance, and the sandy shore sparkled as white as the

Moon under the beaming Sun. And although Europa knew she was flying on the back of this mystical beast, she was not scared. If anything, she felt liberated. She had lived such a sheltered life, never daring to do anything different, but now she was free. She could be anything she wanted to be and that felt wondrous.

Eventually the pair landed, high up on a rocky cliff beneath a shady olive tree. Below them, frothy waves lapped at the shore, and the silvery shapes of dolphins could be seen leaping, catching the ebb and flow of the waves.

"Where are we?" the princess asked.

Taurus lowered his head, and slowly, steadily his shape began to shimmer and shift. The gleaming skin and sturdy form was replaced by a muscular man of godlike proportions, with dark wavy hair.

"Zeus!" Europa exclaimed.

The god stood tall. "Yes, dear princess. I am sorry for the subterfuge, but I needed to meet you, to catch you with an open heart and mind."

There was a moment of silent understanding when it seemed that time stood still, and that even the Earth stopped moving, and then she was in his arms, just as he had always meant it to be.

Of course, that could be the end of the tale, as with so many of Zeus's conquests that had finished as swiftly as they had begun. But as we know, Europa was not like any other woman, and Zeus was deeply smitten. Perhaps some of Taurus the bull had seeped into his psyche and left an imprint there, for he was suddenly in love with the idea of love and compelled to commit his heart to the princess. Loyalty flowed through his veins, and he longed for the stability of a life with her.

From that moment on, he did his best to woo Europa, for fear that he might lose her love to another. He showered her with gifts, the first being Talos, a giant bronze man and a permanent guardian to keep her safe. The second was a dog named Laelaps, a fearsome creature that could run like the wind, and hunt anything the princess might desire. The third gift was by far the most magical—a powerful javelin that could hit any target, anywhere in the world.

As you might imagine, the princess was indeed impressed, but to her the most important gifts Zeus could bring were the qualities of Taurus, who had literally swept her off her feet in the first place. The honesty and tenacity with which the bull pursued its goal, the gentle grace with which it carried itself, and its sweetly melodic voice. Yes, it had stolen her away, thundering through the heavens as it went, but such resilience and grit should always be rewarded. And so Europa wed her god and gave him three handsome sons, who would become the judges of the Underworld when they eventually died. And while their marriage was short-lived, for who can truly share their life with a god— and not just any deity, the father of all the gods—the bond between them was never forgotten.

Europa married again, becoming the wife of King Asterius, and the first queen of Crete, and Zeus, being Zeus, continued to take what he wanted from mortals and heavenly beings alike. That is, until one day, late in the spring, many years after he had first alighted upon the beach in bull form. It was a day tinged with mist and sadness, for although the Sun still shone in the sky and the scent of the olive trees filled the air, it was to be Europa's last day on Earth. Zeus knew this, and he longed to be with her one last time.

As her spirit departed her body, Zeus, too, transformed, taking the shape of the bull and standing at her bedside. His presence was as comforting as it always had been. With ethereal fingers she reached out, and wrapped her arms around his neck, and they rode together one more time through the sky, up beyond the clouds, higher than they had ever been before. And just as she had done many years before, Europa felt free, and at one with the Universe.

There they were together, reunited in death. The princess and the bull, two starry figures dancing in the darkness, forever entwined. Eventually they reached a point where they could see all of the cosmos and the stars shining brightly, and it was here that Zeus gave Europa his last gift. Together, they changed into the stunning constellation named Taurus. There at the very tip of the Earth, where the sky meets the heavens, they sat—a glistening formation of stars for everyone to see and enjoy, and an emblem of enduring love.

TAURUS RITUAL TO PROMOTE WELL-BEING AND BOOST SELF-ESTEEM

You will need: A warm bath filled with bubbles, olive oil, ylang ylang essential oil, a small dish, a lighter or matches, white and gold candles, and candle holders.

This ritual is designed to help you embrace the sensual and romantic nature of this Star sign, while allowing healing energy to flow.

- To begin, run a warm bath and fill it with scented bubbles to make it a sensual experience.
- Add a tablespoon of olive oil and two drops of ylang ylang essential oil to the dish and swirl with your index finger to combine the ingredients.
- Light the white and gold candles in the candle holders to represent Taurus the bull, and gently immerse yourself in the bubbles.
- As you relax and enjoy the warmth of the water, dip your finger in the scented oil and trace a heart shape in the center of your chest, where the heart chakra resides. This symbolizes your intention to take the time and care that you need to love yourself.
- The heart chakra is the energy center that relates to the seat of your emotions and your heart energy. When it is activated in this way it allows you to give and receive love freely, and also to learn to love and accept yourself.
- Pour the remaining oil into the bath, and soak. As you do, engage all of your senses. Think about what you can see, such as the soft light of the candles flickering, and what you can smell, such as the sweet scent of olive mixed with ylang ylang. Also consider what you can hear, such as the gentle lap of the water and how this feels against your skin.
- Relax and let all of the sensations soothe and recharge you.
- To finish, repeat the following affirmation, "I am loved, I am loving, I love myself."
- Enjoy the rest of your bath, but be careful not to slip when you get out, as you may be a little oily.

✸ AFFIRMATION

"I am loved. I am loving. I love myself."

GEMINI
The Dioscuri

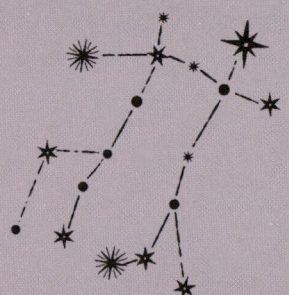

DATES Late May to late June

CHARACTERISTICS Sociable, inquisitive, talkative, engaging, changeable, spontaneous.

ELEMENT Air

PLANET Mercury

Never in the history of deities and mortals was there a twosome as intertwined as twin brothers Castor and Polydeuces. Born to the queen of Sparta, but conceived by different fathers, the two boys suckled together in the womb, connected by their innocence, and bonded for life. But while Castor was the son of King Tyndareus, Polydeuces was the son of the king of the gods, Zeus, and the result of some magical trickery.

Never one to give up on a human conquest, Zeus had set his sights on the queen of Sparta, but he also knew she was deeply in love with her husband, and so he transformed into a graceful swan, and wooed her with his charm and poise. The resulting babe became part of the inseparable duo, tied together by the blood of their mother and an understanding far deeper than their heritage, for Castor and Polydeuces were soulmates, able to sense each other's joy and pain. Some said they were two sides of the same coin, for when one was distraught, the other was elated and vice versa, meaning that together they were in perfect balance. Such harmony cannot be strived for, or fashioned out of love. It is innate in twin souls.

As the boys grew, so did their reputations, for they were both skilled in different ways. Castor was an excellent horseman, with the ability to soothe the wildest stallions and perform such feats of dexterity while riding that he seemed gifted by the gods. Polydeuces cut an impressive figure in battle. Like his father Zeus he had an air of authority, but his particular talent was boxing. No mortal man could outbox him, for he was quick, nimble, and strong, and perhaps a little advantaged, thanks to his father's powers. Together they were an unstoppable force called "the Dioscuri," meaning "Sons of Zeus." It seemed that they could read each other's minds, and sense what the other was about to do. This connection served them well when they joined the Argonauts on their quest for the Golden Fleece.

The Dioscuri were as handsome as they were godly in their ways, and had a string of dalliances that Zeus himself would have been proud of. And so it was no surprise when Castor and Polydeuces became entranced with two Greek maidens called Phoebe and Hillaera. The boys were smitten by the way they walked, their subtle curves, and their shy countenances. Such beauty had not crossed their paths before, and they could not ignore the feelings that had been ignited within them.

"Brother," Castor said, "we must make them ours."

"I agree," smiled Polydeuces, "I cannot go on living without being able to gaze upon those sweet smiles. But are they not promised to two others, twins like us?"

Castor nodded. "They are betrothed to Idas and Lynceus, but that is of little consequence. They may be twins, but they are not the mighty Dioscuri!"

"That is true," said Polydeuces. "We are destined for greatness, and cannot be denied. I say we seize them and make them our own."

And so the die was cast, and the Dioscuri made their conquests, sweeping Phoebe and Hillaera away without a thought for Idas and Lynceus.

Time has a way of calming all woes, and bringing new opportunities, but it failed to soothe the pain or humiliation of the two remaining twins, who had lost their betrothed. Left to stew in sorrow, their anger swelled deep within their bellies. They longed for revenge, and for a way to make the brothers pay—and, as with all things, whatever you feed with focus and energy, you attract, and so their chance would come one fateful day.

During their journey with Jason and the Argonauts, the Dioscuri had proved themselves several times, showing great bravery and honor, as might be expected by such a unique pair of twins. From battling monstrous creatures to saving their fellow sailors at sea, it seemed that there was nothing they couldn't do, and the boys enjoyed the attention they received, the adoration filling them with bravado. Perhaps that is why they continued to embrace a life of adventure and put themselves in harm's way. Maybe they felt invincible, and for Polydeuces this was true. Being sired by the father of the gods gave him certain advantages and made him immortal, but for Castor it was a different story. Though he

30   THE ASTROLOGICAL SIGNS

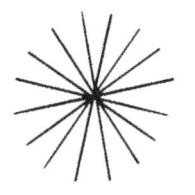

was touched by his brother's magic, he was still mortal, a difference they never forgot but often underplayed.

"I will always protect you, brother," Polydeuces would say. "We are one and the same. We cannot exist without each other."

And Castor would pat his twin upon the shoulder and reply, "We are bonded. Nothing can separate us. We are the Dioscuri."

And so it went on, but their exploits did not go unnoticed. Stories of the duo traveled far and wide, covering all of Greece and Sparta, and even reached as far as the gods on Mount Olympus. While most were enchanted by tales of the brothers, there were two who were less than enamored. Idas and Lynceus had been planning their attack for the longest time, and they found out from word of mouth where the Dioscuri would be. They knew it wouldn't be easy to defeat them, but at least they had the element of surprise on their side, and when the time came and their paths finally crossed, they struck hard.

Castor was the first to fall at the hands of Idas; a fatal blow out of the blue, and a sharp intake of breath was all it took to seize the life and light from his eyes. Polydeuces felt it instantly. His heart lost the drum of his twin's beat, time stood still, and all the fickleness of their deeds, the joy and the laughter, the pain and the pleasure, rushed before him. He saw his own life through his twin's death, and in that moment his soul split in two.

"No!" He cried, rushing to Castor's side, but it was too late. Castor had gone. All that was left was the broken shell of his twin, lying in his arms.

As grief turned to rage, he charged toward Lynceus, fists first, before unleashing his dagger and plunging it into the man's heart. Lynceus crumbled in a heap at his feet.

"What have you done?" Idas yelled. "You've killed my brother!"

"And you killed mine!" snarled Polydeuces, but before he could say another word, Idas was upon him, and it seemed that he might win the fight, for Polydeuces was a shadow of his former self. A twin without a twin, and no longer half of the Dioscuri, he was bereft and seemed to lack all of the strength and skill that had served him so well in the past. Idas stood over him ready to strike a final blow, but before he could meet his end, Zeus intervened, sending a powerful thunderbolt to halt Idas in his tracks.

Polydeuces stood in silence and surveyed the destruction before him. The three bodies seemed to be wasting away before his eyes. Once more he fell to his knees, cradling Castor's head upon his lap.

"My brother, my other half, what am I to do without you?"

He sobbed, letting the tears fall upon his twin's cheeks. Then, turning his face to the heavens, he called to Zeus.

"Father, I do not want to live without my brother. Take my life now, so that we can be together in death."

There was a moment of silence, and then the growling sound of thunder rumbling in the distance, as Zeus responded to his son's pleas. "You would end your life, just because your twin is dead?" he boomed from the heavens.

"I would, in a heartbeat," said Polydeuces. "We have always been together, two in one. We mirror each other. There is no other way."

"But you forget who you are. You forget I am *your* father, and that even in death you will be immortal, and therefore separated from Castor."

Polydeuces thought for a moment. He looked at the pale face of his brother, and then up at the gathering clouds, and an idea came to his mind.

"Make him immortal like me, and then end my life so that we can be together. Please father."

"And why should I do that?" snapped Zeus. "Why should I give up the son I have saved, so easily?"

"Because you are my father and because I have never asked anything of you before this moment." He clambered to his feet then and clasped his hands together. "Please father, let me go, I do not wish to exist in a world without my twin."

The sky darkened, and clusters of clouds merged together to create a sea of charcoal that pressed down upon the Earth. Then the heavens opened as Zeus spoke once more.

"Very well, I will make Castor immortal in death, and I will end your Earthly life now so that you can be together, if that is truly your wish."

"It is."

There was a clap of thunder, and the ground began to tremble, the sky shaking with fervor. A bolt of lightning hit the Earth, cracking the surface, and leaving a web of splinters in the dry soil. Tendrils of light exploded in every direction, wrapping wiry threads around Polydeuces, ensnaring him in a deadly embrace that would steal his last breath. Then in the blink of an eye all was calm again. The Earth was whole, the crevices that had split open were gone and the sky was as blue as the Mediterranean Sea. The only difference was Polydeuces—his motionless body lay at the side of his twin, as handsome in death as he had been in life. The pair were a perfect reflection of each other.

In that moment, Zeus in all his greatness appeared by their lifeless forms. His head bowed in contemplation. "What am I to do with you two?" he whispered.

Tapping his staff upon the ground near their feet, he watched their bodies rise into the air. Gradually, as the two forms lifted higher, what had been flesh and bone transformed into the ethereal: a pattern of tiny stars threaded together in an eternal dance. Slowly, gracefully, they soared up toward the heavens, and the stars grew in size and brightness. Eventually a constellation in the shape of the twins formed and took its position in the night sky. It became known as Gemini. Zeus nodded, at last satisfied with his handiwork.

"It is as it should be—the Dioscuri together forever and shining bright for all the world to see."

GEMINI RITUAL TO CREATE A SENSE OF HARMONY AND BALANCE

You will need: Two yellow candles, candle holders, a pin, a length of ribbon or string, and a lighter or matches.

This ritual will help you unite the light and dark within your psyche, and to create a sense of wholeness while tapping into the vibrant energy of this Star sign.

- Yellow is synonymous with enthusiasm and spontaneity, two qualities associated with Gemini. Take the yellow candles and, on one, use the pin to carve half a circle into the wax. On the other, carve the remaining half a circle, so that when you stand them next to each other, you have a full circle, and the picture becomes whole.
- Place the candles standing upright in the candle holders next to each other on the table in front of you, and then arrange the ribbon or string in a wide circle around them. This circular symbol represents unity.
- Light both candles and gaze at the flames.
- Spend a few minutes thinking about the different aspects of your own personality. Do you have opposing qualities? For example, perhaps you can be impulsive sometimes, but set in your ways on other occasions?
- Think about your behavior and the qualities that you like and dislike. All of these aspects come together to create your unique identity and make you who you are.
- Say, "Light and dark, night and day, together forever in every way. I embrace both sides, to make me whole, and let true harmony take control."
- Let the candles burn down and continue to think about all the wonderful traits that make you so special.

✳ **AFFIRMATION**

"I embrace both sides to make me whole, and let true harmony take control."

CANCER
Gate of Men

DATES Late June to late July

CHARACTERISTICS Sensitive, empathic, intuitive, emotional, expressive, modest.

ELEMENT Water

PLANET The Moon

The primordial source of life, was, according to the Ancient Greeks, an ever-flowing, constant presence. Likened to a body of water, it would continue to exist through time and space, pouring forth to create new life and filling the places in between.

Positioned above Earth, floating somewhere high up in the galaxy, this soup of souls would rain down upon the planet, and each tiny droplet that fell would contain the spark of new life. Those wishing to be born would need to move in this way through the starry realm, to find sanctuary in a living, breathing body upon Earth, but in order to do so, they had to pass through the Gate of Men.

Known as the constellation Cancer the Crab, this network of gleaming stars became the gatekeeper to Earth. Each worthy soul would seek entrance, so that they could unite with the human world, taking shape and form in a flesh-and-bone body of their choice. But what did admission require? Perhaps there was a special word, a charm, or a ritual performed to gain access? And why the crab?

Many have pondered this, for it seems that such a humble creature is a strange choice for this role.

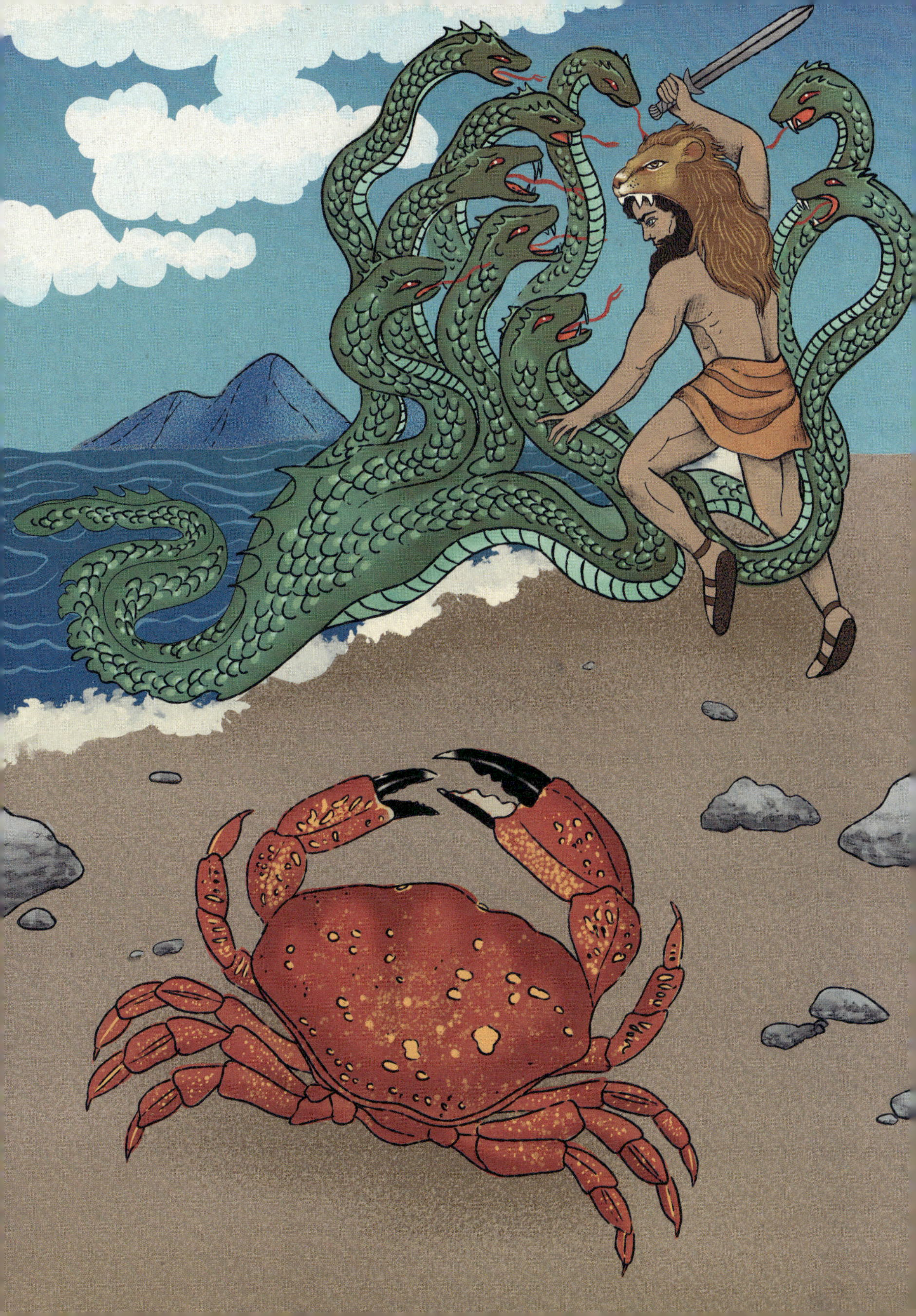

According to legend, it was the perfect selection, for while there were mightier beasts that walked this Earth in ancient times, there were none so pure of heart that they might sacrifice their own life to help another.

Karkinos the crab might have lived an uneventful existence by the shoreline of the Mediterranean if it hadn't been for the intervention of the goddess Hera. As beautiful as she was sly, she was a jealous deity, always hungry for the attention of others, particularly that of her husband Zeus, the king of the gods. Some say she had good reason, for Zeus was renowned for his infidelities, and this surely fuelled the fire of her bitterness.

When Zeus fathered a son with the mortal woman Alcmene, her anger grew into something savage, and she swore she would not rest until the child named Heracles was dead. The boy grew into a demi-god; half man, half deity. He was the epitome of strength and valor, and his reputation grew with him, which only served to enrage the goddess more.

"I will find a way to kill him," she proclaimed. "He will not be able to hide from my wrath forever."

But Heracles was clever, too, and though she tried many times to thwart him, he always seemed to be one step ahead of her schemes. In a moment of utter desperation, Hera resorted to a spell, and one that would have cataclysmic results. She laid upon him a fit of madness that seized all reason from his mind and plagued him with demons. Heracles, sent mad from the dark magic, could not overcome the destructive thoughts in his head. They swirled about him like a black cloak, and he was unable to see what he was doing, never mind understand why he was doing it. His uncontrollable rage finally bubbled over and, in a fit of anguish, he killed his wife and family. Once the deed was done, the cloud lifted and the spell was finally broken, but it was too late. Heracles had destroyed the one thing he loved the most in the world, and there was no way back.

Hera, smug with her success, sat back upon her throne to survey the damage. While she was sad it had come to this, for she had never meant for him to kill his loved ones, she was secretly happy he was out of favor with the gods.

"See, I have been telling you all along—he is no hero, he is just a man, and a weak one at that, for he couldn't control himself," she sneered.

Zeus shook his head. "Do not treat me like a fool, Hera. There is more to this than meets the eye. Did you have a hand in it?"

"Me?" she smiled. "I did nothing. It is he who slaughtered his own kin."

Zeus bit his lip, for he knew that his wife had played her part. "Your meddling will cost you much one day," he said gravely. "As for Heracles, he will be made to pay."

And pay he did, for poor Heracles longed to find a way back into the hearts of men and gods, but to redeem himself he needed to complete twelve labors, treacherous tests of strength and nature. These challenges were so incredibly difficult that they could kill him, or at least destroy what was left of his reputation.

"You said he would pay," Hera snapped, "but this is no punishment, not for a man like Heracles. He enjoys the thrill of competition and will easily meet all your demands."

"Silence!" Zeus yelled. "It is my final judgment. Do not question me, Hera."

The goddess bowed her head for she knew better than to battle with her husband, but inside she was secretly hatching a plan. She would make things as difficult as possible for the young hero, and she would have her way, even if it meant resorting to devious means.

Each god picked a suitable challenge for Heracles. His first labor was to slay the Nemean Lion.

The terrifying beast had plagued the area of Nemea for many years and was under the guardianship of Hera, who had a hand in bringing him to life. Even so, Heracles was not swayed by stories of its prowess and made short work of the challenge, impressing both the gods and the locals with his strength and agility.

The second labor was Hera's choice. Hurt by his swift put-down of her beloved lion, she had scoured the land in search of a horrifying opponent for the hero to fight. Her prayers were answered when she happened upon the Hydra. A nine-headed serpent, it was a monster of epic proportions with acrid venom that seeped through its veins. Each sharp, forked tongue had the ability to slice through anything. Massive in size, and lithe in movement, the Hydra was a fearsome predator and more than a match for Heracles. While he swiped his sword and beheaded it many times, the serpent simply slithered and hissed and regrew more heads. To those watching, it seemed they were equally matched, and at times the hero had the upper hand, but Hera was not leaving anything to chance. She clicked her fingers and muttered a magical chant, summoning some unlikely assistance for the giant beast.

Into the fray came Karkinos the crab, scuttling with a sideways gait beneath Heracles's sandaled feet. His pincers raised, he snatched at the demi-god's toes, pinching at the flesh. And while onlookers must have been amused by this spectacle, it was enough to steal the hero's attention, to distract him and allow the Hydra some respite to heal its wounds. The tiny crab—for that is what he was, compared to musclebound Heracles and the gigantic serpent—knew he had a role to play. He was no match for their strength, and he lacked in size and presence, but he was courageous, and honor-bound to the goddess. A being of the water and a sensitive soul at heart, Karkinos intuitively knew the outcome of the fight, and that he would meet his end, but still he threw himself into the battle with the bravery of a warrior.

The end came swiftly. Heracles stepped upon the shell of the crab, and he died instantly. It was then that the hero realized the secret to the Hydra's survival, and how he could kill the monster. He needed to find the Hydra's weakness, just like the crab's shell had been central to its demise, the serpent had a small amount of time when it was without one of it heads before regrowth. This was when it was most vulnerable. Working quickly and with sleight of hand, each time he beheaded the creature, he took a torch and cauterized the wound, preventing a new head from growing in its place. Slowly, as each head was removed, the serpent finally crumbled. Unable to regenerate, its colossal body curled into the sand in a heap. Heracles was triumphant once more, and from her seat in the cosmos Hera had to concede defeat, as she was forced to when Heracles continued on to complete all twelve of his labors.

Taking a long, deep breath, Hera closed her eyes and, as she exhaled, released the anger that had consumed her body and mind for so long.

"It is done," she muttered, as she fell back in her throne. All the steely fury that had kept her rigid and prone was gone. It was as if a veil had been lifted and she could finally see all that her hate had accomplished.

She gazed down upon Earth at the scene before her, and her eyes fell to the broken body of the crab. Innocent to the ways of gods and mortals, it had been called upon to serve her, which it had done valiantly while almost certainly knowing his fate. A citizen of the sea, governed by the element of water, and now returned to the fluid state through death.

"My little friend," she whispered. "You did not deserve this." A tear formed in the corner of her eye, and she brushed it away. "You were honorable and courageous despite the odds, and I am sorry for the outcome, for it was inevitable. What you have done will not be forgotten. I will make sure of that."

Reaching out from the heavens with soft fingers, she scooped up the remains of the crab in her hand. Cupping it gently in her palm, she lifted it high into the sky, high above the clouds and into the very depths of night, and the darkest part of the cosmos. With one delicate movement, she let it hang in the canvas of the sky. The body of the creature was now whole again, reformed from twinkling stars and reborn in a new and brighter form.

"Here you will stay, and you will be known as Cancer the Crab, forever faithful, a devoted denizen of the ocean and the gateway to Earth."

She paused then, to admire her handiwork, and noticed the gentle glow of the Moon in the distance. Forever changing, this powerful orb's cyclical nature had something in common with the crab constellation. She smiled to herself ruefully, as she realized that while she had brought about the end of the crab, she had also created something new and beautiful from its broken body, just as the Moon shifts and changes.

"The cycle of renewal goes on. As you have been reborn, so those brave souls who venture forth from the primordial well of existence will pass through you to find new life upon Earth and you will intuitively know if their heart is open and if their soul is pure."

And so it was that the Gate of Men was created in the galaxy, and Karkinos, now Cancer the Crab, found a new home and purpose, one that seemed fitting for such a sensitive being. And those upon Earth looked to the stars and gave thanks for its humble presence and the humility it represented.

CANCER RITUAL TO DEVELOP EMPATHY AND PSYCHIC PERCEPTION

You will need: A piece of moonstone, an image of the Moon, and a journal and pen.

This ritual tunes in to the psychic energy of the Moon, which is the governing planet of Cancer, by using the Zodiac sign's associated stone. It will help you intuitively sense the emotions of others.

- Make sure you are sitting somewhere comfortable. Now position the moonstone in front of you.
- If you have a picture of the Moon, place this directly in your line of vision, or sit by a window and gaze at the Moon in the sky.
- Spend a few minutes looking at the image and notice how it makes you feel. What springs to mind as you focus on the Moon? Make a note in your journal of any words, phrases, or descriptions that come to mind.
- Enjoy being in the creative flow and write what you feel. Don't worry too much about things such as grammar or spelling.
- Close your eyes and imagine you're bathed in the Moon's soothing light. Feel it permeate your being and gently ignite your psychic senses. Breathe this in and notice how the energy of the Moon makes you feel.
- Sit with this energy for a few minutes, and let it fire up your intuition.
- Open your eyes and write down anything that now comes to mind. You might feel the urge to compose a poem, to write how you feel, or to reflect upon what the Moon means to you.
- When you've finished, read what you have written and simply enjoy the experience of being creative and in tune with your emotions.

✳ AFFIRMATION

"My inner light ignites my imagination."

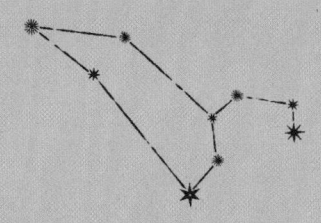

LEO
The King of the World

DATES Late July to late August

CHARACTERISTICS Confident, bold, ambitious, generous, attention-seeking.

ELEMENT Fire

PLANET The Sun

High in the mountains of Nemea, there lived a king, but he was not like any Earthly monarch. This king prowled the dusty landscape, stalking his kingdom with pride, and while he may not have had an ornate throne to sit in, he did have a castle—a lofty cave gouged from the rock, which gave him the ideal vantage point from which to watch and wait.

When the Sun hit the tip of the mountain as it slid from view, this mighty king would throw back his glorious golden mane and roar. The sound would crash against the jagged stone, reverberating through the hillside. Those on the ground or within earshot, would marvel at his magnificence for it could not be denied he was a rare beauty. Resplendent without the need for human finery, he would stand in the amber glow of the setting Sun and accept his praise, for he was the Nemean Lion.

How life began for him is something of a mystery, and there are many versions of the tale, depending on who does the telling. Some of his subjects believe that he was crafted by magic, created out of thin air and the iron will of the goddess Hera as a way to annoy her husband, the king of gods, Zeus. Angered at his many

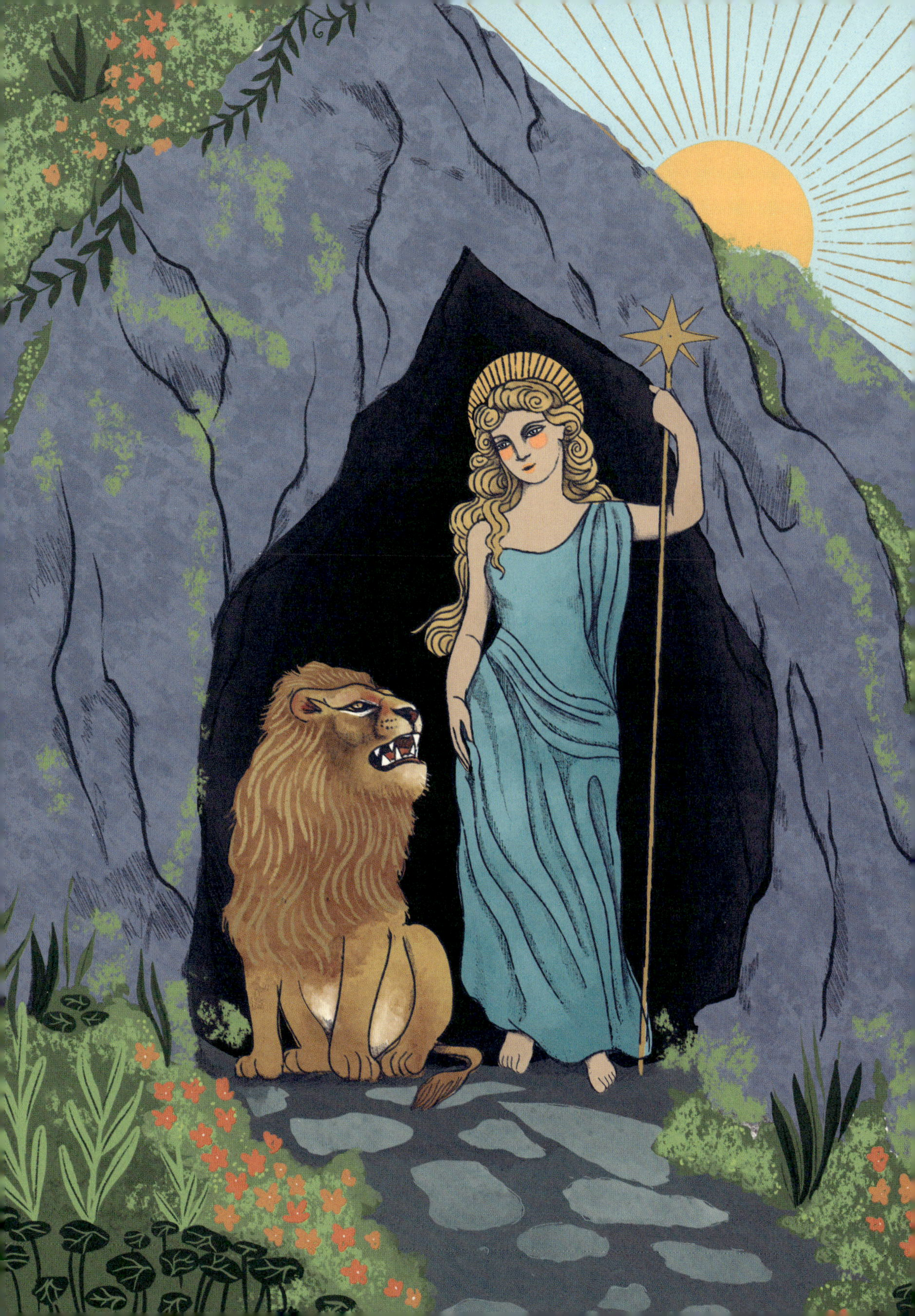

dalliances, she shaped a beast to play with, a fearsome predator that could create havoc upon Earth and cause many problems for him.

Some suggest the lion was born from the loins of Typhon, the terrifying monster god who would go on to slaughter many of the pantheon and cause the gods to flee Mount Olympus. Then there were those more adoring mortals who believed in the romantic version of events, and that the lion was the result of a coupling between Zeus and the beautiful Moon goddess Selene. As the beast grew, he became too big for the Moon goddess to hold within her tender grasp, and so she cast him out of the heavens, and down to Earth under the watchful eye of Hera. The lion, freed from his cosmic prison, grew strong and confident. He wore his newfound courage like a shield, and soon realized that he had command of the land, for though Hera tried to tame him, even she could not control his ego or his lust for life.

And so it was that the Nemean Lion began to prowl the length and breadth of the land, taking in the full extent of his new realm. He understood his role in this place. It was up to him to keep the people in line, to give them something to admire and fear in equal measure, and he enjoyed this immensely. There was nothing like the adoration of his subjects to lift his spirits and make him feel like the king of the world. The other animals looked on with envy for there were none like him, and certainly none who had the power to take him on.

"There is nothing I cannot do, nothing I cannot be. I am the greatest of them all!" He roared.

Being held in high regard kept him happy for a while, but it didn't satisfy all of his needs. The Nemean Lion needed a challenge, something to boost his bravado. He craved the success of victory and was prepared to work for it. Hunting the creatures of the land was easy, and he had much bigger ambitions. So he decided to have some fun. After all, he needed to remain in the hearts and minds of the people, and to do that, he needed to remind them of his presence.

One day he saw his chance. A pretty maid out walking with her friends was the ideal victim. He recognized there was nothing that a warrior loved more than a damsel in distress. Seizing the girl in his enormous jaws, he carried her off into the distance. Her screams echoed across the mountainside as he ran. Leaping over rocks, the lion scaled the stony ground with ease until he reached his hilltop lair. There, he deposited her upon the ground, gently releasing her body, and then tapping her with a meaty paw.

"Do not fear, mistress, I do not wish to eat you. If I did, you would be dead already." The maiden gasped and clutched her mouth. "You are the bait in my plan. I ask only one thing of you." Too horrified to speak, she nodded frantically. "I just need you to keep screaming, so that the warriors know where to come."

The girl paused just long enough for the lion to charge forward; his hot breath seared her face.

"Scream!" he roared and she instantly cried out in fear.

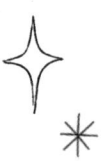

Word of the girl's capture spread, and soldiers from nearby towns gathered, each one taking their turn at the beast and failing miserably. Soon the lion had bested and eaten most of the locals capable of wielding a weapon, and he had little need for the girl, but he realized that he'd hit on something. This was a good ploy, and one that could work all over Nemea. What fun he would have first seizing a captive and then watching as each eager challenger took their turn to face him!

"I am indestructible!" he cried from the top of the mountain. "No mortal man has the power to beat me!"

And it was true, for the Nemean Lion had a secret weapon. His skin, as swarthy as one might expect of such a beast, was impenetrable thanks to the magic that had created him. Gifted with incredible strength and dexterity, he had the ability to enchant almost anyone who crossed his path with his awesomeness.

While the lion strutted his way across the land, leaving a trail of destruction behind him, the gods watched and began to grow weary.

"This cannot go on," they said, imploring Zeus to do something about the situation. "If he continues in this way, there will be no people left to worship us, and then what are we to do?"

Reluctant to intervene, Zeus decided that the best way to deal with the problem was to hand it to someone else, and he had the perfect candidate. Heracles, the disgraced warrior and demi-god, was prepared to do anything to regain his honor, after falling foul of a curse that had made him kill his entire family. Zeus had been looking for a way to punish him without any personal involvement, and this was the ideal solution. He would set Heracles a series of labors—tests of his strength and resilience that could be fatal, and the Nemean Lion would be the first.

Pleased with his decision, he imparted the news to the rest of the gods and goddesses, but Hera was not happy. She had spent many hours with the lion, training it in the ways of the world. She had been the only deity to spend time with the creature and nurture it, and it had proved a willing partner in crime, for it had caused much trouble for Zeus.

"Let me deal with it," she begged, "I know the lion and its ways, and I will be able to stop it doing any more damage."

Zeus, not normally swayed by his wife's sentiment, decided in this case to let her have her moment.

"Very well, you may try, but if you are not successful then I will pass the task on to Heracles. You have till the morning."

Hera wasted no time. Using her magical powers to traverse between the realms, she arrived at the entrance to the lion's cave and beckoned the creature close.

"Goddess," the lion said with a crooked smile. "I have served you well."

"Yes, you have." Hera paused. "You have created a lot of mischief. I am impressed with all your feats, but now it is time for you to stop. The gods are not happy."

The lion shook his golden mane and began to laugh. "I cannot stop. This is what I do, and this is who I am. People fear me. They look at me and they see my glory. I am a god to them."

Hera took a step back. "But you must stop, otherwise they will send one who will end your life."

"I am not afraid," the lion said, "I am the king of the world."

"You are the king of your world, that is true, but it is time to step out of the light. You have had your moment of fame."

The lion was enraged. How dare she come to his palace and tell him what to do? "Do not threaten me, Hera," he spat. "I could finish you with a swipe of my paw."

"And I could finish you with a click of my fingers," she whispered, "but my heart will not let me, for I had a hand in your making."

With that she disappeared, stepping out of the cave and slipping between the layers to reappear at the foot of Zeus's throne.

The god eyed her with suspicion for he knew of her attachment to the beast. "Is it done? Will he stop?"

She shook her head sadly. "I cannot make him. He is a force to be reckoned with, a passionate soul. He will not stop easily."

Zeus sighed. "Then I pass the feat over to Heracles. Let him finish the lion for good."

As expected, the hero Heracles was committed to the cause. He needed to restore his honor, and this was a way he could win the people's hearts. If he could kill the Nemean Lion, they would surely sing his praises. And so he threw himself at the challenge. A lesser man might have balked at the lion's size, at the spread of his jaw or the glistening teeth like razors that snapped at his heels, but Heracles was also blessed by the gods. His strength was like a hundred men, and while he soon realized he couldn't puncture the lion's rough hide with his dagger, it did not faze him. Battling the lion to the ground with his bare hands, he wrapped his arms around the lion's thick neck and quickly choked the breath from him. As the lion's body fell to the ground, the hero stood tall. He had passed the first of his labors and was ready for the next. Nothing would stop him from completing all twelve of his labors, finding favor once more with both mortals and the gods.

Hera watched from her seat in the heavens, tears spilling down her face. The lion had been loyal to her, despite its need for power and attention, and she felt responsible for its fate.

Reaching out from the clouds with her hands like slithers of moondust, she lifted the lion's broken body into the air. Cradling its head softly, she whispered reassurances, and then, with a soothing breath that turned into a gentle breeze, she cast the lion's mighty form into the heavens. Its distinctive shape hung in the sky, where it was visible to both the Northern and the Southern Hemispheres and could be worshipped by all. It formed a pattern of the brightest stars, truly befitting for the king of the world.

LEO RITUAL TO BOOST CONFIDENCE AND SELF-ESTEEM

You will need: Some space outside beneath the light of the Sun, sunscreen, and loose clothing.

This ritual works with the positive energy of this Star sign, and its governing celestial body, the Sun. It helps you step into the light and truly appreciate your gifts, talents, and natural beauty.

- Since you will be standing beneath the Sun's rays, it's a good idea to apply sunscreen first as protection, and to wear loose clothing.
- If possible, find a patch of grass and stand barefoot to help you connect with the Earth. This will anchor you while working with the uplifting energy of the Sun.
- Stand with your feet hip-width apart. Roll your shoulders back and lengthen your spine.
- Picture a thread of light that travels through the center of your body, and exits through the top of your head, and imagine tugging this lightly to stretch and extend your posture.
- Close your eyes and tilt your face upward. Feel the warmth of the Sun upon your face.
- Imagine that for every breath you take, you absorb more of this light, as it filters through each pore and lights you up like a beacon.
- Continue to breathe in the Sun's energy and, as you exhale, imagine the light seeping outward, surrounding you in a beautiful glow.
- Picture the light of the Sun like a spotlight, flowing down upon you and celebrating your uniqueness. It enhances all of your natural beauty and strengthens all of your gifts and talents.
- Enjoy this all-encompassing brightness and know it is your time to stand tall and shine.
- To finish say, either out loud or in your head, "My light shines brighter with every breath I take."

✳ AFFIRMATION

"My light shines brighter with every breath I take."

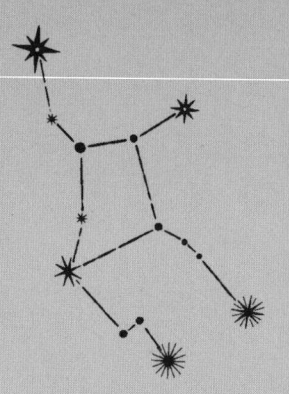

VIRGO

The Goddess of the Grain

DATES Late August to late September

CHARACTERISTICS Self-sufficient, humble, hardworking, practical, diligent, critical, dedicated.

ELEMENT Earth

PLANET Mercury

The goddess of the grain is a nurturing force in all mythologies. Most importantly, she is a mother. She is the great provider, a divine entity that needs no placating or adulation. She simply is.

Self-sufficient in every way, she is a virgin needing only the power within to create new life because she embodies the maiden in all her glory. The innocence of youth is as much a part of her story as the wisdom of age, and never more so than with the story of the Greek goddess Demeter, and her daughter Persephone. Together they formed a powerful union, being one and the same but also two separate entities. While Demeter cultivated the crops, Persephone sprinkled her vivacious light upon them, and they flourished in the sunshine.

In those early days, spring was eternal across the land, and so every shrub and flower was at its best, and it seemed that joy was in abundance. How could the people not be thrilled by the colorful sight that

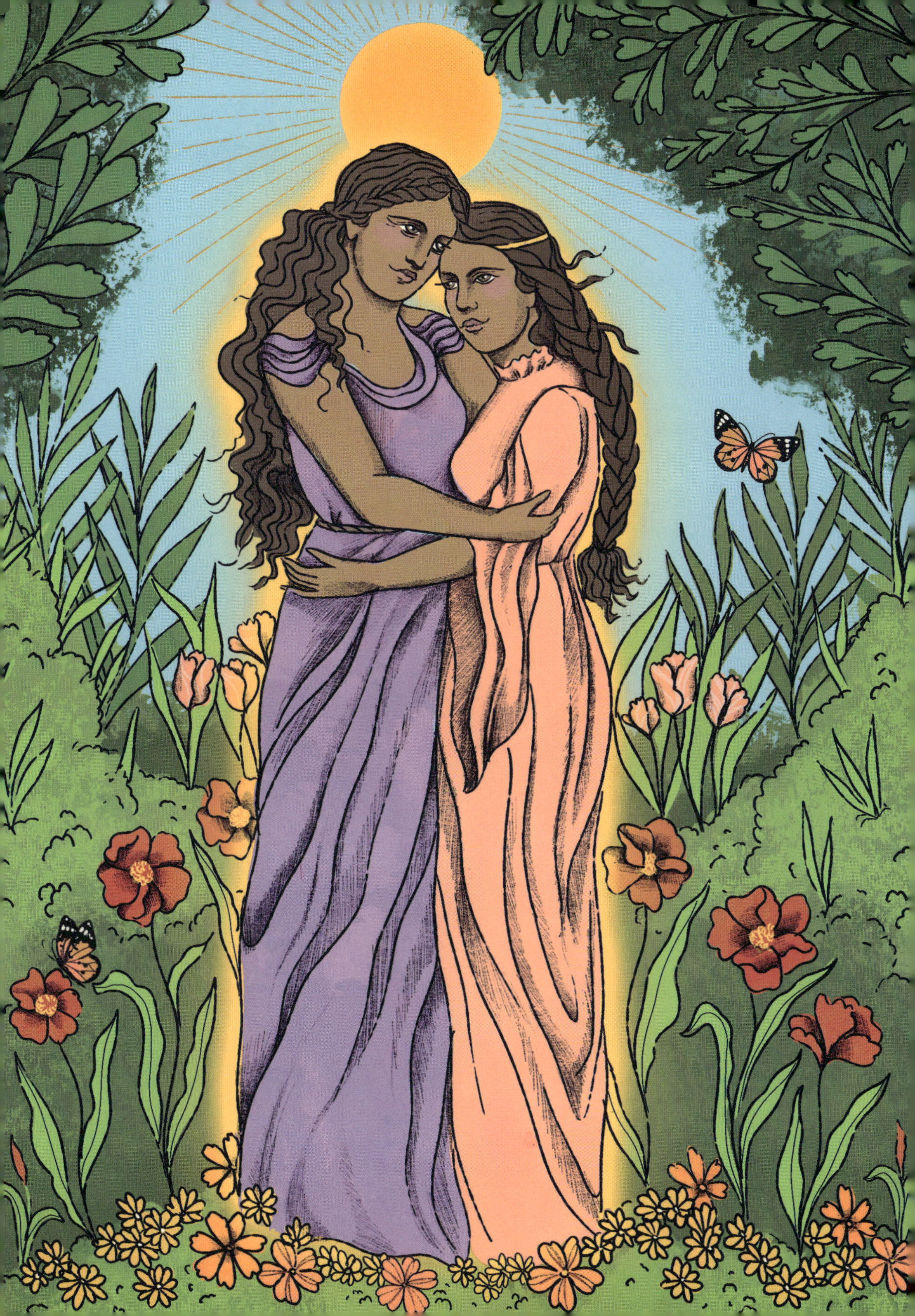

greeted them every day? Nature was generous with its gifts, but as with all things, time has its way, and change, even in the realm of the gods, is inevitable.

And so it was that the beautiful Persephone was coveted by the god of the Underworld, Hades. It was only natural that a being of the dark should be entranced by the light in her eyes. The sparkle of her smile was like the dew upon the buds, ripe and full of promise, and Hades fell deeply in love. He knew that she would never consider him an appropriate suitor, and who could blame her? His domain was the shadow world: a brittle, empty place where the ghosts of the dead wandered, and despair seeped from the cold stone walls. Theirs could never be a normal courtship. He would never be able to enchant her with his smile, or romance her like the other gods, and so, in a fit of desperation, Hades devised a plan. He would whisk her away when she least expected it, keeping her trapped within his realm until she fell in love with him. Then he would offer her the choice of living in the daylight, or the darkness. It was the only way he stood a chance of winning her heart.

Waiting for the right moment, the god kept a close eye on his target. He watched as she wandered the fields and meadows with her mother. He saw them tend to the crops together, and understood the deep bond of love they shared, but it would not deter him from his plan. And so one morning, when the Sun had only just begun its journey through the sky and Persephone was alone picking flowers, he seized his chance. Emerging from the ground in a great tornado, he lifted the goddess into his arms and carried her away to his kingdom.

Demeter knew straight away that something was wrong. It felt like a part of her was missing. The brightness in her eyes dimmed and her heart was heavy, as if wrapped in iron chains. The glow that usually enveloped her skin had become gray overnight and it seemed she was a faded version of herself.

She ran through her chambers, searching for her missing half, for Persephone, but each space was cold and empty. She raced through the fields that they had blessed together, the woods and meadows fresh with flowers and new growth, but there was no sign of the goddess. She called out Persephone's name over and over again like an otherworldly echo, but there was no answer, no words to meet her own and ease the ache within. It seemed that the virgin goddess had vanished from the Earth, for in truth Demeter could no longer sense her daughter's sweet spirit.

The other gods watched solemnly. While they might normally have taken great amusement in the plight of one of their own, Demeter's sorrow was too much for them. It cast a dark cloud upon the heavens and dampened their ardor—even the opulence of Mount Olympus could not lift it. Things on Earth were even worse. Without the magic of Demeter and her tender care, the crops began to fail, and the land struggled to sustain its harvest, for she had abandoned her role. Her head was so full of woe, she could not help her people. Weighed down with the emptiness of her loss, Demeter became almost wraith-like in her appearance, losing all substance and reason, and the environment suffered. The Sun lost its vibrance and the soil hardened, the trees shed their leaves, and the plants withered and died. Winter's cloak had at last come to the land, bringing death and decay.

Zeus addressed Demeter directly and asked what was wrong.

"Don't you see? I am nothing without my daughter, she is the most important part of me," she wailed. "It is only together that we can be as we were, composed, assured in our roles, and complete."

Zeus implored the goddess to overcome her grief. "The people need you; the land needs you. The crops are failing, and everyone will die."

"I do not care," said Demeter sadly.

"But it is what you do. You are the goddess of the grain—a reliable, practical force and the only one who can tend the Earth."

The goddess shook her head. "Not anymore. Not until I get my daughter back."

As Hades was his brother, Zeus knew perfectly well where Persephone was, but he had refused to intervene until that point. Now he realized that something must be done otherwise all of the worlds would suffer. Making his way to the Underworld, he requested an audience with Hades and, once in his company, towered above him.

"The maiden must return to her mother," he instructed, but Hades shrugged and offered a thin smile.

"You know I cannot do that. She is mine and starting to settle here."

"I am the father of the Gods," Zeus bellowed, "and I order her released!"

Hades took a step back. "Brother, I know it is your will and you are the king, but she can only return if she has not eaten any food from the Underworld."

"And has she?"

Hades grinned. "Only this morning she ate six pomegranate seeds."

Zeus bristled with anger. "Six, you say?"

Hades nodded, for he had planned it all along. He knew the rules of his realm and had tempted the goddess with an array of exotic fruits in the hope that she would partake and be tied to the Underworld forever.

Zeus frowned; he could not walk away without the goddess. Stroking his beard he thought for a moment and an idea came to him.

"Then I decree that Persephone will spend six months of every year with you, in this place, to represent the six seeds she has eaten. The remaining time she will be with her mother. That seems a fair resolution."

Hades agreed, reluctantly. While he couldn't have her permanently, at least she would be his wife for half of the year, and that would have to be enough. With an oath made between the two brothers, Persephone was allowed to emerge into the daylight once more, where her mother was waiting with open arms.

"My daughter, my other half, I have missed you so much!" Demeter cried, and together they embraced tightly, and it seemed for a moment to onlookers that the two deities merged, the edges of each blurring to form a whole, and then shimmering apart again.

The people of the land rejoiced too, for at last it seemed that the darkness of winter was lifting. The ground beneath their feet had softened almost instantly and was warming beneath the light of the Sun. A deep rumble could be felt coming from the Earth's core, an awakening as the sky brightened from charcoal gray to powder blue. And slowly, tentatively, tiny shoots began to appear, poking from between clumps of newly formed grass. Saplings stretched their fronds to meet the warmth of the Sun's rays, stems thickened, and plump buds formed. The dry soil, now velvet rich with moisture, was able to sustain new life, and the crops began to grow in an abundance. Flowers spread in every direction, to create a blanket of color more vivid than ever before, and the joyful scent of their sweetness filled the air.

"Spring has returned!" the people cried, and began to dance arm in arm. "We are saved!"

Demeter and Persephone looked on. Standing together they radiated light and a myriad of blessings, which enveloped the Earth. And while they were only able to spend half of the year together, it was enough time for both to fulfill their role, to be practical and tend to the land, to nurture and create new life, to pay attention to every detail, and ensure that all needs were met. When the time came for Persephone to return to the Underworld she did so dutifully, knowing in her heart that she would always be able to return, when it was cyclically right. Each time she left, she took with her the light, allowing winter to return and the Earth to recharge beneath a blanket of snow and shadows. Then, as the seasons changed, so Persephone would re-enter the world, greeted at first by her mother, who was always there to embrace her, and then she would be met with the praise of her people.

In honor of this diligence, a constellation in the heavens was mapped for the virgin goddess of the grain, called Virgo. The largest of the Zodiac signs, this grouping of stars shines brightly, and her appearance in the sky marks the re-emergence of Persephone as she steps from one realm into the other and brings with her the spring. As Virgo the Virgin, she is committed and willing to work the land, fostering the fruits of labor and unleashing her light so that the crops continue to grow.

VIRGO RITUAL FOR STRENGTH, MOTIVATION, AND TO CONNECT WITH THE EARTH

You will need: A couple of slices of stale bread, a bowl or bag, access to a yard or park.

This ritual, which uses wheat associated with the grain goddess, taps into the fortitude of this Star sign, and also helps you engage with the environment and feel connected to the Earth.

- To begin, take the bread and break it up into smaller pieces, into the bowl or bag.
- Continue to knead the pieces to create even smaller crumbs with your fingers. As you do this, think about the Earth and how it sustains new growth. Think about the energy of nature and how it works with the seasons, being a continual influence upon the land.
- Consider the kneading of the pieces of bread as a practical application and meditative practice to improve your focus.
- When you're ready, take the bowl or bag outside, either in your yard, or to a communal patch of land, and begin to sprinkle the contents around you in a circle.
- As you do this, think about the cyclical nature of the Earth and consider how that works in your life. Your strength and motivation will ebb and flow, but it will continue on.
- Once you have scattered the bread in a circle, sit in the center, and spend some time meditating.
- Press the palms of your hands into the Earth and feel the connection.
- Close your eyes and draw strength from the Earth. Imagine the energy flowing through your hands, up your arms, and into your chest every time that you inhale.
- As you exhale, imagine you are letting go of anything that impedes your motivation, releasing it back to the Earth.
- Continue breathing in this way for a few minutes and let the power of nature recharge and revive you.
- When you are done, collect as much of the bread as you can to dispose of at home. You can leave a few small pieces for birds or other animals.

✷ AFFIRMATION

"I am in tune with the natural world, and move with each transition."

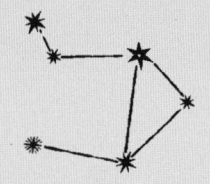

LIBRA
Lady of Good Counsel

DATES Late September to late October

CHARACTERISTICS Easy-going, balanced, fair-minded, persuasive, indecisive, charming.

ELEMENT Air

PLANET Venus

Wherever you are in the world, when you stand beneath the night sky and breathe in the silence, you can feel the gentle weight of justice upon your shoulders. The scales that measure the rights and wrongs and define what is fair and honorable hang loosely in the sky, but they are more than a pretty pattern of stars.

They are a reminder that balance is required to live a joyful, fulfilling life. They also signify that every last thought, word, and deed, can be seen in the heavens. For it is there in the sparkling cosmos that Themis, first wife of Zeus and goddess of justice and reason, would hold court. And while she might not be seen with the naked eye, that doesn't mean her presence cannot be felt, every time your conscience speaks within your soul.

Themis, and the many other deities like her, do not force their opinions upon us. Instead, they take a step back and allow our better judgment to rise to

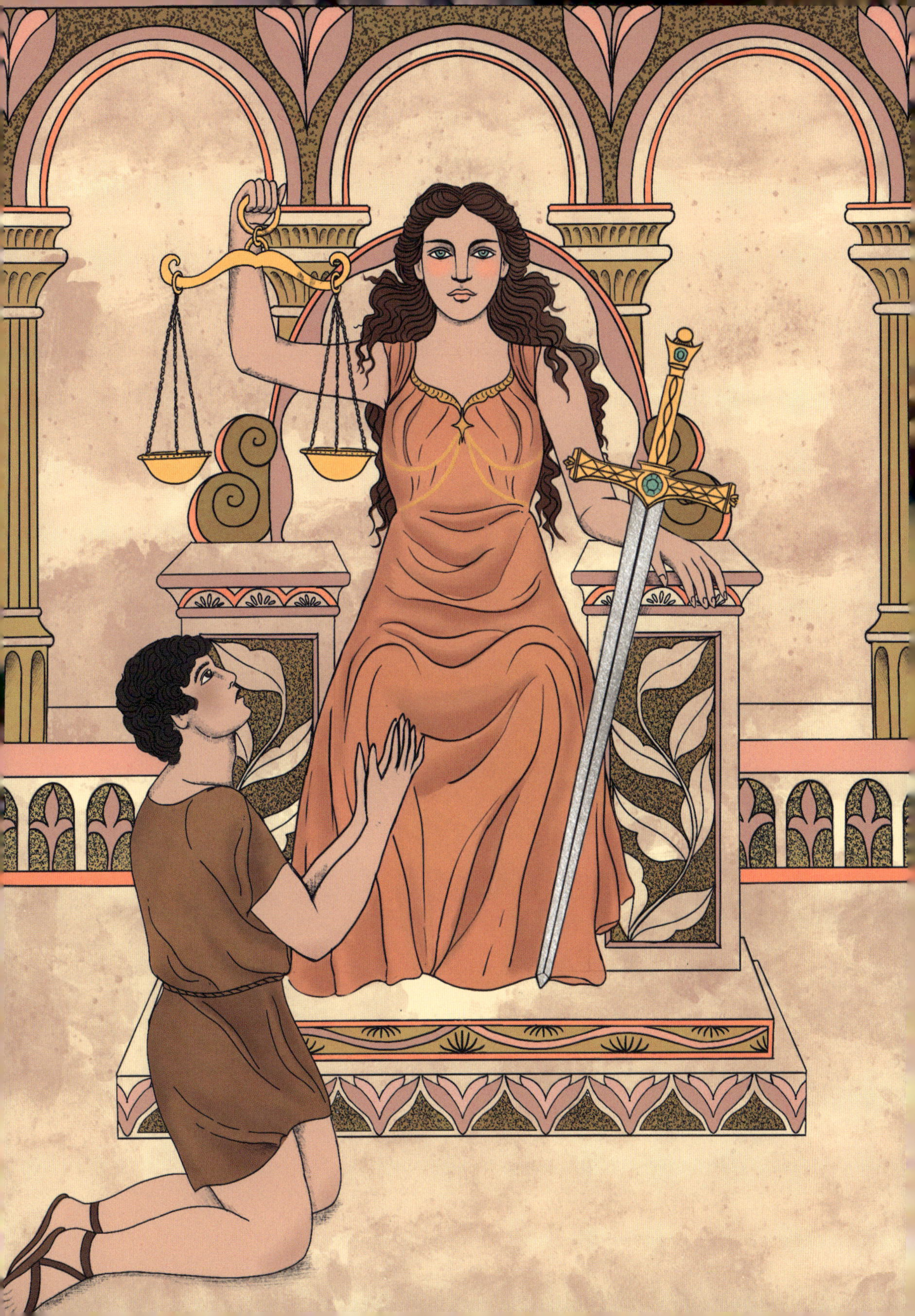

the surface. But should you need a reminder, a symbol to help you along the way, then you should look to the stars, to the constellation known as Libra, and the scales suspended in its place, for it is there you will find the answers.

Once upon a time, although in that moment time did not exist, there was a goddess so radiant she caught the eye of the king of the gods, Zeus. She was extraordinarily beautiful, but she held herself with grace, and her face shone with the light of understanding. Zeus was intrigued by such honesty, for it seemed that when she spoke, everyone listened. Her words were calm and reassuring, but they were also without judgment and, unlike the other deities, she didn't find fault, or fall prey to her innermost passions. She simply was there in the moment, present and accepting. It was only natural that Zeus should be drawn to such an authentic beauty, and so he married her. She was named Themis.

While so many of Zeus's romantic conquests were happy to slip into the shadows or stand at his side with little input into the daily doings of the people, Themis was different. She genuinely cared about the welfare of those upon Earth. Truth was at the heart of her every action, and she used it like a sword, to cut through the murky sludge of human deceit.

"I have a calling," she would say to her husband. "I must teach what I know, and share my truth with humankind."

"But we are not here to make their lives better, without their adoration. It's their job to petition us, to worship at our feet."

"Perhaps for you, my love, but for me, it is different. I must speak as I find, and I must show them the way and help them see that there are many sides in an argument. We cannot expect them to do right if they have no awareness of the primal laws of justice, or of each other. We have to give humanity a chance."

Whether Zeus entirely agreed, or just preferred to humor her and keep the peace, it's hard to tell, but he could see that his wife wasn't a woman to be silenced. Her words were meaningful, and it was one of the many things he loved about her, and so he conceded.

"If that is what you want, then I will allow it. Let the temple of Delphi be the seat of your power, and the place they visit to learn from you."

And so it was that Themis inhabited the temple at Delphi, and made it her place of worship, where she would deliver important life lessons such as reason, fairness, and the ability to listen and learn from each other. She would sit upon her marble throne, holding the Scales of Justice aloft, which was both her symbol and a way to weigh the fates of people and the choices they made. She also used her powers to deliver prophecies, and the people would call on her when they needed an insight or a vision. The Oracle of Delphi became her tool of choice—she would speak through it and gift those who asked with psychic perception.

But while Themis worked for the good of her people, many of the other gods were jealous. After all, it seemed that Zeus had given her so much, and that the people adored her for her insights.

"She speaks of fairness but has more power than any of us!" grumbled the Sun god Apollo. "Why should she be the keeper the Oracle? Wouldn't it be more fitting to give that role to the god who illuminates all life? I am the natural choice for that position."

Zeus, wanting to keep the natural order and placate the other deities, eventually decided to pass this role on to Apollo, but that didn't stop Themis from receiving petitions, or interacting with the humans. In fact, it made her more determined to keep the peace and bring balance to the Earth, and this did not go unnoticed by the rest of the pantheon.

"Why does she have to intervene so much? By being there, and teaching them the difference between right and wrong as she does, she is making herself more popular than *any* of us!" they said.

"It is simply her way," Zeus would argue. "Themis means no harm. If anything she is trying to restore balance."

"But she shows off her power, too!" they cried. "Have you not seen her wield the Sword of Truth, and cut through their lies?"

"Should they do anything wrong, she calls upon the goddess Nemesis to administer punishment."

"Surely, that is a role reserved for you as father of all!"

On it went, their petty complaints and jealousies filling the air, and giving Zeus an almighty headache. Even so, he was still enamored with his wife, and more than that, he trusted her. She had become his advisor and, because of this, he called her the Lady of Good Counsel. She tempered his ardor and helped him see things from every perspective. She also guided his morals, which were easily swayed.

"Would it not be a good idea to take a step back from humankind, now that you have opened their eyes to the rights and wrongs of the world?" he asked her one day.

But Themis gazed upon her husband's face, and whispered, "Why?"

Zeus could not answer, for in truth there was no good reason why. It was only because of the other gods and their constant moaning that he had made the suggestion. Themis, for her part, was a good wife and, in those early days, bore Zeus two sets of children. The first was the Horai, three sister deities who governed the seasons and the division of time, then the Morai, also three girls, who would be known collectively as the "fates." As their family grew, so, too, did the order of things, and the ebb and flow of time. Each sisterly grouping had a role that shaped daily life, giving it structure and movement, while also influencing the choices that humans made, and this soon reflected upon Themis, and her need for balance. After all, time and tide brings change, a change in attitude, and new feelings that surface, and so it worked that way with Zeus, for he had fallen for the goddess Hera and longed to make her his wife.

But even though Themis was swiftly replaced by Hera, Zeus could not cut ties with Themis completely. In truth he needed her, and had a great respect for the way she carried herself. Not only that, he valued her opinion more than any other of the deities, and Themis remained a trusted part of his pantheon, even though she was no longer his queen.

"Look at her," the other gods would mock, "sitting at his side, with her Scales of Justice. Does she not see how ridiculous she looks!"

But Themis ignored them. Name-calling had never bothered her and she would not let their opinions color her motives or change her morals.

When eventually it was time for the gods to retreat from their seat on Mount Olympus, when new laws and ways of being came to pass upon the Earth and the Greek pantheon no longer held a place in the hearts of humans, the gods fled in great numbers. Even the great Zeus was no more, and his closest followers and cohorts crumbled with him.

The heavens were abandoned and the once glorious palace in the clouds was an empty shell, but for one lonely deity, Themis. She remained, refusing to abandon her post, or her role in Delphi. It didn't matter that she was alone or, even worse, unwanted by the people. It seemed they had forgotten all she had taught them, and were less interested in upholding truth and harmony, preferring to take what they wanted without thought, and to live in conflict. Even so, Themis stayed to overlook events and to dispense justice and restore balance wherever she could. When she couldn't, she simply watched, prayed, and hoped that a resolution would present itself for humankind. And those who felt her presence and saw something of her dedication and strength of spirit, looked to the skies and decided to reward her steadfastness by mapping a constellation in the shape of the Scales of Justice. They positioned it in the heavens as a twinkling reminder for those on Earth, to show that balance is the key to a happy life. They called the constellation Libra, a moniker synonymous with good reason.

It is impossible to tell whether she is still there, filling the space between worlds and watching over us. Perhaps she, too, has finally fled the cosmos, or faded away over time, like the others of her kind. Perhaps she rides through the night sky, with her Sword of Truth raised in one hand, ready to dispense justice upon the Earth, her scales held high in the other, as a reminder of what is most important. And perhaps when we look within and listen to the beating of our heart and our own conscience, it is then that we find the meaning of Libra and the Lady of Good Counsel.

LIBRA RITUAL TO PROMOTE HARMONY AND BALANCE

You will need: Some space to move freely, a yoga mat, and a piece of lapis lazuli.

- Stand upon the mat with your feet hip-width apart and your weight equally balanced between both feet.
- Lower your center of gravity by bending slightly at the knees, and bounce lightly in this position, keeping your back straight and your shoulders back and relaxed. Notice how this gentle movement makes you feel, and how your body supports you.
- Lapiz lazuli has a lovely, balancing energy and is also linked to the Star sign Libra. Hold the lapis lazuli in both hands in front of you.
- Take a deep breath in and straighten your posture. Feel your spine lengthen and your chest expand.
- As you exhale, squat down so that you're bending at the knees. Keep your buttocks tucked in as much as possible and hold this position as you release your breath.
- Notice how the ground supports you and aids your balance.
- Inhale again and straighten your legs, returning to an upright posture, then repeat your downward lunge, bending at the knees and sinking as low as is comfortable for you.
- Notice how the lapis lazuli feels in your hands, and let the steadying, uplifting energy of the stone imbue you with lightness.
- Continue to repeat this cycle of breathing and notice how your balance improves each time you lunge toward the floor.
- To finish, say, "I am centered and happy."

✷ **AFFIRMATION**

"I am centered and happy."

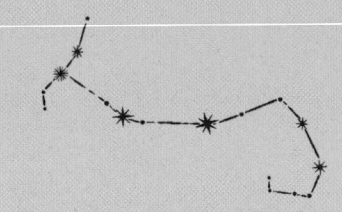

SCORPIO
The Hunter and the Hunted

DATES Late October to late November

CHARACTERISTICS Passionate, secretive, ambitious, enigmatic.

ELEMENT Water

PLANET Pluto

The Earth, also known as Gaia, mother of all, was a bountiful goddess, creating all living things, giving them shape, form, and purpose. Each voluptuous curve of her body provided sustenance, forming hills and valleys, tumbling rocky shorelines, and the sweetest scented meadows. She rose from the Earth and was a part of the Earth. In truth, she was the most beautiful being that ever existed, draped in her emerald finery, and wearing a garland of flowers around her head, but more important than that, she was generous and kind.

Every creature that walked the planet, every tiny flying insect or sleekly plumed bird, was hers, and she cared for it, lovingly watching over her creations as they lived their lives. Unlike the other gods. she didn't make a big show of her power—she didn't have to. Gaia was everywhere, and that was enough.

And so the Earth grew, and the animals thrived, and all were none the wiser to her presence, believing that their existence was simply down to fate and a need to survive. As with all things, as the creatures multiplied so, too, did their predators, some with clashing jaws and sharply slicing claws, and some in

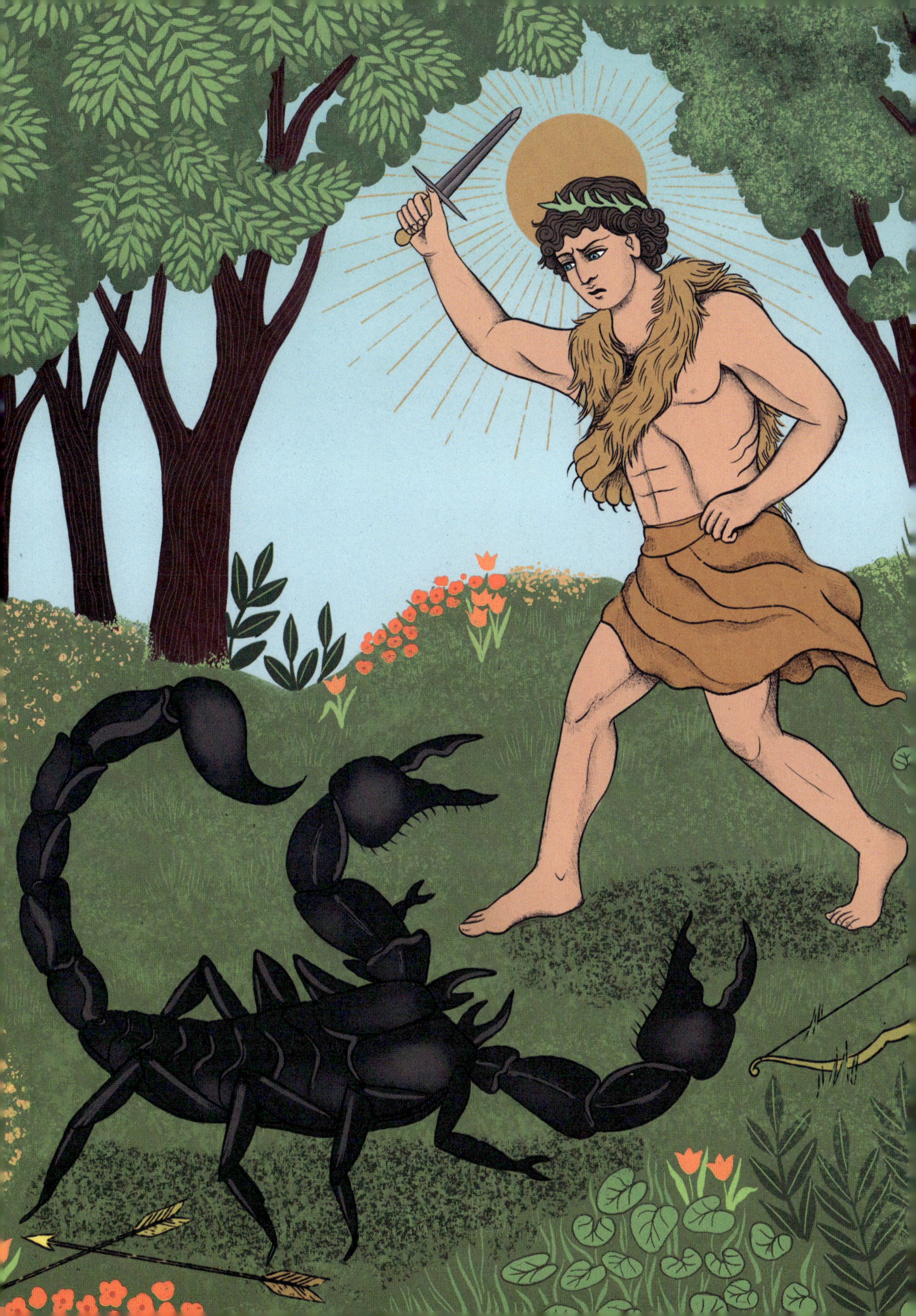

human form. Even the gods enjoyed the hunt. It brought them great joy to show off their skills, and illustrate how powerful they could be, and what better way to prove to humankind that they really were above reproach than to demonstrate their prowess against some of the fiercest creatures. From deer to bears, pheasants to boars, it was good sport and a way for them to occupy their time while keeping an eye on the people.

Artemis was by far the most gifted hunter in the Greek pantheon, and while she loved the challenge, she was not governed by bloodlust or ego, like her peers. She would hunt for what she needed, and to keep the wild creatures in check, but she was also protective and kind-hearted, believing that everything in nature had a place and a right to exist. Slight in build and boyish, but with the gentle curls of youth and bright eyes, she was fast and nimble and a match for any of the gods, and soon became bored of their hunting parties.

"Is there no one in the Universe who can best me, or at least match me in agility and skill?" she would laugh. And, of course, she was always met with silence, for there was no other like her. Until one day, her call was answered by the giant, Orion. His voice bellowed through the heavens.

"I am your equal," he said, "I can beat your kills easily."

"Big words from a big man," she grinned. "I accept your challenge."

The giant laughed. "This is going to be fun. You may be a goddess, but I am the best hunter in the world."

"We shall see," she beamed.

And so it was that Orion and Artemis became firm friends, and partners in the hunt, for it was true that they were equally matched when it came to skill and athleticism. Artemis adored the fact that Orion could keep up with her, that his large strides would power through the undergrowth, and keep time with her brisk pace. She loved that he would challenge her, and that they would keep count of their kills together, buoying each other onward. In return, Orion loved her company. He was more than a little enamored with the goddess, but also impressed by her strength and vigor. They would set daily targets and encouraged each other to excel in every way. It was a dynamic relationship, and one that worked for a while. But as with all things, change is inevitable and what started out as friendly competition became more aggressive over time.

Artemis valued the wild creatures. She enjoyed running with them in the woods, and learning their ways. She would not kill without good reason, but for Orion it was all about winning.

"I could slaughter every animal within these woods, I am sure of it."

Artemis frowned. "And what would be the point in that? We do not need to do that for sport. Do we not have fun and adventures together, and isn't that what it's all about? The freedom of nature, of feeling the Earth beneath our feet, and running with the wind?"

"Perhaps, but I am growing tired of doing the same thing, of sticking to small numbers, and culling. I want a challenge, something worthy of me."

"It will not make you more of a man," Artemis sneered.

"I am man enough," Orion gloated, "I do not need to prove myself to you." He paused then. "I am sure, if I set my mind to it I could hunt and kill every animal upon this Earth. Imagine that! What an achievement that would be."

Artemis frowned. "That would be a big mistake. You cannot do that Orion, you will destroy the Earth."

"I do not care about the Earth, and anyway the gods will simply magic up more creatures. No harm done."

"No!" Artemis cried, but it was too late. Orion had disappeared deeper into the forest, and while she could easily have caught up with him, she no longer wanted to. Her heart was full of fear for the land and the wild things that lived upon it. She knew that Orion's words were tinged with truth, and that he was a threat to the world around them. And so did Gaia, for she had been listening.

Rising from her slumber beneath the Earth, she smoothed her lush green skirts and shook her golden locks, scattering petals and moss in every direction. She cast her eye over the planet, from the wooded places to the dry and barren deserts and the brittle rocky outcrops that seemed to reach to the heavens—so many different landscapes, and all home to an array of creatures.

"No more," she said defiantly, her glare fixed upon Artemis. "He will take no more from this Earth." And then with a twist of her slender fingertips, she pulled an enormous, monstrous creature out of thin air. It was a scorpion, with gigantic spider legs, a large swarthy body that rippled as it moved, and huge crablike pincers that snapped and clicked hungrily. Its tail, long and segmented, curled over its body, the stinger poised to attack.

Artemis took a step back in horror, but Gaia simply smiled and softened her gaze. "Do not be afraid, it means you no harm. It is a creature like any other—clever, feisty, and honorable too, for it protects the Earth under my instruction. But should it be crossed, betrayed, or attacked by another, then you will feel the deadly sting of its tail."

Together they watched as the scorpion moved with ease, its company of legs carrying it speedily to its destination. Once in front of the giant Orion, it came to a halt, presenting itself to the great hunter. Orion, for his part, was bemused, and a little in awe of the beast.

"What manner of ghastly creature are you?" he asked, stroking his beard. "Never mind, as wretched as you are, you will do for my first kill today!"

Unsheathing an arrow, he took aim and fired, but the pointed end seemed to bounce off the shell-like surface of the scorpion. Its skin was thick, but its heart was as fragile a butterfly's wing, and as easily hurt by harsh words as sharp arrowheads. The scorpion lunged forward, raising its magnificent tail, ready to attack. And while Orion fired again and again, even charging with his trusty dagger in a last-ditch attempt at slaughter, it was too late. The tail thrashed down, knocking Orion off his feet. The stinger pierced his flesh, and the poison sank deep into the heart of the hunter. Within seconds he had withered to a husk upon the ground.

"Orion!" Artemis gasped, but it was too late. He had fallen, there was nothing to be done.

The scorpion, though still in one piece, bore the injuries of Orion's attack, and began to retreat. Forever faithful, he searched for the safety and familiarity of his mistress Gaia and collapsed at her feet.

"There, there," she whispered stroking the wounded creature. "Despite your hard exterior, you feel things keenly, don't you? I will soothe you of your pain, and honor you, as you have honored me by serving with passion and dedication."

With that she cast its lifeless body up into the heavens, and there it sparkled as the many patterned constellation Scorpio, a reminder to all who would gaze at the night sky of the value of the Earth and all its beautiful creatures.

Artemis stared at the twinkling image of the scorpion, and how it lit up the darkness. "It is a fitting tribute to the hunted, but what about the hunter?" She turned then and called upon the father of the gods, Zeus. "Father, hear my plea, for though Orion was bested by the beast and rightly so, he was a good man at heart, and an outstanding hunter."

Zeus looked down upon Artemis and the scene before him from his throne enshrouded by clouds. He had been watching the events unfold with great interest. It was true that Orion was an exceptional hunter, and a friend of the gods, and he hadn't always been so bloodthirsty. He had died doing something he loved, and while fate, and the goddess Gaia, had decided his end, the least he could do was celebrate the giant of a man Orion had once been.

Waving his hand in a sweeping motion over the Earth, he muttered some words in ancient tongue, and slowly the body of Orion began to transform. The bulk of his enormous frame glistened, becoming almost translucent. The weight of his body seemed to evaporate, replaced by a scattering of stars that together held his shape. Gently he began to rise into the sky, twisting and turning, until eventually he found his place in the blanket of darkness that had now settled. Orion the hunter, a constellation so bright that it was possible to see him most nights, prowling the cosmos.

Artemis and Gaia looked on, and then took a moment to acknowledge each other, before the younger of the two disappeared into the dense woodland. Gaia stood a minute longer. Breathing deeply, she caressed the Earth, the mound of her belly and the folds of her flowing garments. She gave thanks for all she had created, for the flora and fauna, from the tiniest to the greatest, and then she sank back into the Earth, reclining with a deep sigh of satisfaction that all was well once more.

SCORPIO RITUAL TO MOTIVATE AND INSPIRE YOU TO FOLLOW YOUR HEART

You will need: A piece of either yellow topaz or citrine, a glass, and some fresh water.

This ritual works with the passionate energy of Scorpio, by connecting with the stones associated with this sign. It will help you channel your emotions and promote focus and determination to make your dreams come true.

- Yellow topaz is associated with ancient wisdom and, like citrine, has a high energy vibration. Both stones generate positive energy and will help you manifest your wishes. Place the stone of your choice in the bottom of the glass and cover with the water.
- Half fill the glass and then place it in the fridge to chill overnight.
- In the morning, retrieve the water and remove the stone from the glass.
- Hold the stone in your left hand, which is linked to your heart, and close your eyes. Ask the following question: "What do I want the most right now?"
- Relax, breathe, and let thoughts and feelings rise to the surface.
- Don't try and force anything—just be aware of any ideas, or thoughts that seem to stand out. Breathe into them, and really feel what it will be like to make this happen.
- Add the stone-infused water to a bowl, or a sink. Dip your hands in it or use it to refresh your face and neck by splashing it upon the skin. As you do this, focus on what you want to create and how you want to feel.
- To finish, say, "I embrace my inner desires, and work toward making my dreams a reality."

✵ AFFIRMATION

"I live with passion and follow my heart in all things."

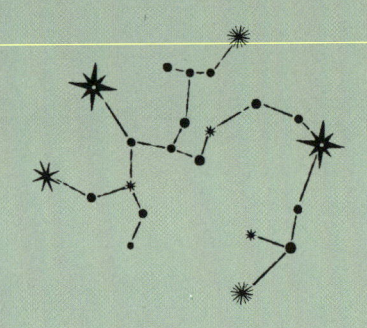

SAGITTARIUS
The Starry Steed

DATES Late November to late December

CHARACTERISTICS Adventurous, freedom-loving, spontaneous, fickle, playful.

ELEMENT Fire

PLANET Jupiter

The ancient world was full of mystical beings, creatures that might never have seen the light of day but for the imagination of the gods, and some hybrid parenting. Among the plethora of beasts, one was wilder than most, but this was hardly surprising when you considered his makers.

Being the son of the Greek god Pan, and the Naiad nymph Eupheme, his heritage was tempestuous. Nature in all its riotous beauty flowed through his veins. His father Pan was a notorious rebel rouser, who liked to express himself through music and celebration. A being synonymous with fertility, and a lover of pleasure, Pan was spontaneous. He could not be tamed by rules and had no need for other luxuries. He ran free through the forests, and that's where he happened upon Eupheme, nurse to the Muses, and a kind-hearted nymph. She embodied most of the qualities Pan lacked. Taking time and care to look after her charges, she was responsible and diligent. It seemed that they were polar opposites and yet the attraction between them was strong. Together they formed a union, which, while it did not last, was enough to conceive a child, a boy called Crotus.

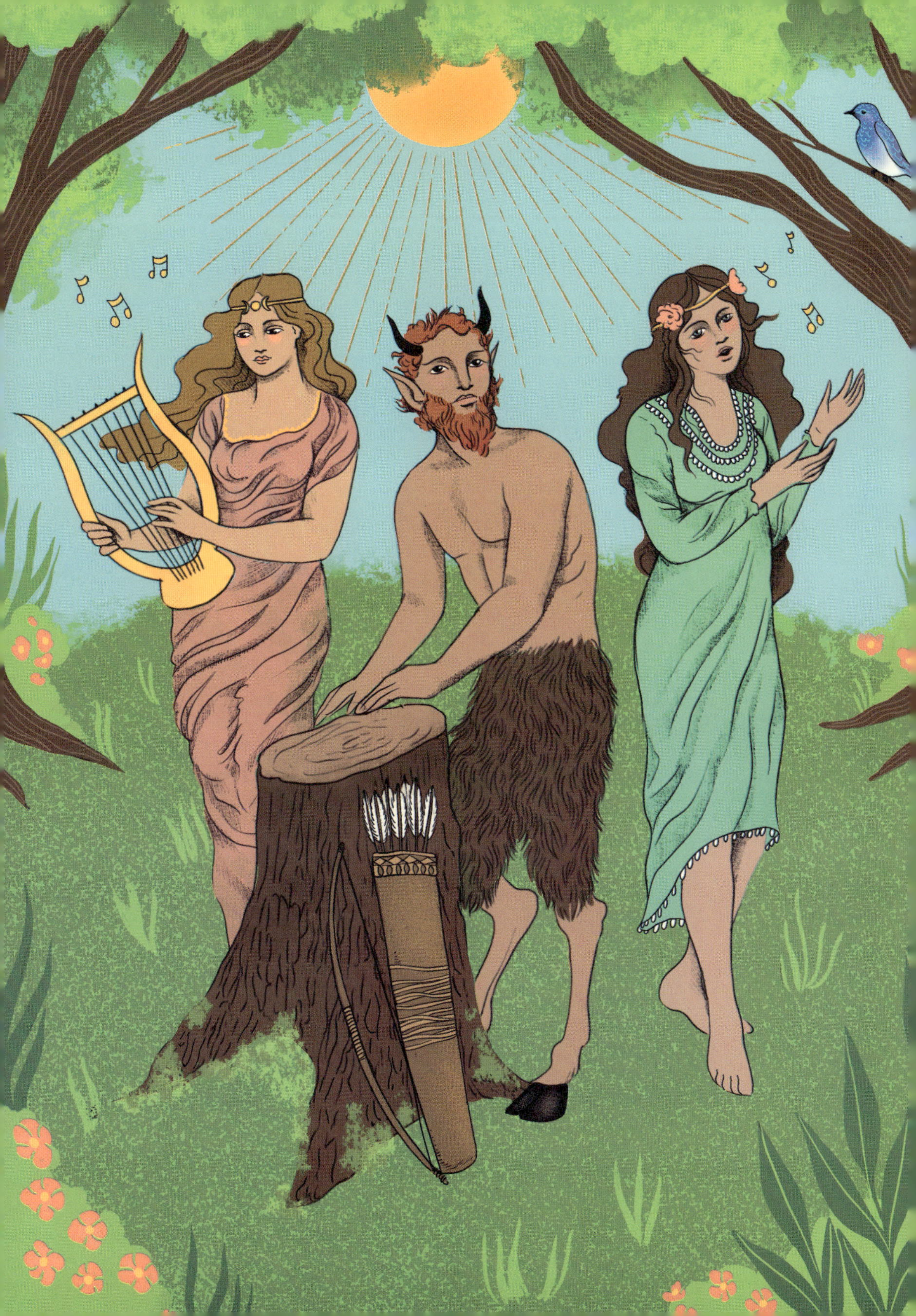

Like his father, he was a satyr. The upper part of his body was like a man, but he had goat legs and cloven hoofs that were sturdy and more than capable of carrying him through the unkempt undergrowth. And there was nothing Crotus liked more than to forage in the woodland. Immersing himself in nature, he embraced his wild spirit, and while he loved the freedom of the hunt and being able to escape into the deepest, darkest parts of the forest, he also enjoyed the company of the Muses whom his mother nursed. They were different to any of the other children of the gods. Their energy was ethereal and timeless, and in their presence he felt inspired.

In truth, Crotus was a little in love with these beautiful beings and, as he grew to adulthood, he spent as much time as he could with them. Each one had their own gift, whether it was music, words, poetry, or new ideas—being with them all together, it felt like he could explore each gift to the fullest. When he'd had enough of indulging his creative side, he would take to the woods with gusto, leaping over tree roots and galloping at speed. He would run with the deer, and tussle with the wild boars. He would climb the tallest trees, and sit with his head in the stars, listening to the owls hooting. He would prowl through the foliage, belly to the floor so that he could hear the rustling of the night creatures going about their business. And he would hunt, not for fun, but to survive and be at one with the land, and it was this that he excelled in.

Crotus was a gifted hunter because he understood nature. Rather than setting himself apart from it like the gods and mortals, he was feral in his ways, and knew the rhythms of the natural world. He also knew that hunting with his own hands seemed barbaric, and was not a swift resolution for the animal in his sights, and this bothered him greatly. He would ponder the problem and consider how there might be a different way to hunt without unnecessary suffering. Unlike Pan, he had a conscience and had inherited his mother's sensitivity, even if he didn't show it on the surface. And so he called upon his friends the Muses and spent time in their company upon Mount Helicon. He let them feed him berries and serve him wine, and in return he listened to their chatter and let their gentle voices unlock his imagination. It was then he came up with an idea for a hunting tool, something that would aid him but cause less distress to his prey. The invention could be fashioned out of wood and yarn and used to propel a weapon through the air.

"I shall call it a bow and arrow," he said triumphantly, "and it will serve me, and others like me, well."

The Muses were impressed, for while they visited many and tried to impart their gift of inspiration, few seemed to be open to their powers, and most didn't appreciate what they had done for them. Crotus was different. Unlike the mortals, who took their gifts for granted, and the gods, who believed they were above them, he acknowledged their part in every decision he made and their influence in his life. This, in turn, meant their admiration for him increased and, by way of recompense, his talents grew.

Soon Crotus developed a flair for music. He loved to play the lyre and to sing, and he would sit in a coppice of trees and create magical melodies to match those of the birds that peeped from the branches. Sometimes words were his gift, and he would compose the sweetest poetry, speaking from the heart, and reciting his verse for the rest of the Muses to enjoy. Sometimes he would make things, using the gifts of nature that he found scattered around the forest floor. And always he would be true to himself and his whims, finding freedom in expression and acknowledging his wild side.

The other gods looked on from their seat in the clouds, and they sneered. They failed to understand the attraction of spending so much time in the woods, with the Muses.

"Why does he not want to enjoy the fruits of his heritage? He is part god, after all!" they would say. "He could be sitting here on Mount Olympus with us instead of running with the wild things."

But Crotus would not conform to their ways. He didn't need their approval—he wanted to be independent and make his own decisions.

"What is he doing down there?"

"What value does he bring to the world?"

"Why is he not like us?"

The gods grumbled on, until eventually Zeus decided to see for himself what all the fuss was about.

Sneaking down to Earth in the guise of a songbird, he flitted between the trees in search of Crotus and his Muses. Drawn by a slither of sound that curled upon the breeze, he found himself in a small clearing, watching the satyr and the Muses perform. The music they made was so enchanting he almost fell off the branch he was perched upon. It seemed that Crotus had managed to capture the essence of nature and harness the underlying beat of the forest as he tapped out a rhythm to accompany the Muse's song. The beat had no pattern, and yet it stirred something deep within the Earth.

Zeus watched as Crotus continued to drum with his hands, picking up tempo and volume, and then gradually slowing things down, until the last of the Muses stopped singing. In that moment of silence Zeus felt obliged to say something, to make them aware of his presence, but before he could transform, Crotus stood, bowed to the Muses and began to do something he had never seen before. With his bare hands, he clapped, bringing them together in a hard, slapping sound, over and over again. He clapped, and he clapped, with a big grin upon his face.

"I applaud you!" he said, to which the Muses clapped back to show their appreciation.

"What manner of magic is this?" Zeus asked, stepping from the shadows in his godly form.

Crotus looked then at the god but didn't seem surprised that he was there. He shrugged, "It is my way of giving thanks, of saying I like what you have done, you have made me happy."

Zeus smiled. "I see. Well I like it very much." And he began to clap along. "What do you call this?" he asked.

Crotus looked at the Muses, and then back at Zeus and smiled. "We call it the gift of applause."

"Then let applause be a thing. From this moment on we shall all applaud when we are happy." And with that he left Crotus and the Muses to continue making music together.

The other gods couldn't wait to hear what Zeus had to say on his return. They gathered together in the great hall, laughing and muttering, for they were sure the god would be enraged by what he had seen.

"Is he as ridiculous as he looks? Are you going to smite him for being useless, or at least punish him for not following the rules?" they asked.

Zeus was quiet for a moment and then, standing, he looked at each one in turn. "Actually, I am going to applaud him for doing what he loves and doing it well, for not following the crowd, and being true to his own heart." And he began to clap loudly.

The deities gasped and looked at each other. They felt sure that Zeus had lost his mind, that he had been infected by Crotus's feral ways. Even so, after a time they followed suit and began to clap their hands—for what else was there to do?

Crotus, unaware of the confusion he'd caused in the heavens, continued to roam free and embrace his gifts. He was an exceptional hunter, a great musician, and well-loved by mortals, animals, and the Muses. When the day finally came for him to take his last breath and move on to the next life, he was sad to be leaving his Earthly family behind. He was such an integral part of nature, and he loved the freedom that this gave him, but he also knew that his time on Earth had come to an end.

The Muses were heartbroken. Although they had enhanced his gifts, he had given them so much in return, not least a way to praise them and give thanks, and so they decided to petition Zeus on his behalf.

"We must not let the mortals forget him, or what he has done," they said. "He is well-loved for his adventurous spirit, his sense of fun, and for his skill as a hunter."

Zeus agreed. He had a soft spot for the satyr despite what his peers thought. It seemed that in following his own path, Crotus had managed to balance the wildness of his father with the kindness of his mother and create a legacy of goodwill that impressed the god greatly. And so, as he had done with many others who had made their mark, he placed Crotus in the sky as a twinkling constellation, but he made some changes to the satyr's appearance. He gave him the hind quarters of a horse to denote his strength and speed while hunting, and placed his beloved bow and arrow in his hands.

When he finished, he stood back to admire the bright pattern of the stars.

"There you are, for all to see! Sagittarius the Hunter and now a starry steed, may the world applaud your good nature and may you continue to roam free through the heavens!"

SAGITTARIUS RITUAL TO PROMOTE SPONTANEITY AND HELP YOU BROADEN YOUR HORIZONS

You will need: Three drops of bergamot essential oil, an oil burner or a small bowl of hot water, some of your favorite upbeat music, and some space to move freely.

This ritual connects with the vibrant energy of this Star sign, allowing you to step outside your comfort zone in a safe space and have some fun. It uses movement, rhythm, and music to help you harness the power of Sagittarius.

- To begin, add three drops of the bergamot oil to your oil burner or bowl of hot water. This invigorating scent captures the energy and enthusiasm of Sagittarius.
- Close your eyes and inhale the sweet aroma, letting it lift your spirits.
- Play your favorite dance track, making sure to choose something that makes you want to tap your feet.
- Clear a space on the floor and begin to move. Don't worry too much about your steps, or what you're doing. It doesn't matter how you look. This is about feeling the rhythm of the music and going with it.
- If it helps, close your eyes and just sway in time with the music. Let it lead you away, and see what thoughts arise.
- Imagine the spotlight is solely on you, and that you can do anything you want. Lose yourself in the beat and just enjoy yourself.
- This ritual is about tapping into your passion, and allowing yourself to let go and do what feels right for you.
- When the track has finished, wind down by slowing your movements until you reach a standstill.
- Place your hands upon your heart, take a deep breath in and, as you exhale, say with confidence, "I allow my spontaneity to flow, I embrace new adventures!"

✴ **AFFIRMATION**

"I allow my spontaneity to flow and I embrace new adventures!"

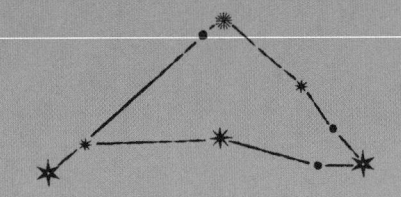

CAPRICORN
Father of Souls

DATES Late December to late January

CHARACTERISTICS Honest, responsible, pessimistic, logical, focused.

ELEMENT Earth

PLANET Saturn

When the world was first created and the sea began to flow, a new kingdom sprang to life. This underwater world was a vibrant, fluid space where many creatures thrived. Vast azure chasms that sparkled and appeared to move with each breath were threaded in between cavernous chambers littered with an array of treasure.

Billowing seaweed raised its frothy tendrils to praise the Sun, giving thanks for the gentle rays that filtered through the inky depths. Pretty shells danced among the coral, while an assortment of silky finned fish sought refuge in the ever-expanding reefs. Sometimes larger creatures appeared, floating into unknown territory, often lost or seeking sanctuary in the emerald depths. Each new being brought a different kind of light and their own magic to this dazzling realm. It was a kingdom fit for a king, and while the gods languished in Olympus, little did they realize what glories lay beneath the waves.

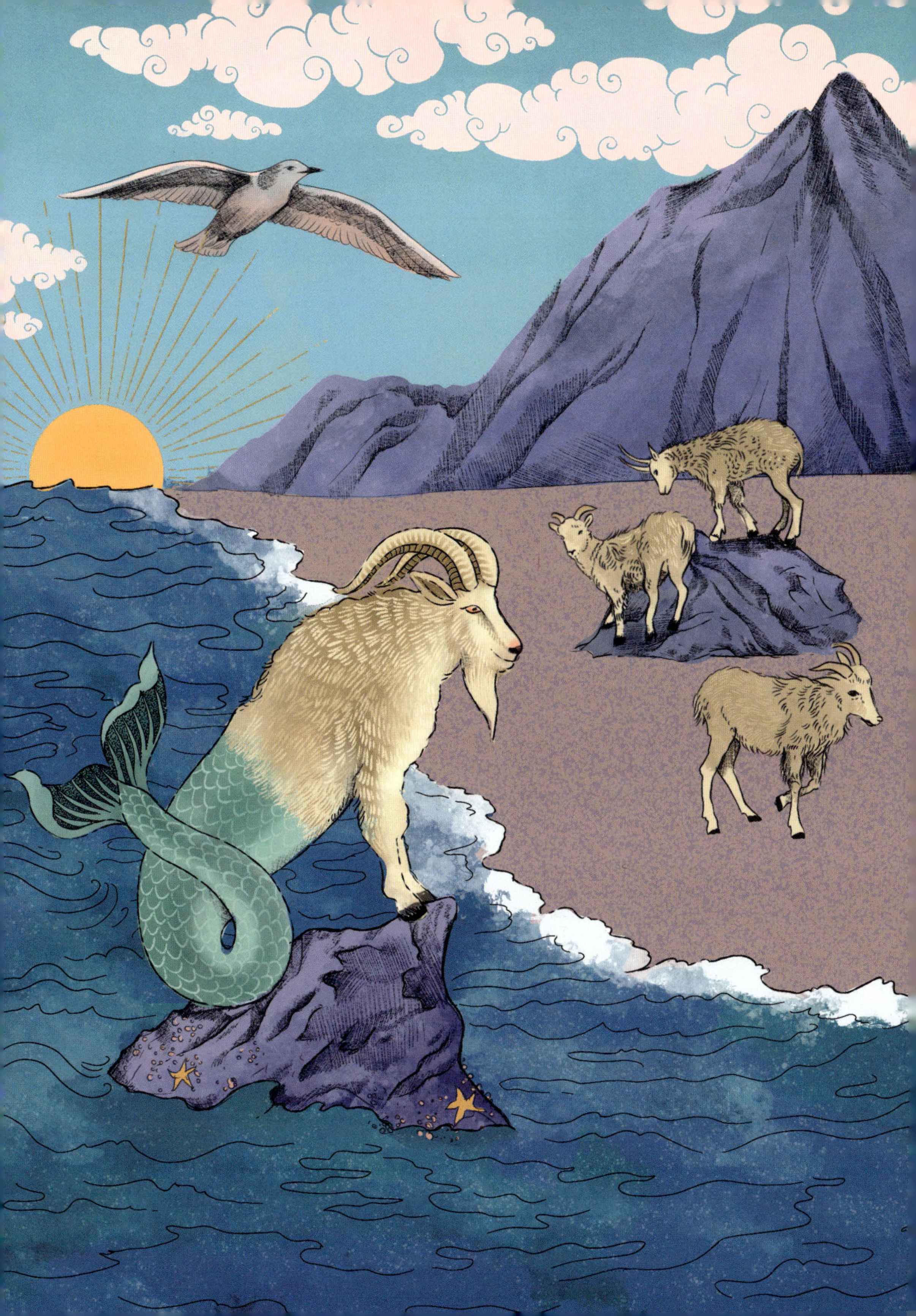

Within this domain there lived one who had taken on the role of leader, bringing order and structure to the subterranean world. He was a strange creature by all accounts, for he was made of the Earth but able to breathe in the water, and this made him unique. His name was Pricus and he was the father of the sea goats, and a master of time, for he had the power to control the way it moved. From the waist up he looked like a mountain goat, with swarthy thick fur, a slender muzzle, and horns that curled outward from his furrowed brow, but where his back legs should have been, there grew a glimmering fish tail that he used to navigate the ocean.

Able to swim with the dolphins by the coast of Crete, and cover large stretches of the Mediterranean, Pricus loved the water. Although he was a beast of the land, the sea gave him respite and time to think. It was a space where he could lay and ponder, and there was nothing the goat loved more than to think deeply on matters close to his heart and formulate plans. Not only that, but Pricus and his kin could converse as humans, another talent that seemed to be part of his magical heritage and a gift from the gods.

Despite the freedom that his powers gave him, Pricus knew there were certain rules he had to follow. If he ever wandered too far from the sea shore, then he might lose his gifts forever, but this had never bothered him. Pricus was a creature of habit who loved the benefits of routine and the stability that this provided, and he wanted to ensure that his family would always have everything they needed. He knew that being born from land and sea was a great honor. Unlike other animals, he would always have two homes, and be able to flit between them. If there was danger on land he sought the sanctuary of the sea, and should a watery predator such as a shark attack, he would always be able to escape on foot. He also knew, however, that too much time upon land could ultimately end things, for his fish tail only had a certain amount of magic to sustain it. Pricus made sure that his hundreds of sea goat offspring were aware of this, but his lectures often fell upon deaf ears. His children listened, but didn't really hear the true message their father had for them. While his words were full of authority, there was little love and understanding of their needs, and it seemed like he was giving out orders.

"He just doesn't want us to have any fun!" one of the older ones cried. "He thinks he can boss us around, but there's more to life than rules. There's a whole new world out there. We should sneak to shore one morning and explore!" he suggested, and his siblings agreed, for what could be more exciting than a secret adventure?

And so it was that Pricus's brood ventured onto the sandy beach without him knowing. Under the baking heat of the Sun their fish tails slowly dried out to reveal spindly back legs with hooves. While they were shaky at first, they soon began to master their land legs and enjoy the grainy feel of the sand against their fur.

"What a brilliant idea this was!" they squealed, as they rolled upon the damp land, and wandered further afield. "We should stay here, there is so much to see and do!" they agreed, and as time moved on, the day stretched into the evening and the young sea goats still had not returned to the ocean.

Pricus was beside himself with worry. Where could his children be? They knew the routine and what was expected of them. They should have been tucked up in their sea beds. As he traversed the tumbling waves, growing more anxious, a seagull happened to fly by, and call out his name.

"Your children have left you; they are on the beach having lots of fun!" it cawed.

Pricus cried out in rage. How could they do this to him? They knew the dangers, but it had not stopped them. Forever practical, he set a plan to get his children back, for while he couldn't control them, he could ask the god Zeus to assist him and appeal to reason.

"They need to realize what could happen if they keep doing this," he said to the god.

Zeus replied, "I know what to do. Tell them if they do it again, they will no longer be able to return to the sea. There will be no more chances. If they stray from the beach and disobey your orders, they will lose their tails for good, and all of the magical benefits I have given them."

"I have told them this many times," said Pricus.

"But this time is different. If they wander away from the shore, then my threat becomes a promise."

And so Pricus made his way to the beach and waited for his children to return. He knew that eventually they would seek the security of their watery home, and it was then that he warned them of Zeus's threat. The children, now tired from their exploits, lowered their heads, and followed their father back into the sea. Whether they fully understood the implications of Zeus's promise and the weight of their father's concern is highly doubtful, because two days after their original foray, they decided to escape again.

This time, they went even further and for longer, scrambling beyond the beach and up into the rocky outcrops. They gathered in a cluster and surveyed the sea.

"What a view!" they cried as they looked down and watched the waves crashing against the shore.

"This is surely the kingdom of the gods!" one of them yelled, and his voice echoed upon the wind.

"It is. . . ." another replied. "It's. . . ."

For a moment all that could be heard was a weird, muffled cry of anguish and, as the other goats tried to join in to ask what was wrong, they, too, struggled. It seemed that their words were being choked down, swallowed by air and secreted away. The only sound to be heard was a strangled bleating that rattled in their throats.

Panicking, the young goats staggered to the sea, waiting for their legs to transform, and their scaly tails to return, but the change that usually occurred when they hit the water didn't come. Again they tried, rushing into the waves, bleating their prayers to the heavens, but nothing worked. The gifts they had been given from the gods were nothing but a memory.

Eventually they returned to the mountains where they had lost their voices, in the hope that the setting was key to their salvation. Believing at least that they were closer to the gods, they tried to raise their voices, to beg for their father's forgiveness and a chance to follow the rules he had set so diligently. But nothing could be done. Without their sea tails they were now solely creatures of the Earth and would need to learn the ways of the land and become mountain goats.

Pricus was devastated. He knew what had happened and realized that even without Zeus's threat they would have continued to rebel, to seek freedom and a life away from him. Even so, he tried to intervene, using his power over time to return to the moment when his young were still sea bound. Once more he urged them to behave, to listen to what he was saying. He told them in no uncertain terms what would happen if they disobeyed, how they would become mortal mountain goats and lose their powers for good, but it mattered not. His young were unable to remember what had happened the last time and could not be tamed. They did exactly the same thing again, fleeing to the mountains in the belief that they knew best and, just as before, they lost their gifts.

"You cannot change their hearts and minds," Zeus said softly. "You cannot keep turning back time, in the hope they will learn. It will never happen."

Pricus agreed. He knew there was nothing he could do and that he had lost his family, and although he was heartbroken, he also knew that he needed to be practical.

"I cannot live without them," he said sadly. "I cannot turn back time again, and I cannot change them either. There is nothing for me here in the ocean or on land. I no longer wish to live."

Zeus sighed. "You are immortal Pricus, that is a part of your gift. You cannot die."

"But I cannot go on either. If I can't be their father, what am I to do?"

Zeus turned his face to the heavens and thought for a moment. "I shall make you a father of souls instead. You will be a gateway in the sky, which those who have departed the Earthly realm must pass through to reach the other world. It will be your job to soothe their souls, and give them the strength they need to move on to the next realm."

He paused then. "You will remain there forever, as a reminder of the value of rules, structure, and order."

With that he flicked his fingers, and Pricus became a being made of starlight, a twinkling vessel, and the constellation known as Capricorn the Horned Goat. Placed high in the heavens, he was formed of five stars that shone brightly to mark his mythical status as a master of time and the father of souls.

CAPRICORN RITUAL TO PROMOTE CLARITY AND FOCUS

You will need: Rosemary essential oil, a small bowl of hot water, a towel, and access to some space outside.

This ritual combines the Earthy practical elements of Capricorn with the watery influence of the original myth in order to bring clarity and strengthen the mind.

- Find a spot where you can sit in comfort outside and you won't be disturbed, ideally on the ground so that you are close to the Earth.
- Half fill the bowl with the hot water and add in several drops of rosemary essential oil. Rosemary is an invigorating scent that helps to strengthen focus and bring clarity. Coupled with the fluid element of water, it will help to rejuvenate your mind.
- Place the bowl in front of you and lean over.
- Cover your head with the towel, to help you focus solely on the scent.
- Inhale deeply and let the vibrant fragrance infuse you and alleviate any fatigue.
- As you exhale, imagine that you are purging your mind of any clutter, letting the debris slip away with each breath. Picture it being absorbed by the Earth, where it can be transformed into positive energy.
- Continue to breathe in this way for at least five minutes.
- If you find your mind is wandering as you do this, try and bring your focus back to your breathing and the aroma of the rosemary. Imagine it enveloping you in a cloak of stars and see them twinkling brightly.
- When you've finished, stand up and give your body a shake to get the energy moving again.

✳ AFFIRMATION

"Every breath I take imbues me with clarity."

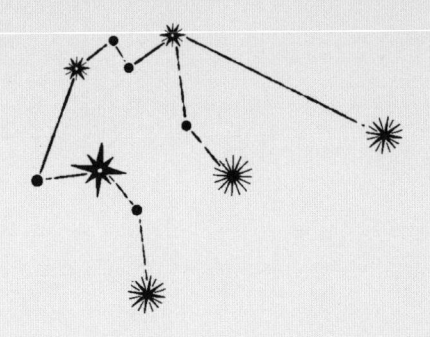

AQUARIUS
The Cup Bearer

DATES Late January to late February

CHARACTERISTICS Independent, intelligent, inventive, friendly, attentive, truthful, assertive.

ELEMENT Air

PLANET Uranus

The Greek god Zeus was many things during his reign. Father of the gods, carrier of thunderbolts, wielder of lightning, and a lover of deities and mortals. As such, he was considered the strongest of them all, for who could compete with his exploits? But he did have a weakness, a compulsion that could often lead him into trouble.

Zeus craved beauty in all its forms. He loved to surround himself with pretty things, from objects and trinkets to jewels from the four corners of the globe. Most of all, he coveted being around beautiful people. He considered them to be of a higher standing because of the way they looked and, as superficial as that was, he didn't care. Zeus enjoyed luxury, and, to him, a handsome face and a winsome smile was by far the most expensive treasure.

It didn't matter what it was, or how hard it was to obtain, once Zeus had set his mind on something or someone, he would do everything in his godly power to attain it. Once claimed, it would take its rightful place in his chambers, whether as a prized possession, a unique relic, or to serve him as one of his many nymphs and pleasures. Zeus was a collector

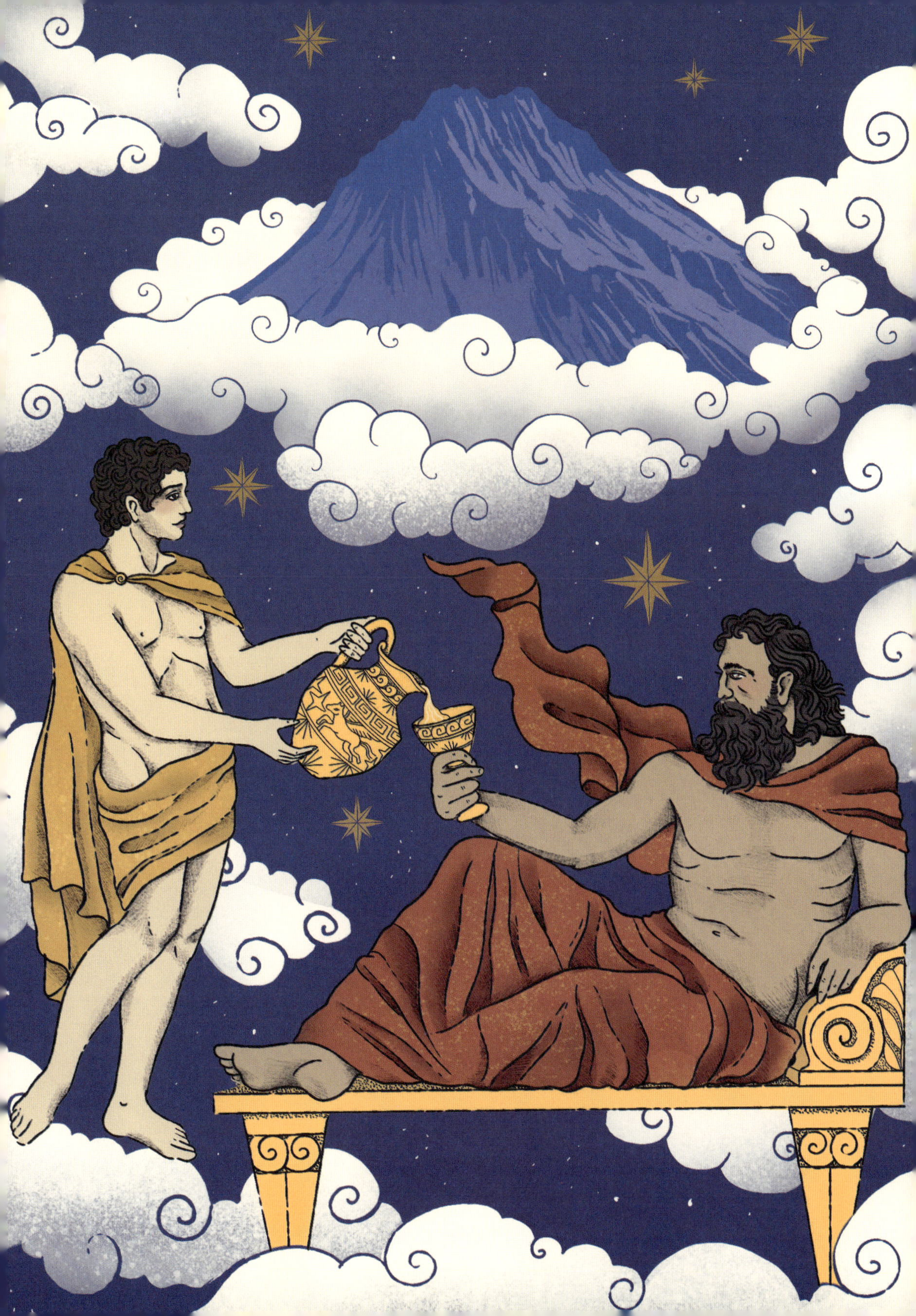

and had an appetite for taking things that weren't his. He saw it as a divine gift, for what purpose was there in being the leader of all, if you couldn't have some fun along the way?

And so, when he saw the young Trojan prince, son of Tros of Dardania, herding sheep high on a mountain one day, he knew that he had to have him. While he had seen many impressive mortals, there was something distinctly different about this one. The young man, called Ganymede, had a gentle way about him, a nurturing essence that could be seen in the way he tended his flock. It was as if he was created to serve and this made Zeus smile, for he had the ideal role for him. Not only was Ganymede fair of face, with sparkling blue eyes and a smile that lit up the heavens, he also had dark hair that curled about his handsome features, framing them like a picture. Zeus was instantly beguiled.

"How can this young man stir so many feelings within me?" he pondered.

It seemed to him that the prince was his ideal match, and that he would happily spend many days finding the key to his heart. But how to attract his attention in the first place?

Zeus knew he could take Ganymede if he wished. It would be easy—after all, who could fight the king of the gods? But force seemed the wrong approach for one so tender. It would only steal the sweet smile from his face, and that would not do. Zeus wanted Ganymede to be happy, to radiate the same warmth in his company that he did when addressing his sheep.

"Of course!" the god cried out. "I have the answer!"

The prince loved nature and had a natural connection with the land and all its creatures, and so it made sense that Zeus should use this to his advantage, and so he transformed, shifting from a hulking, god-like man into something equally as mighty.

"Let the king of the gods be the king of the birds!" he yelled, as his flesh became feathers, and his mouth a magnificent, hooked beak.

Swooping down from Mount Olympus, he circled the young man's head, just high enough to let him see his extraordinary wing span, then when the prince seemed fully enchanted by the display, he landed a stone's throw away on the mountain top.

Ganymede was astounded. He had never seen a golden eagle in such proximity, and this one seemed strangely inquisitive.

"What manner of angel are you?" he gasped, as the bird settled and then extended its wings.

"Look how you shimmer in the sunlight!" he said, taking a step closer.

He expected the bird to lift from its perch as he approached, but it remained. Their gazes locked, and it seemed in that moment that some kind of magic was afoot, for Ganymede's head felt light and his legs buckled beneath him.

"What are you?" he whispered, as he fell to the ground.

The eagle didn't answer. Instead it wrapped its vast wings around the young man like a cloak and scooped him up with muscular claws.

Ganymede tried to resist, to fight the creature off, but it was no use—the bird was stronger than he'd imagined and in his woozy state there was little he could do.

Up and away they flew, higher than the clouds, higher than Ganymede had ever imagined the heavens to be, and, while he was scared and somewhat stunned by what was happening, he felt excited, too. He had always been adventurous at heart, the kind of man who liked to explore and invent new ways of doing things. He enjoyed unique experiences, and the thrill of flight was out of this world.

"Where are you taking me?" he said, finally finding his voice.

But the bird remained silent until they reached their destination—Mount Olympus.

As he landed and shook himself down, the bird stood before him, and slowly the air began to blur and shift. The eagle's eyes became wide and blue, and the feathers morphed into flesh and bone, until gradually Zeus appeared.

Ganymede bowed low. "The king of the gods!" he cried, "What have I done to offend you, that you would take me from my home?"

Zeus smiled and held his shoulder lightly. "It is the opposite, young prince, I am deeply honored to have you in my company, and I have a proposition for you."

Ganymede listened earnestly as the god explained that he was in need of a cup bearer, a mortal who would be happy to serve him and his kind on Mount Olympus, with the nectar that would sustain them.

"But why me? Surely you have your pick of servants."

Zeus nodded. "It is true, I do. But none are as intelligent as you. I want a cup bearer who will thrill me with their charm, who will question me, and challenge my views. I want a cup bearer who is independent in spirit, but also willing to serve me."

"And what happens when you tire of me?" Ganymede asked, for he was well aware of Zeus's whims.

"That will *never* happen."

"But if it does, I need you to promise that I will not be forgotten," the prince said, "for if I am to leave my father behind upon Earth, and all that is my birthright, then I should at least be given some honor for my role here."

The god grinned. "You want to strike a bargain?"

"I do," said Ganymede defiantly, for he had always been outspoken and truthful.

"I agree to your terms," replied Zeus, "and as a gesture of goodwill I will see that your father the king receives some recompense for his loss."

"And my honor?" the prince asked.

"You will have it, but there is no need, for I *will not* tire of you."

The deal was done, and Ganymede's future was set in the stars. Zeus stuck to his word and ordered Hermes, the messenger god, to pay a visit to Tros of Dardania. He took a selection of the finest horses, magical steeds that could gallop as fast as the wind, as a gift and a payment for his son's service. The king was speechless and conceded that it was an honor for his son to be so prized by the gods. Being one who only considered how things looked to others, he was rather proud of himself for siring a son so special.

While on Mount Olympus, Zeus did his best to make Ganymede feel adored. He gifted him the finest of garments and blessed him with eternal youth and immortality.

"See," he said, "is that not a testament to how much I think of you, and that I will never grow tired of you?"

The prince nodded, but deep in his heart he was weary. As the god had always known, he was clever, and had a novel way of thinking about life. He could not be fooled by grand gestures, and he knew that Zeus had an eye for beauty and a need for excitement. That said, he applied himself with gusto to his new role as cup bearer to the pantheon. He carried the nectar between them and listened to their conversations. He relayed messages to Zeus and paid him compliments, which the god adored. He served him diligently and with warmth, as was expected. Until one day, when the god's head was turned once more.

It wasn't that he meant to go back on his promise to Ganymede, but he simply couldn't help himself. His addiction to beauty was something he couldn't control, and while he had tried for many years, the need for something new and pretty in his life had become too much, so when he saw the nymph playing in the sea, he was smitten. To be fair, he had also grown a little tired of the prince's questioning. What had in those early days been such a revelation, to be challenged and to engage in witty conversation, was now exhausting. Ganymede was inquisitive and constantly so, and his eternal youth meant that with age it did not lessen.

"And so the time has come," the prince said, pouring one last cup of nectar for Zeus. Astute as always, he realized that his days were numbered.

The god smiled. "You never cease to surprise me with your quick intelligence."

"Do you remember your promise?" Ganymede asked, looking him directly in the eye.

"I do," said Zeus solemnly.

As he drained the last drop of liquid from the cup, he looked lovingly at the cup bearer one final time. Then, placing a hand on his shoulder as he had done many years ago, he closed his eyes and cast a spell.

The prince, still holding the jug from which the nectar fell, collapsed, and as his spirit departed, Zeus flicked his fingers, and transformed him into a constellation of stars known as Aquarius the Cup Bearer.

Gracefully, he danced into the night sky, until his profile could be seen from Earth, the tilt of the jug as the water fell a reminder of his role among the gods. Some said that when Aquarius rose in the southern sky at night it was a sign that the heavens were about to open and the rain would come, that Ganymede had once more assumed the role of cup bearer so that the nectar of life could continue to flow.

AQUARIUS RITUAL TO FIND YOUR TRUE VOICE AND FOLLOW YOUR HEART

You will need: A fennel tea bag, a cup, hot water, a pen, and a piece of paper.

This ritual taps in to the authentic energy of this Star sign, using an herb often associated with Aquarius, and also the elements of water and air, to help you tune in to your inner desires.

- Find somewhere comfortable to sit.
- Place the tea bag in the cup and cover with hot water. Fennel is a refreshing herb that invigorates body and mind and will help you unleash your inner truth.
- As the teabag steeps, inhale the scented steam. As you breathe in the air, imagine your mind clearing so that you can see and feel what is important.
- Write the following questions at the top of the paper: "What is important to me right now? What do I need to focus on?"
- Once the tea has brewed, remove the bag and sip slowly.
- As you raise the cup to your mouth, imagine that with every taste, things become clearer to you.
- Focus on the tea's taste and aroma, and how you feel as you drink it.
- When you have finished, breathe deeply, and put pen to paper. Let your thoughts spill forth and don't worry too much about sense or reason—simply let your mind speak through the pen.
- Take a moment to read what you have written and consider any thoughts or feelings that have surfaced.

✸ AFFIRMATION

"My heart guides me toward my true purpose."

PISCES
A Fish Tale

DATES Late February to late March

CHARACTERISTICS Imaginative, intuitive, artistic, romantic, intense, anxious, generous.

ELEMENT Water

PLANET Neptune

Heroes come in many shapes and are not always recognizable. Sometimes the hero within must fight to get out, and often it is a change of events or a cause dear to a hero's heart that sets them on the path to victory. Heroes can be born in the moment, displaying uncharacteristic bravery, and sometimes they're just waiting for the right time to unleash their inner light. The heroes of this story are an unlikely twosome, but being in the right place at the right time set them on a path to stardom.

A long time ago when the world of humans was inhabited by gods and goddesses and the Earth gave birth to all manner of magical creatures, there lived a god more powerful than most. He was a match for the father of the gods, Zeus, and more potent than any other deity, because he was more than just a god. He was a monster, too, and his name was Typhon. Born from the womb of the goddess Gaia and the venomous hell hole Tartarus, it was no surprise he was such a beast and made up of so many different creatures. While at first glance he looked like a man, those who dared to take a second look were struck dumb by his horrific appearance. As tall as a mountain, with a swollen head

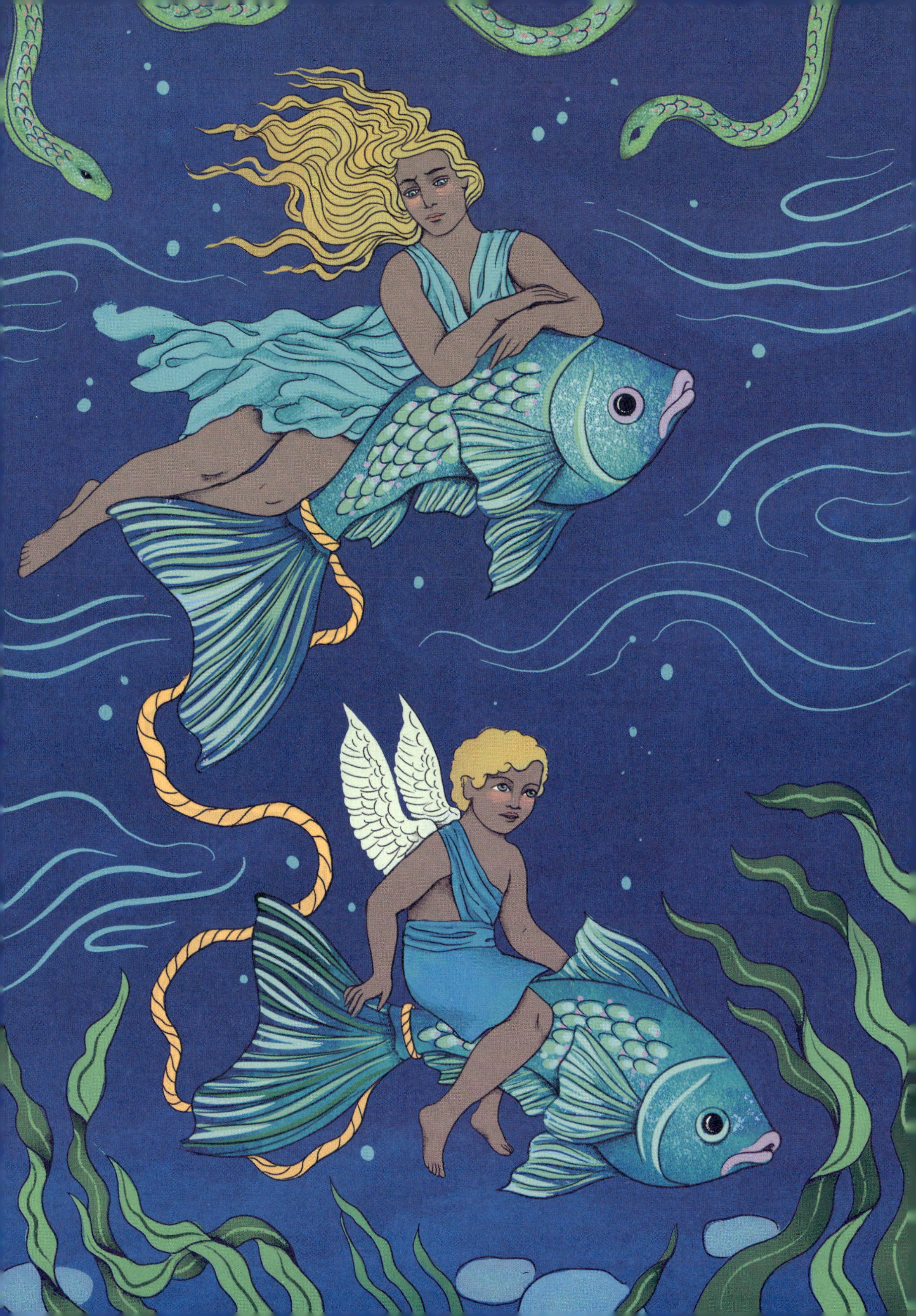

that scraped the sky, his face was a seething mass of rage. His eyes burned red and scorched the flesh of those he encountered, and when he opened his mouth to consume his victims it seemed that the caverns of Tartarus were upon you, for his jaw split his face in two. A hundred snakes coiled from his scalp, spitting and hissing, and his legs were sheathed in scales that rippled as he walked. His body carried a hundred snapping dragon heads and was cloaked in as many wings, which propelled him foward, and his voice was like the stampede of a thousand wild beasts. Typhon was the most fearsome monster that had ever existed, and while he was banished to the Underworld for most of his life, in truth, there was no stopping him.

The gods knew this, and Zeus most of all secretly feared the beast from below, but while Typhon was entombed beneath the Earth, all remained calm. But, as with all things, change comes when you least expect it, and Typhon had been growing restless for some time. He was well aware that the rest of the deities lived a charmed life up on Mount Olympus. He knew of their great riches, and how they played with the people of Earth for their own amusement. He knew of the father of the gods and how he lived as he pleased, sitting upon his throne in the heavens. And he knew that somehow this wasn't fair. He was a god, too, and yet he never saw the light of day.

As his unrest grew, he began to pace the confines of his prison and, being of such an enormous size, caused the walls to splinter and crack. His heavy footfalls rumbled through the core of the Earth and eventually carved a path into the cold rock. His head burst through the surface in a seething, wriggling mass of vipers. Tilting his chin upward, he breathed deeply of the air and let it fill his lungs. The wings that were so tightly bound to his oily flesh began to loosen and extend, until, at full stretch they lifted him upward, pushing his body from the Earthly tomb that bound him. And within a matter of moments, he protruded from the Earth and unleashed his fury in a wave of snake venom that washed over the land.

"I am Typhon and I have come to claim my birthright, for there is none more powerful than me."

He hammered his fists against his mighty torso and roared with such animosity it seemed the ground might split in two.

His words were charged with years of repression, and the sound that emerged was a tormented war cry that could be heard high in the cosmos, to the tip of Mount Olympus.

"What was that?" the gods cried, for they had never heard anything as terrifying. Each looked to the other for reassurance, and for the first time in the long history of the pantheon, they were truly unnerved. Murmuring and wailing, they ran to each other for support, causing a commotion within the heavens.

Zeus however, knew exactly what was coming and who the perpetrator was. He slammed his staff into the ground. "Quiet! All of you, listen to me now." As the deities calmed down, he explained what would happen. "You need to gather your things and flee, as fast as you can. You must leave

Mount Olympus now! The beast that is coming is part god, part monster and a match for me. I will fight him, but I may not win. The only way to ensure your safety is to get as far away as you can."

Silence fell upon the gathered beings, swiftly followed by the understanding that they were in great peril, and quickly, one by one, the gods and goddesses fled the halls of Olympus.

As he watched them go, Zeus counted each one, happy in the knowledge that they would be far away when the final battle commenced, and that's when he realized that Aphrodite, the goddess of love, and her son Eros were nowhere to be seen. In a panic he called out to her, praying that she might hear his cry and seek safety, but he couldn't be sure that she'd heard his words. Closing his eyes, he made a wish to all of the creatures upon the Earth to help the goddess and her son, wherever they were.

"If you see them, help them," he prayed. "Let them find refuge with you, and lead them to a safe place. In return, I will pay you the greatest honor."

Upon Earth, deep in the heart of an ancient forest, Aphrodite had been bathing in a stream with her son Eros, unaware of the chaos in the heavens. Reclining upon the riverbank, she let the gentle afternoon sunshine kiss her skin and soothe away any worries, as her son played by the water's edge.

"What a beautiful day," she smiled to herself, and let the rejuvenating energy of nature lift her spirits. It was then that her son yelped and caught her attention. "Whatever is the matter?" she asked.

"A fish, mother. Two fish, in fact!" he squealed with delight. "They nipped my fingers!"

Rushing over to the stream, she looked down into the glistening water and, sure enough, there were two giant fish, emerging from the ripples.

"What have we here?" she asked, reaching out with her slender fingers to stroke their scales.

"You must come with us," the fish spoke into her mind. "It is not safe here, for Typhon is free and he seeks to kill you."

Looking to her son, and then up into the sky, she felt a shiver run through her.

"There is no time to spare, goddess," the fish whispered. "He is coming!"

Sure enough, the Earth began to quiver and shake as his thunderous hoofed feet clambered against the soil and mud. The undergrowth seemed to part, bowing down to his immense presence.

"Quick," she said to Eros, "climb upon the fish now!"

"But what if we are separated, mother?" the cherub cried.

"Tie our tails together," the fish urged, "and we will swim in unison to freedom."

And so Aphrodite did as she was instructed, binding the tails of each fish together to become whole, and then slipping upon the back of the other fish, they slipped deftly into the water. The creatures, though small in comparison to the beast that was Typhon, were far faster in the stream. Moving like arrows, they carried the goddess and her son away, their fins charging through the water and sending a spray of droplets in every direction. And although they were scared and unsure of the outcome, the fish did not waver in their purpose, being sensitive souls and blessed with intuition, they knew exactly where to go to escape Typhon's glare.

The monster watched them go, helpless to strike because they were too quick for his lumbering gait. Instead, he turned his attention to the sky, and to the realm of Zeus. At least there, he would fare better. Leaping upward, he charged to the summit of Mount Olympus, in the hope that he would be able to destroy at least some of the gods, but when he reached his destination he found that it was deserted. Only Zeus remained to face him.

Together the gods fought in a battle which lasted for what seemed like an eternity. The war raged in the heavens, and those upon Earth would testify that it looked for all the world like the sky was about to collapse and that the clouds were made of rocks and all the light had been vanquished. The great hulking shadow that was Typhon swallowed everything and it seemed there was little chance of a resolution. But Zeus was not easily deterred and would not give up his mantle without a fight. Drawing upon every last reserve of strength and will, he summoned his thunderbolts and, in a final attempt, hit the monster right between the eyes. The spear of lightning dazzled him, sending him careering from the heavens and giving Zeus enough time to strike at his heart with his staff.

Typhon cried out in pain, and then toppled to Earth. His broken body tumbled, eventually reaching Tartarus, where it lay in a crumpled heap upon the rocks. There, it was sealed beneath many layers of stone, sandwiched so deep that it would be impossible for the creature to breathe again. The deed was done, and the battle had been won. Zeus was triumphant and, in a moment of joy, he called to his pantheon to return to their heavenly home. One by one they did, cautiously emerging from various hiding places, and taking up their positions in the stars.

Last to arrive was the goddess Aphrodite and her son Eros. Throwing herself at the feet of Zeus, she clasped at his ankles and said, "My lord, you saved us. You sent the fish to rescue us!" And then, turning toward the creatures, she said, "So brave and kind they were, and so creative, for they carried us deep into the ocean, where we could not be seen by the monster."

Zeus listened and nodded. "It seems that I owe these fish a debt of gratitude." Taking his great staff in his hands, he pointed it at the fish, who were still tied together by their tails. "I place you in the heavens to become the constellation known as Pisces the Fish. You will be forever intertwined to represent your dual nature, and how you balance the realm of the imagination with the reality of your emotions."

And so it was, that the fish transformed into an array of twinkling stars, and a beautiful constellation for all to see. A reminder to the people of Earth that true heroism lies within us, and can be revealed at any moment, when we choose to swim into the light.

PISCES RITUAL TO RELEASE ANXIETY AND BOOST THE FLOW OF LOVE IN YOUR LIFE

You will need: Access to free-flowing water such as a river, stream, or even the sea, and a white flower of your choice.

This ritual works with the gentle, fluid nature of Pisces to soothe away anxieties and open your heart, so that you can give and receive love.

- Stand by the body of water and hold the white flower in both hands.
- Spend a few moments breathing in the peaceful, fluid energy of the space and watch how the water flows steadily toward its destination.
- Now close your eyes and hold the flower to the center of your chest, where your heart chakra, the energy center associated with love, resides.
- Breathe deeply and bring to mind anything that is worrying you, any fears, or any doubts.
- As you exhale, imagine pouring all of those emotions into the flower.
- Continue to breathe in this way for a couple of minutes.
- When you are ready, open your eyes and toss the flower into the water. As you do this, you might want to say something simple, such as, "I release these emotions and open myself up to the flow of love."
- Watch the flower being carried away and continue to breathe deeply.

✳ **AFFIRMATION**

"I release these emotions and open myself up to the flow of love."

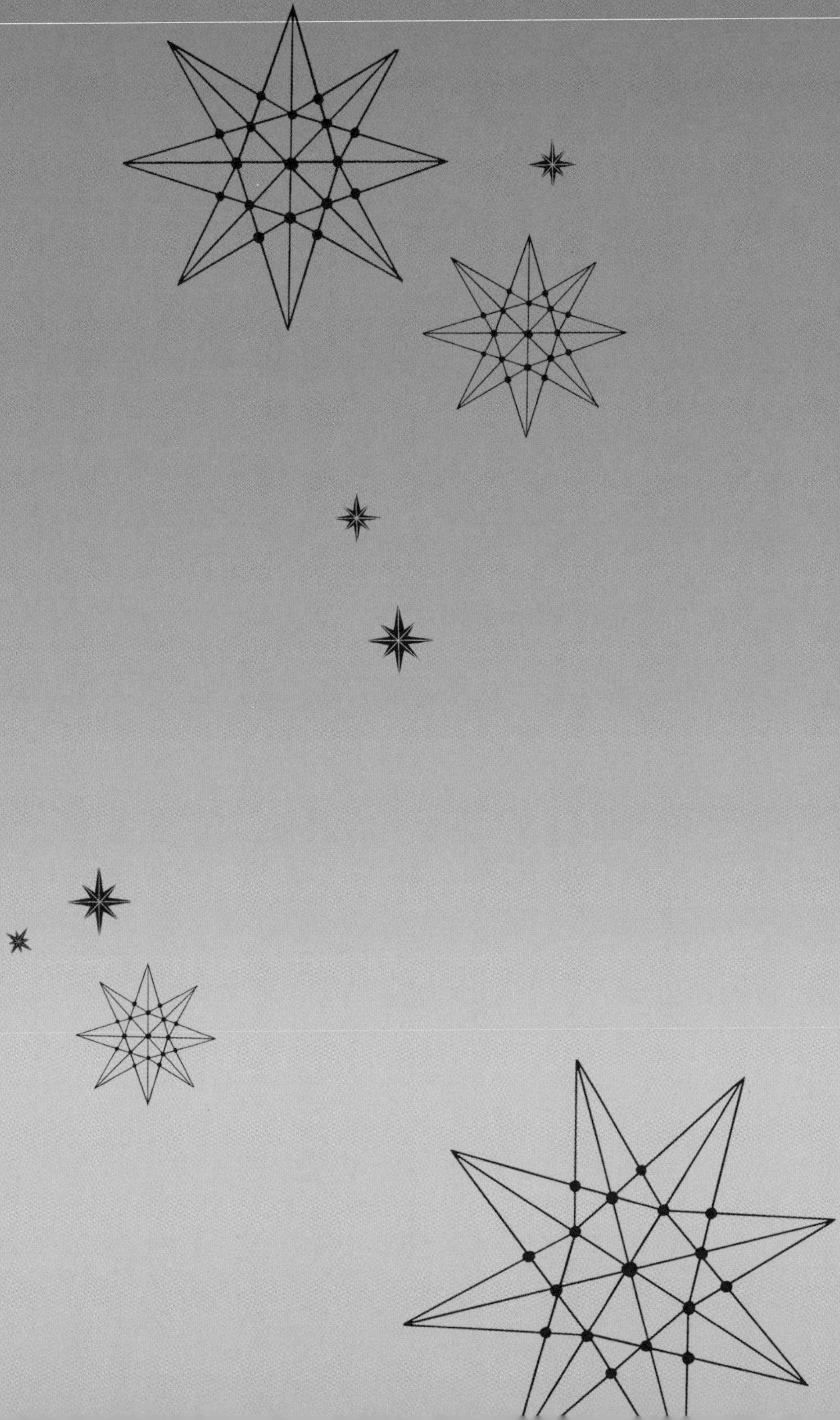

THE PLANETS

We live in a solar system that exists in a seemingly endless galaxy known as the Milky Way. Born around 4.6 billion years ago, our planetary system came into being after a cloud of interstellar gas collapsed, causing an almighty explosion. The resulting swirling mass of debris began to cluster together, and the pressure at the center of this vortex caused hydrogen atoms to fuse and produce helium. Slowly, steadily, the bright burning mass of the Sun was formed. Further out, other allegiances were made. Dense material began to solidify and stick together, and, over time, these clumps grew so big that gravity shaped them into spheres. Some became planets, dwarf planets, and moons, while other clumps failed to make the grade, and were transformed into what we now know as asteroids, comets, and meteoroids.

The Earth was among this cavalcade of newly born planets; a lump of rock tied to the Sun's orbit, but it was not on its own. Being one of the first, and closer to the fiery orb, it was formed of rock and could withstand the heat, but those planets further away were made of gas and liquid that had settled in the outer reaches of this fledgling solar system. And so the galaxy began to take shape, and the planets arranged themselves in a structure based on when they were formed.

As human life came to fruition upon our planet and people evolved, so, too, did new ways of thinking. Ideas and concepts to explain the human experience, along with what we could see and feel, were developing into narratives. The Ancients looked up to the night sky and they saw things they could not explain, stars that burned brightly, and shapes that moved and changed location. They began to question what they could see. Astronomers of old studied the system in depth and uncovered its structure and pattern. They attributed meaning to such celestial phenomena as the planets, believing there was some significance in their cosmic placing and the way they looked. The Romans, in particular, were fascinated by the movement of the constellations, and what this meant for them. They studied the sky and mapped the stars in detail, and eventually named the planets, as a way of organizing them and giving each one greater significance. It made sense to them to choose monikers based on Roman deities—after all, it was commonly thought that they ruled over everything and were heavenly entities, so it made sense that they would take a celestial shape. With this in mind, they gifted each one a title that resonated with a characteristic of a god or goddess.

The largest planet was called Jupiter, after the king of the gods, and the red planet was named Mars, a fitting epitaph to the blood-soaked god of war. The brightest planet was a natural choice for the goddess of love and beauty and became Venus, while the super-swift orbit of Mercury around the Sun meant it was associated with the fleet-of-foot messenger god. Soon, all of the planets within the solar system had names and attributes associated with the Roman pantheon, and each one had its own mythology to complement its namesake. Astrologers were quick to run with this idea and link each planet to a Star sign based upon a constellation, and so the Zodiac was fully formed, and each astrological birth sign had a governing planet that influenced traits and behaviors.

Within this section you will find a selection of stories relating to each of the planets, based upon myths and folklore associated with its deity. While the stories are focused on the Roman pantheon, it is interesting to note that some other mythologies have their own versions of these gods and goddesses. Some tales are centered on a specific myth, while others draw upon the deity's folklore to create a story that brings the planet's attributes to life. The tales, like those of the Star signs, are a representation of meaning and symbolism, given voice and structure to help you connect with the mythology and understand each planet's nature. You will also find a ritual alongside each narrative to help you harness the energy of each planet, taking elements from the story.

Most of all, these tales encourage you to take a moment and look up at the night sky. See what the Ancients saw before you and embrace the beauty of the cosmos. Learn more about the planets within our amazing solar system and lose yourself in their enchanting stories.

MERCURY
Gods, Humans, and Tricksters

PLANETARY ASSOCIATIONS
Self-expression, communication, negotiation, ideas, curiosity, trickery, fickleness.

ASTROLOGICAL SIGNS Gemini and Virgo

DAY OF THE WEEK Wednesday

Among the vast and growing pantheon of deities, there was one more human than most. Gifted with frailties, and the need to deceive, he could also be incredibly kind, but he was a god of contradictions and a storyteller at heart. He understood the human need to communicate, to express what lies deep in the soul, and to make connections with others, for it was inherent in his make-up.

Some called him a trickster, and it was true that he had done his fair share of mixing things up, causing chaos out of calm, and bringing confusion to the table. Perhaps that was because he enjoyed attention, but in truth he simply liked to play, to throw a curveball into the pot and watch it bubble and bluster. Yes, Mercury was a master of mayhem, but he also had the ability to smooth the waters and bring resolution with the right words and some quick negotiations. If all else failed, a wave of his Caduceus, a magical staff gifted to him by the Sun god Apollo, could heal any rift. Because he was the patron of merchants and traders, and the king of thieves, this was an essential tool.

The people of Rome had always known about his questionable talents, but they still petitioned him

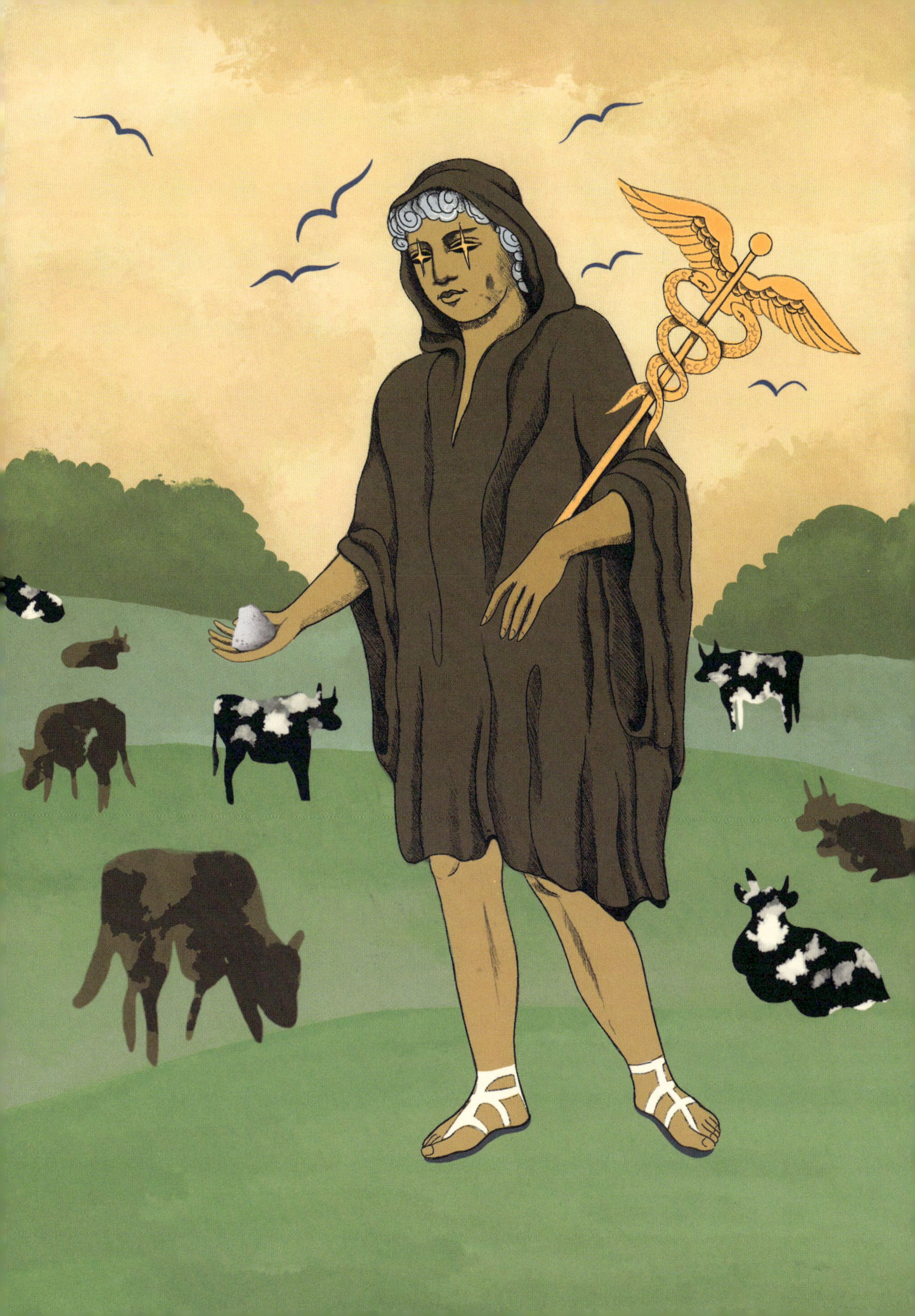

for help, for while he was unpredictable, he almost always answered their prayers, even if the outcome was not what they expected. Sitting with the stars in the sky in his planet form, he was a powerful presence, but unlike the other deities he preferred to spend his time on Earth, to rub shoulders with the peasants and exchange pleasantries, which he could only do wearing a disguise.

The other gods despaired at his need to mingle.

"What is the attraction? These people are not your equals, they are not gods, and they do not have our powers."

But he just shrugged. "They are more like us than you think. They deceive, they manipulate, and they control their destiny, as much as we control it for them."

And so it was one fateful day, in a small village outside of Rome, that Mercury decided to don the baggy, dirty apparel of a poor man and prove his claims to the rest of his heavenly peers.

With a weary gait, and carrying the world upon his shoulders, he staggered forth. It was a hot day, and the swathes of crude material chafed at his flesh, making his discomfort even more apparent, but he didn't mind. It simply added to the subterfuge. As he entered the village, he was met with hostility. The people stared and jeered, some turned their backs, and were even more horrified when he approached them with his hands out.

"Please, a little food for a traveler—a morsel of bread, a sip of wine?"

But those he encountered ignored him, or insulted him, and then turned and went on their way.

Mercury smiled beneath his cloak; it was as he thought. Humans were fickle and unkind, for while they could be gracious and caring, they could equally turn their backs in disgust. Just as he was about to retreat, a bearded man approached with a small loaf of bread in his hand.

"Take this. I am happy to share what I have."

Mercury, stunned by this admission, took a moment to gather his thoughts. "Thank you, kind sir. I appreciate this."

The man shook his head, "It is nothing. I have enough."

"You have enough, you say?"

The man nodded and seemed to stand even taller as if to demonstrate his wealth.

"Yes, my name is Battus. I am a servant, but I do well, and I am content with what I earn."

"You are?" Mercury enquired, an idea forming in his mind. "What is it that you do?"

"I stand guard over a herd of mares for my master, and he pays me well."

"That is indeed a good vocation, but do you not want more?"

The man shook his head. "I am not bothered by Earthly gains. I like to think that I am honorable."

Mercury took a bite from the bread, and chewed thoughtfully. "It seems you are a better man than me, and I thank you again for your kindness."

With that, he ambled back along the path and out of the village, but his visit wasn't done, for he still had a truth to prove to the gods watching above, and he wouldn't leave without doing it.

Waiting in the shadows as the Sun began to set, Mercury watched the man called Battus take his staff and trundle toward the pasture, where the mares he guarded were grazing. Setting up a perch on the tree stump, Battus surveyed the land before him. He looked out onto the meadows, beyond his own, and gazed at a huddle of cows belonging to his master's neighbor. As the Moon cast its silvery light upon the landscape, a figure appeared in the far field, as tall as he was magnificent, with dark curls and eyes that shone like the stars. He seemed to grow in stature, despite being in the distance. Battus sat up, paying close attention to this enigmatic intruder. He watched as the man began to lead the cattle away and, taking each by the neck, guided them out of the field. In that moment, Battus had a choice. Should he intervene and stop the thief, or look away? After all, it wasn't his charges that he was stealing. Before he had time to make a decision, Mercury appeared before him.

Without his disguise, his true splendour shone, and Battus recognized him to be the thief in the moonlight, a man of wealth and means.

"Do I know you, sir?" he asked, and Mercury shook his head.

"You do not, but I know you, or at least I know your sort, and I would ask a favor."

Battus was enthralled. "Anything, Sir."

"Do not speak a word of this. Do not mention what you have seen to your master, or his neighbor, and in return I will reward you with a prize heifer, and a purse filled with gold to see you as your own master."

Battus's eyes widened. "You stole the cattle."

"I did, what of it?"

"I don't know what to say."

"That's easy," Mercury whispered, placing a finger on his lips. "Say nothing to anyone, and you will reap your reward."

Battus swiftly nodded. "I will not say a word of what I have seen. I promise."

"Very well, we have a deal," said Mercury extending a gloved hand. "I will return in the morning, with what you are owed."

And with that, he quickly merged back into the forest.

Battus sat quietly for the rest of the night. Whether his heart was heavy or not, it was hard to tell. Perhaps he was picturing his new life as a man of substance, imagining the things he could buy and do, for this one deception. As the Sun began to rise over the brow of the hill, Battus heard footsteps approaching, and turned to find his master's neighbor before him.

"My herd has gone, seized in the night! Did you see anything?"

Battus looked at the ground. "No sir, I did not."

But the neighbor was undeterred. "Please, I urge you to tell me, if you saw who took them. I will pay you well. I will bring you two prize heifers from my herd when they are returned, and not one but two purses of gold."

Battus scratched his beard; this was a magnificent offer, and too good to refuse. Would it really matter, going back on his word to a thief? There was surely no honor between them, and he was doing the right thing, by revealing what he had seen. At least, that's what he told his conscience.

"I accept your offer, and I will tell you all you need to know," he smiled.

The Sun was high enough in the sky to bathe the fields with its golden glow when Mercury finally returned to the pasture to find Battus, and the neighbor, waiting for him. He looked from one man to the other, and spoke.

"Ah, Battus, you disappoint me. It seems you have gone back on your word and been tempted by an even greater offer."

"How do you know my name?" the peasant asked.

"I know many things," the god replied, shifting shape and form, between that of the lowly beggar from earlier, to his fully resplendent self.

Battus gasped. "I recognize you; you said you were poor! You tricked me!"

"It really shouldn't matter what I look like, or who I am. Your word is your word. You said you were an honorable man who had enough, when in fact you are nothing more than a chancer who is easily swayed by the promise of more. All I had to do was make an offer and you hungrily accepted with little thought for anyone else."

Battus tried to speak, to open his mouth and say something of value that could demonstrate his innocence, but the god silenced him with a flick of his Caduceus.

"Do not worry, I am actually glad, for you have proved my point perfectly."

He turned then, his face gazing up at the cloudless sky.

"See, brothers, and sisters, what I have been trying to tell you for so long. Humans are just like us. They manipulate and they can be manipulated. All it takes is the right kind of offer, the right choice of words, and an ability to communicate your message with ease."

He turned then to the neighbor. "Your herd is waiting for you in the next field, I am sorry for any inconvenience I have caused."

And then with one last flourish of his Caduceus, Mercury pointed it straight at Battus and turned him into a lump of stone.

For a moment he stood, looking at the cool, gray granite that had once been a man. Then, patting his hand lightly upon the stone, as if to brush away some dust, he chuckled, "Now, my friend, you truly do have enough, for you are stone, and have no need for anything."

He walked away, his sandaled feet skimming the blades of grass and giving away his godliness. As he went, he pondered the human condition—the goodness and grace, coupled with those more negative traits that seemed inherent in the people he met. The frailties and quirks that made each individual unique, and the stories they told to others, and to themselves, as a way of making sense of the world and their actions. There was no denying it—gods, humans, and tricksters, they were much the same.

MERCURY RITUAL TO HELP YOU EXPRESS YOURSELF EASILY AND WITH CONFIDENCE

You will need: A piece of peridot or green tourmaline, a pen, and some paper.

This ritual helps you tap in to the planet Mercury's mercurial energy, which will help to trigger the imagination, boost creativity, and aid all of your communications.

- To begin, spend a few moments in quiet contemplation with the stone of your choice. Peridot captures the positive, creative energy of the planet Mercury, while green tourmaline is an uplifting stone, which clears negative energy and boosts confidence.
- Find somewhere comfortable to sit and hold the stone in both hands.
- Close your eyes and focus on the feeling of the stone against your skin.
- Take a long deep breath in and imagine you're drawing the energy of the stone along each arm, and up into your chest.
- Hold this breath for a few seconds so that you can absorb this energy, then slowly release it through your mouth. As you do this, imagine you're releasing any fear associated with the way you express yourself and what you really feel.
- Repeat this breathing cycle for two or three minutes, to clear your mind and imbue yourself with positive energy.
- Now open your eyes, take the pen and paper, and begin to write. Don't worry too much about the words. Simply ask yourself: "What do I want to express right now?" Let the words flow.
- Consider the pen in your grip like Mercury's Caduceus, a mighty magical wand that can help you communicate through your own unique voice.
- When you've finished, spend a few minutes reading through your work. Don't worry if it doesn't make much sense. Instead, give thanks for the opportunity to communicate and unleash your thoughts and feelings on paper.
- To finish, hold the stone again and repeat the breathing exercise at the beginning of the ritual, to help center yourself, and to infuse your body with positive energy.

✳ **AFFIRMATION**

"I express myself with creativity and flair."

VENUS
The Morning Star

PLANETARY ASSOCIATIONS
Beauty, love, grace, wisdom, divine feminine energy, creativity, fertility.

ASTROLOGICAL SIGNS Taurus and Libra

DAY OF THE WEEK Friday

The Ancients would often ponder the question of real beauty. What makes a woman unique? Is it the curve of her hip, the wave of her hair, or the sparkle and shape of her eyes?

For some it was the way she spoke, and for others how she moved. Many said it was an indefinable quality and the essence of her soul. If she was good and kind, a nurturing wife and mother, then this made her more pleasing to the eye because these qualities accentuated all her other charms. There were those who suggested it was a superficial construct, and only skin deep, and those who argued that beauty was so much more than symmetry, or one outstanding feature. It was a myriad of things that could not be put into words, although many poets and scholars tried.

The question caused much debate, as you might expect, for Rome was an appealing city, a place where the rich got richer, and used their wealth to excess. The women adorned themselves with the finest garments and indulged in various rituals and practices to enhance their gifts and talents. Ultimately, though, true beauty was always synonymous with one. The founding mother of the capital, and the goddess of

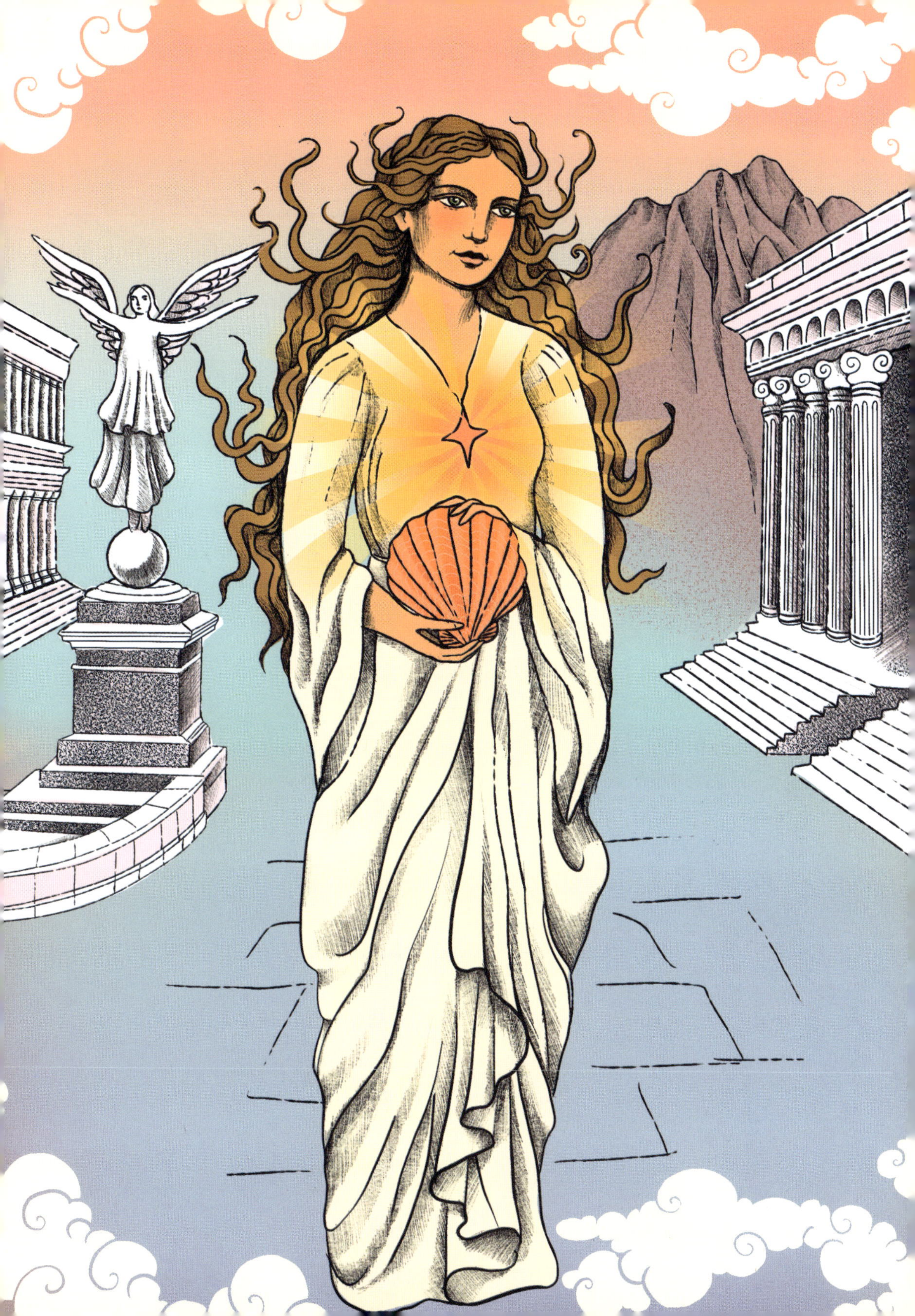

love, Venus was the epitome of perfection, but the essence of her loveliness came from her creative spirit and the gifts she bestowed on others.

They called her the Morning Star, and she was certainly the brightest sight in the sky. Wherever she roamed, a rosy, pink glow followed, as delicate as the prettiest bloom but also strong and ever present, just like the woman that she became. And really, it's no wonder when you consider her beginnings. Unlike the other deities, she was not born in the traditional way, from a mother's womb, but created from sea spray and her father's genitals. As the waves parted, she sailed to shore, her voluptuous glory cradled within a giant scallop shell. A fully formed woman, she stood with pride and looked out at the land that would become her new home, and all of the creatures, the gods, and the beings that had gathered at the water's edge, bowed down.

When she stepped to shore it seemed that the Earth swooned. The sky raced down to meet her, sending a gentle breeze that tugged playfully at her golden curls, and the ocean released its grip reluctantly, watching her stride forward with confidence.

Venus was not a woman to be trifled with, and not just because she was a goddess. She knew her own power and was not afraid of it. She was rarely afraid of anything. Such surety made her even more attractive, and the love she felt for herself exuded from every pore. Those who were lucky enough to cross her path were almost blinded by the light that shone from within. Her allure became a thing of legend, and mortals and gods were helpless in her presence, for what else was there to do? Venus was the goddess of love and beauty and would not be denied. That said, she returned the favor, making those she chose feel treasured and adored. Her love was generous and her heart big enough to embrace the entire world. This was just as well, for she had many lovers and did not distinguish between gods and humans. It mattered not whether her beau had magical abilities, as long as he was prepared to worship at her feet. In fact, she often found that mortals were more willing to do this, having less of an ego than some of the more powerful deities.

Her marriage to the god Vulcan was fated from the start. He was a jealous man who longed to control his wife, but being born from the ocean she was a part of nature and longed to be free to do what she wished. Her love could not be contained or saved solely for him. She was the Morning Star, and the brightest in the sky. She could not dim her light even if she wanted to, and this bothered him greatly. How could she truly be his if she shared her beauty with everyone? His steely ways could not tame her, and she embarked upon a string of affairs; some sweet and simple, others as tempestuous as the stormy sea.

"I love," she would say. "That is what I do. I radiate love to my people, to the heavens, to everyone."

And then she would smile, and that one expression was bright enough to compete with the Sun's rays.

And so it was that Venus met Anchises, or rather she watched him from afar. A mortal prince of Dardania, and an ally of Troy, he was held in high regard, but despite his royal lineage, he preferred the simple things in life. Anchises was a keen shepherd and loved nothing more than to stroll the hills with his sheep. Venus was instantly smitten by his caring nature, and this, coupled with his youthful good looks, made him the perfect conquest.

One day, as he wiled away the hours with his flock upon Mount Ida, she came to him, but rather than reveal her true nature, she decided it would be more appealing if she took on the guise of a Phrygian princess. At least then he would see her as his equal and give the romance a chance. In white robes, and with her hair flowing around her head, she looked every inch the noble maiden. Her eyes sparkled with mischief, and when she smiled it was with innocence and hope. Anchises was beguiled and didn't question her sudden appearance in such a remote spot. He was only too happy to entertain her, taking her on a walk and sharing a picnic. He regaled her with tales of his exploits, of the places he'd been and his life as a Dardanian prince, and in return she listened, laughed, and offered a glimpse of her life and her ancestry. It was all too easy for Venus to win his affections, and soon they embarked on a passionate affair.

Anchises, for his part, was smitten. He wanted to make her his bride, and when she revealed that she was carrying his child, he was thrilled. The boy was born nine months later, and named Aeneas, and it was only then that Venus decided to unveil her true identity to the prince.

"You lied to me," he yelled. "How could you do that?"

"You would not have looked at me in the same way, if you had known who I really was."

The prince sighed. He knew she was right, and a part of him was excited to think he had caught the eye of the goddess of love and beauty. How special did that make him?

"I would still have loved you," he said. "In fact I would have loved you even more, because of who you are!"

Venus shook her head. "And that is why I couldn't tell you. Love is not based on a person's status or magical ability. It is not about power or greed."

"But it helps," said Anchises.

Worried, Venus tried to appease him. "Please do not say anything about who I really am. You must keep my identity secret. Do not boast of this conquest, for if you do and the gods find out, they will be angry."

While Anchises was a good man and promised he would never brag about his romance, the thought that he had been singled out was a boost to his ego. He grew confident and proud, and wanted everyone to know that he had won the heart of the goddess of love, and so he talked, and he gossiped, and he spread the rumors. And the gods were listening.

Jupiter, enraged by this revelation, sent a mighty thunderbolt in his direction. Whether he intended to kill or scare Anchises didn't matter, for the bolt hit him directly, and he died instantly.

Venus was heartbroken. She had a soft spot for her Dardanian prince and loved their child deeply, but there was nothing more to be done. Her only mission now was to ensure the boy grew into a fair and honest man, a prince who knew the true meaning of love and how to share it with his people. While she could not be with him permanently—her place was in the heavens—she watched over his progress daily, guiding him in visions and dreams. Sometimes she would visit him and pretend to be a distant relative. Other times she would speak to him and whisper suggestions and advice on how he might act, and what he should do to win favor. She knew he had the potential to be a great man and, with her influence, they could create empires together.

It is this she had in mind when she gave him the idea to build the city of Rome. "It will be a wonderful place, a safe place where people can strive to be the best that they can be. A city of industry where people can learn, they can educate themselves, and devise new ways of thinking."

"And what will it look like?" he pondered.

"It will look like another world," she whispered into his mind. "It will be the pinnacle of the Earth, with temples and statues and ornate palaces fit for a king. It will have squares and lined walkways, roads, and fountains. It will be just how you imagine paradise, and you can make it happen. It is down to you, Aeneas."

The young prince smiled, as his thoughts ran away with him. Could he do this? Could he create such a place?

"Yes," she said again. "Yes, you can, and you will, for beauty and love lives within you.

And so he did. Aeneas went on to found the city of Rome, and he created it to fulfill all of the needs that his mother had instilled in him, and many more. The city flourished as expected, and the name of Aeneas became synonymous with its conception. He achieved what he had set out to do, completing his destiny and making his mother proud, and in this one act he became almost godlike.

"Look at this beautiful city!" Venus said, shining her powerful light upon the Earth so that all the gods might see her hand in its creation. "Is it not a shining example of what people can do when they are imbued with passion?"

The gods could not deny that she was right. Looking at the world through her rosy light, they could see that there was beauty in everything, and that the planet was a place of wonder. And so Venus, known as the Morning Star, became a symbol of love and a dazzling reminder to all, that it is your actions and deeds that make you truly beautiful.

VENUS RITUAL TO HELP YOU SEE THE BEAUTY IN THE WORLD AROUND YOU

You will need: Access to a window that looks onto your yard (or an outside space), a pink candle, a candle holder, and lighters or a match.

This ritual works with the loving energy of Venus, to help you see the true nature of things. It uses candle magic and some mindful meditation to help you connect with the beauty of the world around you and boost positive energy.

- To begin, find somewhere comfortable where you can sit, relax, and look out at the outside world.
- Take the pink candle (the color associated with the planet Venus), place it in the candle holder, and light it. As you do this, make a wish to help you see and connect with the wonder of your surroundings, and the wonder within yourself.
- Now take a minute to breathe deeply and reflect on the view. Look out at the environment and let your vision soften.
- If something catches your eye, linger upon it. See the beauty and examine it. If nothing jumps out at you, simply let the vista inspire you, and let your mind drift.
- After a few minutes and when you're feeling relaxed, hone in on one thing, for example, a beautiful flower, a tree, or a cloud in the sky. Imagine this is all you can see for a few seconds, and let it fill your mind.
- Take in as much detail as you can, and then close your eyes and recreate the image in your mind. How does this make you feel?
- Think about your own world and your place in it. Know that you are a part of that landscape and a thing of beauty, just like the flower, tree, or cloud, and that you have your own unique shape and loveliness.
- Say: "I see beauty, I am beauty."
- Let the candle gradually burn down.

※ AFFIRMATION

"I see beauty. I am beauty."

MARS
War and Peace

PLANETARY ASSOCIATIONS
Passion, action, movement, energy, aggression, success, resilience.

ASTROLOGICAL SIGNS Aries

DAY OF THE WEEK Tuesday

His military cloak falls like red mist cascading from the heavens. It swirls about him in swathes of rust, to create an air of mystery and mayhem. After all, he is the god of war, and he wears it well.

Sometimes he rears his head, crowned with a helmet of steel, to hint at the strength and fortitude within, and you can see it peep across the skyline, but there is nothing timid in this slow reveal. He is simply assessing the situation, just as a general would assess the field of battle before he charges. And while he seems to take up most of the sky with his impressive presence, he does not wish to intrude. Instead he watches over the landscape like any protective father, for he is tied to the Earth, and to its creatures.

Once upon a time, there was a goddess called Juno. Considered the queen of the pantheon, she was the wife of Jupiter, the king of all. She was honest to the core, and believed in fairness. Her countenance was such that others came to her for advice, and she had the power to deliver justice and create order. Juno was a homemaker, and family was at the heart of everything she did. While she was well aware of her husband's indiscretions during their marriage, and

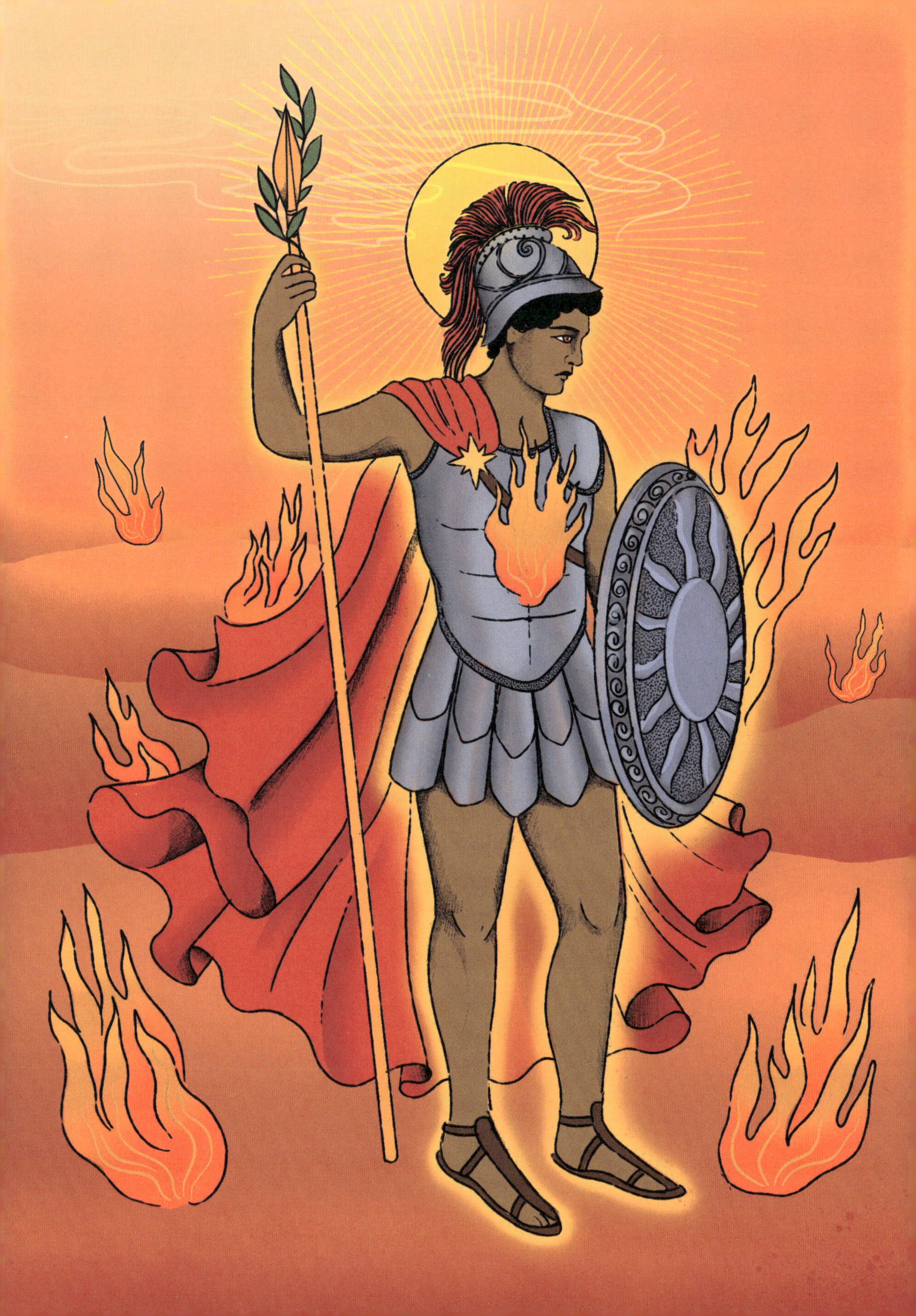

often turned a blind eye to his infidelities, she still cared about what others thought. To her, it was important to show strength, and to redress the balance that his dishonesty had created. And so when the goddess Minerva came forth into the world, bursting from the forehead of her father Jupiter in an act that would defy all convention, Juno was deeply troubled.

"It is not right that Jupiter should have this gift, that he should be able to conceive and create new life without the nurturing force of a woman."

She confided in her maids, "It makes me look weak, and it makes all women appear less important. I must do something to change this."

A seed of an idea formed in Juno's mind, for she was also jealous of the new arrival to her husband's brood. She wanted her own child, a babe more powerful than any other, to prove her worth and restore the equilibrium. But how to do this? While she was magical in her own right, she did not have the ability or knowledge to make this happen.

"How to make a child grow without its father. . . ." she pondered, and in that one statement she had her answer, for grow it must, like a tiny sapling seeking the nurturing light of the Sun.

"He will be of the Earth and from the Earth, and he will bloom like a flower!" she gasped. "That is my answer."

And so she traveled to the realm of flowers, to seek counsel with the beautiful goddess Flora, and she explained her plight, asking that the goddess might bless her with a seedling in her belly or at least give her the knowledge she needed to make this happen.

"I cannot gift you what you want directly," the goddess said, "but I do have a flower that, when consumed, will make you pregnant."

Juno gratefully accepted the colorful bloom, but being cautious by nature, decided she would test its magic first upon a cow. Within seconds of consuming the tiny bud, the cow's lower carriage began to swell, and within the hour, it gave birth to a calf. This was all the proof she needed to try the magic for herself.

Placing her hands upon her stomach, she felt the first kick of the child within. It was solid, mighty, and imbued with the kind of strength that could only come from a god in the making.

"You will be great, my child. You will be a force to be reckoned with," she smiled.

And so Juno, queen of the heavens, gave birth to a son, Mars. His name was a fitting acknowledgement of his fortune, for simply put it means "man," a powerful being who would make his mark upon the world. His birth made a statement to the rest of the pantheon, and to Jupiter specifically. It was a call to arms and a way that Juno could show she was his equal. In that one act, Mars had already fulfilled his purpose. Through dynamic action he had resolved the conflict that simmered between husband and wife and restored the balance. This was to be a common theme in his life.

As the child grew into a man, he learned the difference between right and wrong, but he also learned that goals must be strived for, that action sometimes speaks louder than words, and that discord is a part of life that can either be ignored or tackled head on.

Mars was forthright and fair just like his mother, but he was also impulsive and quick to anger, and he gained a reputation throughout the world. Wherever he went, whatever country or time, there was general devastation and bloodshed, and battlefields stained rose red by the fallen. Soldiers who feared for their lives would call upon the god to bestow bravery in the face of adversity, and he would always respond. The sound of their pleas ignited a passion within him, a need to protect his people, so when the battle horn blew, Mars was there, standing shoulder to shoulder with his men. He would whisper in their ears words of courage and fortitude, but also words to feed the flames of animosity. He would push them forward, an invisible hand upon the back, the tug of an arm, just enough for them to sense his presence and feel his fervor. But was it enough? Mars was well aware that more often than not, he was leading the men to their doom, but in the heat of the moment he got carried away.

"Is this what I am meant do, Mother?" he would ask the goddess Juno. "Is death and destruction what I am about?"

"My boy, you may be a man, but you still have a lot to learn."

"Then teach me," he implored.

"I cannot teach you—there are things you must discover for yourself."

But soul-searching was not his strong point. Mars was a man of action. In youth he was hot-headed, making swift decisions that only served to fuel the fire within. From ill-advised choices made in the heat of the moment, to lusty liaisons that only served to cause chaos among the other gods, Mars could not be tamed. That was, until he met the goddess Minerva.

She was everything he was not: calm, collected, and controlled, a symbol of the state of Rome and the goddess of wisdom and commerce. She embodied the qualities that he so desperately needed, and perhaps that is why he was so enthralled, for she would complete him in every way.

He asked for her hand in marriage, but she refused. Minerva wanted to maintain her virginal status. "You have no control of your emotions; you do not think things through," she said sternly.

"But I want you, I need you," he begged.

"And so you think you can take me?" Minerva shook her head. "You will only fulfill your true potential when you act with compassion and strength, and you truly listen to others."

"But I do!"

"You hear, but you do not take the words to heart. Instead, you think you can fight your way to success, whatever the result of your actions."

The love Mars had for Minerva ran deep, and her rejection left him bereft. In a bid to make her love him, he sought the help of the goddess of time, Anna Perenna. An elderly woman, wizened and bent with age upon the surface, but bright as a new flame within, she was sharp and witty and could see that the god needed to be taught a lesson.

"Why go for her, when you could have the wisdom of age and all the benefits that offers, with me?" She flashed a toothless grin.

Mars pulled a face. "Do you not see me? I am young and strong; I am the god of war. I need a beautiful woman by my side, not an old hag. I must have Minerva!"

"Very well," Anna smiled calmly. "I will give you what you deserve; I will cast a spell that will change her heart and make her love you."

That night, Minerva came to him, her head bowed low, her eyes filled with affection. She agreed to marry him, and, even better, she would do it the following day, for what time was there to waste? The spell had worked, and Mars was victorious. How easy it had been to change her mind and what did it matter if a little magic and manipulation were involved? He had achieved his aim, and that was what counted.

But what Mars failed to realize was that Anna Perenna had tricked him. Taking the shape of Minerva, she had come to his bedside and promised to be his wife. Once the wedding was over, she revealed the truth, instantly transforming back into her elderly form.

Aghast, Mars yelled, "You witch! How could you do this?"

"Oh, it was easy," she beamed. "You weren't prepared to listen, or consider your options. You let your passion take over and made a bad decision just to get what you thought you wanted. But it wasn't what you needed."

Her words stung, but they were also true. In that moment, Mars realized how foolish he had been, not only in this one endeavor, but in every misjudged moment of his life so far.

"War is not always what is needed," he said, sadly. "I see that now. Resolution—listening to others to find middle ground—is more important."

"Yes," Anna smiled, "you are beginning to understand. You don't always have to be the aggressor."

And he did understand, for it seemed that calm, assertive action could be the way forward, the way to help his people overcome conflict. And while he would always be the god of war, that didn't mean he couldn't use his powers to help build bridges and bring balance, just as his mother had illustrated all those years ago, when he was born.

From that moment on, Mars made a pledge to use his powers for good, to be assertive when needed, but to think before acting. To show restraint, and to use his passion in a positive way. Instead of purging the battlefield he would remain an observer, seated in the heavens, a gently spinning scarlet ball of light, and a reminder to those upon Earth to take their time, to think and take positive steps and actions when faced with challenges.

If you're lucky, just after sunset on a clear night, you might see him watching over you from his celestial throne, his cloak around his shoulders, his aura bold and bright. You may also see his spear, once used so liberally in battle, now covered by a laurel leaf at the tip—a symbol of peace, and a reminder that harmony is the ultimate goal.

MARS RITUAL TO BOOST CONFIDENCE AND HELP YOU ASSERT YOURSELF

You will need: Hot water, a piece of ginger root, a mug, honey or sweetener, and a red, thin scarf.

This ritual taps into the fiery energy of Mars. It helps to boost courage and confidence by combining warming spice with the hue red, which is associated with the planet.

- Boil some water and place the ginger root in your mug.
- Half-fill the mug with the hot water and let the ginger steep for five to ten minutes.
- As the spice is infusing, spend some time inhaling the aroma from the steam. Close your eyes and feel the warm, uplifting scent imbue you with courage.
- Remove the ginger carefully, and stir in a spoonful of honey or sweetener, if needed. The honey has mood-enhancing properties that will improve your self-esteem.
- Place the scarf loosely around your neck or shoulders and sip the ginger brew.
- Imagine that with every sip, your confidence grows. See it as a red ball of light that sits in your belly, and steadily fills you with strength.
- When you've finished, say the affirmation: "With every breath my personal power grows."
- Whenever you need an extra boost of bravado, wear the scarf, and repeat the affirmation in your mind.

✳ AFFIRMATION

"My personal power grows with every breath."

JUPITER
The Twelve Shields

PLANETARY ASSOCIATIONS
Spirituality, abundance, success, power, order.

ASTROLOGICAL SIGNS
Sagittarius

DAY OF THE WEEK Thursday

Every empire begins somewhere. Sometimes all it takes is the seed of an idea or a collection of people who bond together, to create a society in its crudest form. Even the largest empire in the world, the most ancient and predominant, will have started as a spark before it spread to a flame. And so it was that Rome was conceived, and first ruled by Romulus.

In those early days, the kings held the power and the throne, and they made the decisions that could bring change. However, Romulus was happy to take his seat and let the empire unfold without interference. And while the power fed his ego, he thought little of the implications of a structureless empire, or how society might evolve and go from strength to strength. Order and religion were yet to be realized. The old gods still ruled, and the beliefs and rituals that aligned with them were at the heart of any big decisions.

This suited everyone, particularly the king of the gods, Jupiter, who was a mighty leader and only too happy to influence humankind. When Romulus inevitably took his last breath and passed to the otherworld, it was down to the pantheon to produce a new king.

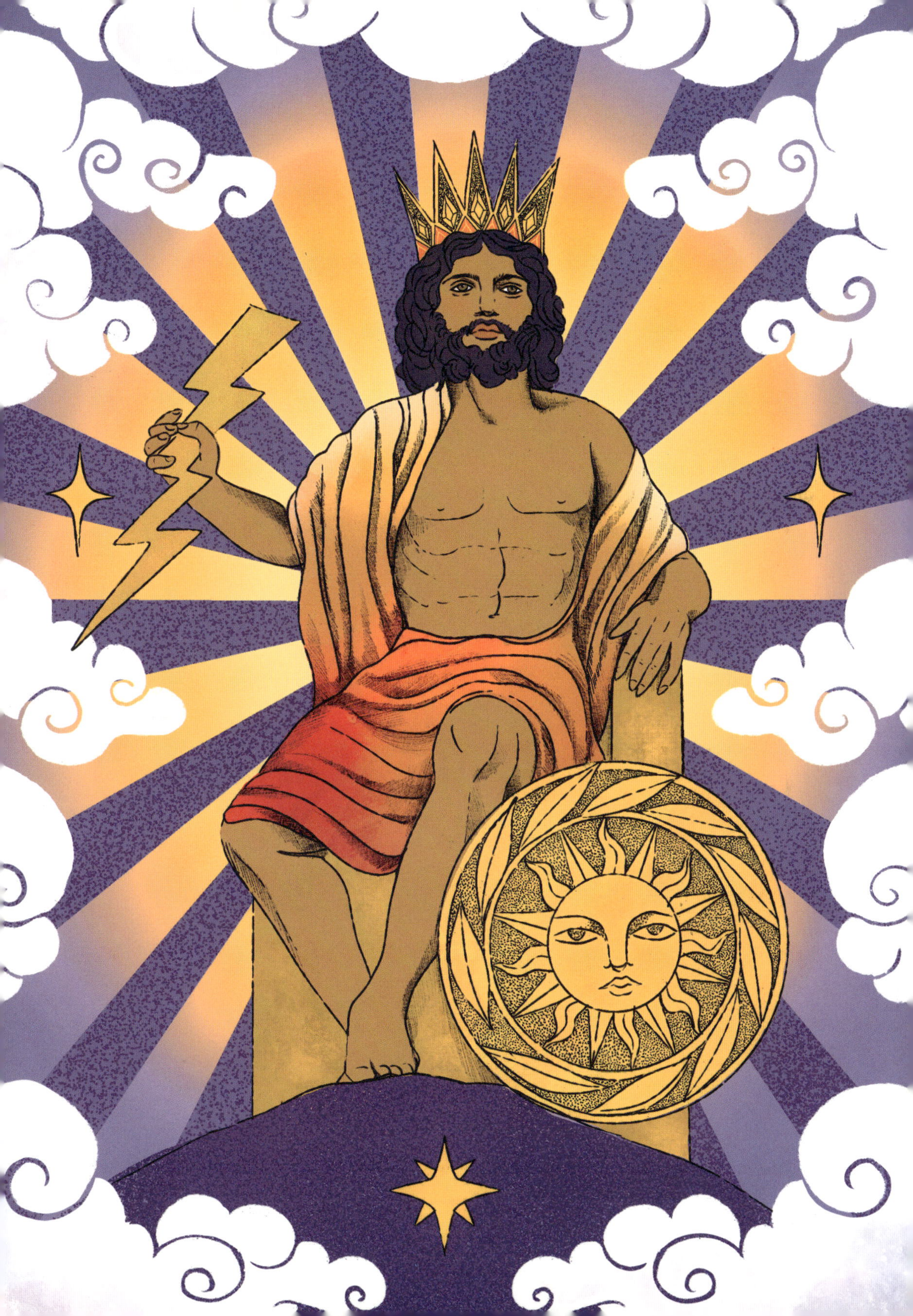

Jupiter did not take this decision lightly. He knew the consequences of such a position in society, having usurped his own father for his seat in the heavens. Despite this, he was notoriously successful, and had a degree of wisdom that the other deities lacked. When he held court among the clouds, it was possible to see him from the Earth in all his magnificence. For while the other gods wore their colors defiantly, Jupiter chose an array of hues to match his temperament. Some days he wore white, gold, and sandy brown, and was bathed in a burnished glow; other days, he wore threads of red and orange, brighter than the Sun, which blended seamlessly with his flowing robes. His changeable moods were part of his charm and a way to connect with the people, for he had seen that humans, too, could be flexible, and fickle, taken with whims and fancies and often lost in their emotions.

He had been watching the Earth for quite some time, looking for a man who could be the kind of king the empire needed, and that's how he first happened upon the youth, Numa. Born in the far southeast of Rome in the Sabine town of Cures, Numa Pompilius was a clever boy, and the son of a wealthy noble. But while he had all the makings of a good ruler, he was hardly on the radar of those elderly statesmen who would choose the next king.

Nevertheless, Jupiter had been listening in on the child's dreams for a long time. The boy yearned for greatness, but his ambition was coupled with a desire to be fair and honorable. He was open to new avenues of thought, and flexible in the way he coped with everyday challenges. Most of all he had an ear for the gods and would often petition them for advice, which meant he would listen and act in their favor. And so, when the time came for a new king to be crowned, Jupiter intervened.

He visited all of the key decision-makers in their sleep, infiltrating their dreams, and urging them to seek a king in the nearby town of Cures.

"Look for the man named Numa," he ordered, "he is the new King of Rome."

The elders shared their thoughts and vision with the people, and it was agreed they should heed Jupiter's words, for hadn't he always provided for them? And so they traveled to Cures and asked Numa to be their king and he accepted, for he, too, had been visited by Jupiter in a dream.

In his slumber the god had appeared as a giant ball of color in the sky, a glistening orb that spun ever closer to the Earth, bathing him in brightness.

"I am with you, Numa; I will help and protect you. You just need to follow my lead," he had said.

"But what if I fail, or make the wrong decision? This is too much responsibility for me."

Jupiter wrapped his light around the sleeping man like a shield and smiled, "Numa, you are not alone. I am by your side in all things, do not fear. Accept this gift and let us work together to create an empire worthy of gods and mortals."

And so, Numa Pompilius was crowned the king and slipped easily into his new role. It seemed it was made for him. After all, he was a pious man who believed in order and establishing rules, and while the people might first have rebelled at these ideas, they soon came to realize that every decision he made was for their benefit.

Numa had the gift of foresight, and he was incredibly wise. Some say he gleaned his knowledge from the heavens, and that he had a team of cosmic advisors who consulted the stars. Others believed it was his keen insight and the way he could read people.

Over time, he introduced a series of religious reforms and established an office that oversaw the rituals and prominent ceremonies of Rome. On the instruction of the gods, he devised a new calendar based upon the cycles of the Moon, which divided time into twelve months, and this eventually replaced the Julian calendar that had once been so popular. His new organized way of marking the seasons proved helpful for the people, particularly those who worked the land, and key decisions were made at certain times.

It seemed that all was going well, until it didn't. For Jupiter wanted more. He wanted the adoration of his people, and physical proof of their love for him—and as Numa's star was rising, Numa was taking all the credit. Jupiter felt it was time to re-establish the balance of power, and his influence on this modern world. And so the wind of change brought conflict and strife to Numa's door. He felt under attack, and his people were restless. Numa's new reforms were causing issues, and industry struggled as a result. The atmosphere was tense, and even the weather was tumultuous. The city had been hit by a stream of powerful storms that had left it battered and bruised, and even Numa had suffered, almost being hit by a lightning bolt aimed at his palace.

Feeling increasingly unsettled and facing potential hardship, Numa knew he would have to petition the gods for aid, and not just any of the pantheon—Jupiter himself. Traveling to Aventine Hill, one of seven mighty hills within the surrounding landscape, he enlisted the help of two lesser deities to call upon Jupiter.

Laying down with his arms outstretched, and his face pressed into the dry Earth, he let his tears fall.

"I do not know what is happening, or why I am under attack. It feels like the heavens are conspiring against me, and my own people are restless. I was almost killed by a thunderbolt. Have I displeased you in some way?"

Within seconds, Jupiter stepped from the sky to the tip of the hill and spoke to Numa. "You have been a good king, but you must remember, it is I who put you in this position, and I can take it all away, too."

Numa nodded and bowed again. "I know, my lord. What can I do to show the weight of my gratitude?"

Jupiter beamed. "That is easy. You must introduce me to your people and make me an essential part of their daily life. Let them worship me and make their offerings at a great temple in my honor. In return I will ensure you are always protected. I will show how to avoid the storms in life, and those that batter at your door. I will teach you how to avoid lightning bolts. I will be your shield."

And with that, he produced a giant circular shield from the sky. It shimmered in the morning light and hovered above Numa's head.

"This is an ancile, and my gift of protection to you."

Numa clasped his hands together in thanks.

"I will return the favor, great Jupiter. I will have eleven more identical shields crafted like this one. Together, they will be known as the Ancilia, and this will become a symbol of the Roman Empire, and of your status here among the people."

Jupiter grinned, "That is a fitting dedication, King Numa."

"You will not be forgotten; I will make sure of it. The people will worship you every day, and I will build the most amazing temple in your honor where they can go to do this."

Numa was true to his word, and a grand and opulent temple was built upon Capitoline Hill in honor of the god. During the Ides of March, the people would visit and offer their sacrifices, as a way to celebrate Jupiter's enduring influence in their life.

Inspired by the god's wisdom, Numa went on to write the sacred laws of Rome, and to create the legal system that kept the people safe and helped to build relations between rich and poor. Everything he did was under the watchful eye of the ever-shifting, always colorful, King Jupiter.

When the time finally came for Numa to take his last breath, Jupiter was at his bedside once more. Whether it was a vision, a dream, or a hallucination as he slipped from one realm to another, who can tell. But for Numa, the god was there bathing him in a shield of brightness once more, and those who looked on would note the light that came in from the night sky, and how it seemed that Jupiter was even more prominent among the blanket of darkness. Perhaps this was one of the many reasons why Numa became almost deified and considered a saint among his people.

As Jupiter watched the king slip away, it was with sadness but also joy. Theirs was a partnership between the mortal and divine that had truly worked over time. It had allowed the father of the gods to show his true colors, which were often misconstrued. He had been able to lead and nurture, to offer his wisdom, and promote victory and success. He had ensured abundance for the people of Rome, and given them the gift of his protection in the form of the twelve shields, a symbol of the divine pact made on Aventine Hill. As a result, they had built an empire between them, a thriving state that would be significant within world history. In addition, both man and god were given their rightful place among the stars.

JUPITER RITUAL TO TAP IN TO YOUR INNER WISDOM AND HELP ACHIEVE YOUR GOALS

You will need: A piece of citrine, a piece of paper, and a pencil.

This ritual combines the circular shape of the shield and the crystal citrine, which are both associated with the planet Jupiter, in a practice to help you attract success.

- This ritual is best performed on a Thursday, the day associated with this planet and god.
- To begin, spend some time thinking about what you would like to achieve. Do you have any specific goals, or are you looking for success in a particular area? Perhaps you're looking for inspiration, or to get things moving on the career front.
- Draw a large circle in the center of your piece of paper, big enough for you to write inside.
- In a few words, summarize your goals and what you're looking for. If you can't be specific, simply write the words, "success," or "abundance," in the center of the circle.
- Hold the citrine in both hands and close your eyes.
- Breathe deeply and imagine harnessing the stone's energy, drinking in its power with each inhalation. The golden hue of the stone is similar to one of the colors associated with this planet, so, as you breathe, imagine this wrapping around you like a cloak of protective energy.
- Continue breathing and let your mind wander. If any thoughts or ideas come to mind relating to your goals, make a note of them by writing them on the paper, somewhere around the circle.
- To finish, place the stone in the center of the diagram you have drawn and leave it on a desk or table overnight.
- Pay particular attention to any dreams you have during the night, since these may provide insight or inspiration for the future.

✷ AFFIRMATION

"I strive for success in everything I do."

SATURN
The Golden One

PLANETARY ASSOCIATIONS
Rules, structure, equality, peace, abundance, harmony.

ASTROLOGICAL SIGNS Capricorn

DAY OF THE WEEK Saturday

When the Roman people needed reassurance, there was always one place they could look. Tilting their heads to the heavens, they would drink in the night sky and wait for the god Saturnus to give them a sign. More often than not, his golden glow would permeate the cosmos and that was enough for them to feel acknowledged. He was there watching over them, dissolving the boundaries between rich and poor, so that every man, woman, and child could be equal.

It wasn't always that way. Though Saturnus was richly favored by the people of Earth, he'd had a rocky start. Luckily, there is nothing that humans love more than a leader who admits their faults and strives to be better, and so Saturnus was re-invented in their eyes. But his beginnings were more questionable than most.

As a young god he had sworn to do right by his people. His father, the supreme sky god, Uranus, was a cruel deity who enjoyed inflicting pain upon others. His tyrannical reign brought destruction to the Earth, and Saturnus watched in horror as his father decimated kingdoms, drowning the land and swallowing entire buildings whole. He knew in his magical heart that

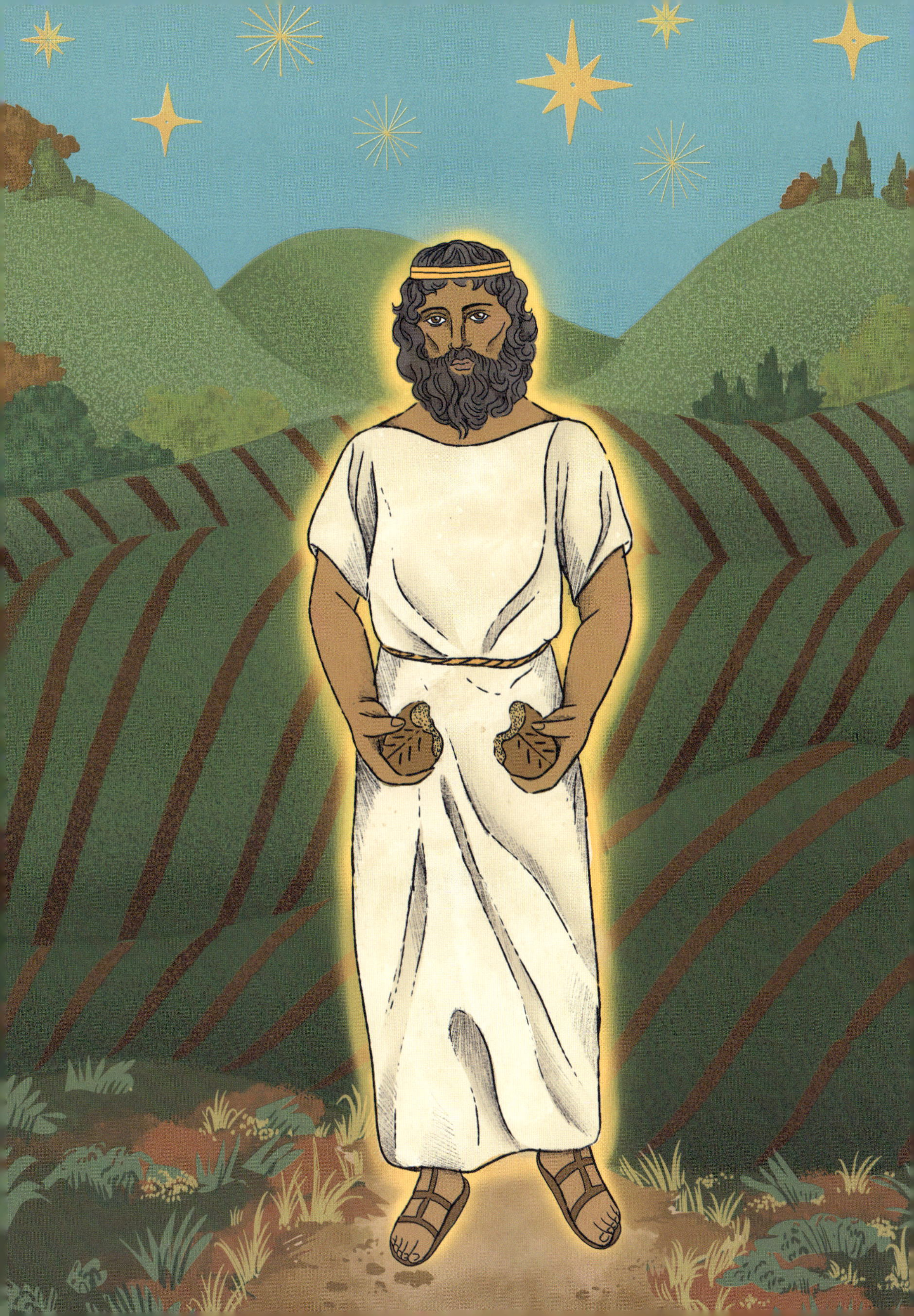

this wasn't the way to rule, and that he had to do something to save the planet. And so he seized the throne, usurping his father in the process.

The people of the Earth rejoiced; at last it seemed that the gods were working in their favor, and that sense and reason had been restored. Saturnus was blessed with patience, and dedication. He brought order to the chaos with his analytical approach, and while most of the other gods seemed to enjoy an argument, he preferred to negotiate with diplomacy. But over time, the power of his position changed him. Where he might have once used measured thought to weigh up a situation, his emotions now governed. His actions were erratic and often fueled by insecurity. He realized just how vulnerable the king of the gods was, for there were always others ready to topple you from your seat in the clouds—and that's how the paranoia began.

Poor Saturnus succumbed to the madness, letting it infiltrate his brain until all of his thoughts were tinged with terror. Even his own children weren't to be trusted, for they might seize his throne at some point! As such, he made a pact with himself. Every time his beautiful wife Ops gave birth to another child, he would swallow it whole, saving himself from the fate of his own father.

The pantheon watched in horror, for though they were a bloodthirsty lot, even they were appalled by his revolting behavior. What had happened to the stoic god who had vowed to lead with honor? And what could be done about it? Luckily, the goddess Ops was clever and, having lost too many children to her husband's madness, decided to secrete her last child away. It was this one act that would bring about the god's downfall and also give him the chance to re-invent himself. The child, Jupiter, grew into a powerful god who was a worthy match for his father Saturnus. When the time came, and with the backing of his siblings after he rescued them, he cast his father out of the heavens, dethroning him in the blink of an eye.

Saturnus was a broken being. Shamed for his actions, and belittled by his own flesh and blood, he wandered the cosmos in search of salvation. As time passed, the parts of the god that were born from ego began to slip away. The irrational thoughts that had plagued his brain were replaced by an emptiness that began to eat at his soul. His body weakened and his pallor faded. His eyes became red blotches from all the weeping he had done. Saturnus was lost in remorse, and also lost in the vastness of the Universe.

It was then, at his lowest ebb, that he stumbled upon Janus, the god with two faces. Some say he meant to find Saturnus. Others believe it was an act of fate. Either way, Janus was gifted with the ability to look into the past with one face, and to see into the future with the other. This meant he could see into the heart of the god, to the core of his soul, and understand where he had come from, while also being able to envisage a brighter future for him.

Taking his hand, he led him to the ancient land of Latium, a part of central Italy surrounding the Alban Hills.

"You will be safe here. You can rest and make this place your home," Janus said kindly.

Saturnus, barely able to look him in the eye, shook his head. "Why help me?"

"Why not?" Janus replied. "You have learned your lesson, and now you can draw upon it and use the skills and traits you have been blessed with to make the world a better place."

Latium, the land of the Latini, was a beautiful stretch of mountainous land, and the host of Rome, the capital city. Rugged and wild in parts, there were plenty of remote places for the gods to hide, but while they might be tucked away from city life, they were still able to see and feel the plight of their people.

Saturnus was only too glad to have a moment of respite, to roam the rocky hills and beaches, and feel at one with the nature. The environment calmed him and gave him time to think, while Janus helped him see the error of his ways. He also gave him foresight: the ability to think ahead and consider the outcome of each action, something which Saturnus had once had before his power hungry ways took over.

It seemed to the disgraced god that time was the answer to everything, and if he could pause it somehow by being present in the moment, then he could make things better and sway opinions in his favor. Nature, too, had much to teach him. He realized that each season had its own gifts, and that these could be harnessed to help the people. As he walked the fields and spoke with the trees and rivers, he learned enough to know how to forage and tend to the Earth. He understood what was needed to harvest the land, to plant crops and nurture them, to give them the best chance to grow in abundance. He also realized there were more practical ways to do this, using tools and technology. These had yet to be invented, but he knew that with a little godly inspiration, they could be created and used in propagation. And so he began to work with the people, at first tentatively, for they were nervous of his influence, and then, as they began to trust his magic, with confidence and care. He taught them everything he knew and imparted his wisdom and blessing so that the crops would grow, and they would reap a good harvest.

Soon the people praised him. "Hail Saturnus, for he has shown us how to work with the land and increase our bounty!"

"Saturnus is god of all, the most powerful!"

"Let us worship him, for all he does for us."

Their cries echoed through the city walls and, as the temple bells rang, it seemed that Saturnus had turned over a new leaf. He had managed to win hearts and minds, and in turn had restored his own sanity. But he was not done.

The class divide bothered him deeply, and he despaired at the way the rich lived in splendor, squandering what they had, while the poor suffered, with nothing. He could see the resentment this caused and knew first-hand what it was like to fall prey to base emotions. He watched the peasants working and saw the appalling conditions that some of them had to contend with. He saw their struggles and it touched his heart.

"I must do something," he said to Janus. "If I do not, then there will be a revolt, and discord will rule over harmony. But what to do?"

"If the divide bothers you so much, then the only way forward is to remove it," whispered Janus.

Saturn, as he was now known, smiled, "Yes! I see that. As always, my friend, you are the voice of reason. I must find a way to make all mortals equal again, if only for a short time."

With that in mind, he went to his temple in the Roman Forum, to pray and impart his knowledge to the scholars and scribes. Planting the idea that was now bearing fruit in his mind, he watched as the learned began to discuss the suggestion between themselves.

"I've had a wonderful idea! Let us have a festival in honor of the great god Saturn. It will be a way to thank him for all of the things he has done for us."

"Yes, yes! But if it is in his honor then it must be fair, for Saturn is a reasonable god who likes order, and all things to be equal."

"Then we shall make it that way. It will be a time when the servants become the served, and we do their bidding. They will be the masters, and everyone will feast at the same table."

"It will be a time of celebration and there will be no distinction between class. The poor shall be treated as the rich, and vice versa."

And so the die was cast and the deal was done, and the festival, known as Saturnalia, was born. The people embraced the idea, for it gave them a chance to be together without resentment or fear—master and servant alike, breaking bread and sharing wine. Among the poor, a king was crowned and given the right to demand anything (within the realm of possibility.) The rich and poor exchanged gifts, and for a day (which soon evolved into a week) of festivities around the Winter Solstice, they were a family. The harmony this created lasted throughout the year, and unbreakable bonds were forged. Peace reigned within Latium, and Rome, the center of commerce and industry, became a happy place to be.

Word of this Golden Age of peace soon spread, and even more people gave their thanks to the god who watched over them from the sky. Honor was heaped at his door, and the people dedicated a day to him known as Saturday, meaning "day of Saturn."

Astronomers, too, were in awe of the god's presence and grateful for the gifts he had bestowed. They paid homage to him, believing that the sixth planet from the Sun, the one that seemed furthest away, was the god of the Golden Age and the one who had helped them find the path to peace. Wearing his usual golden hue and a crown of sparkling rings that encircled him in the sky, he looked magnificent. Being the slowest planet to orbit the Sun, he marked the steady passage of time, just as the people had come to expect. And so Saturn turned his fate around and became the Golden One and a lesson to those on Earth that, given time, love, and forgiveness, harmony will flow again.

SATURN RITUAL TO RECHARGE BODY, MIND, AND SPIRIT

You will need: Access to an open space such as a park or yard, and a notebook (optional).

This ritual taps into the calming power of the planet Saturn to restore harmony and lift the spirits. It will help you connect with the energy of nature, and the environment, and engage at a deeper level.

- This ritual can be carried out at any time of year, since each season has its gifts. It's also something you can do regularly to enhance your connection with the natural world and create harmony.
- You are going to go on a mindful walk and explore your yard or the local park. The key is to take your time and engage all of your senses as you stroll.
- Before you begin, take a minute to address how you feel in the moment, and sum it up in a word, such as "stressed" or "tired" if you are feeling under the weather, and in need of energy.
- As you walk, think about what you can see. If something catches your eye, spend a few minutes focusing on it in detail. Breathe in its beauty and commit it to your memory as if you were going to recreate it later.
- Think also about what you can hear, from the sound of your own footsteps and your breathing, to the sounds of nature.
- Consider what you can smell—the earthy scent of the soil, the sweetness of the flowers, and so on.
- Finally, engage the sense of touch. What can you feel as you walk?
- Drink in the experience and let it inspire you. You might want to bring a notebook and describe how you feel, or sketch something that you see to remind you of your walk.
- When you've finished your walk, consider how you feel and if anything has altered. Sum up your emotions in a word and notice if there has been any change in your mood.

✴ AFFIRMATION

"Each moment of the day offers me the chance to reflect and recharge."

URANUS
The Rainmaker

PLANETARY ASSOCIATIONS
Inventiveness, imagination, eccentricity, progressiveness, rebellion, recklessness.

ASTROLOGICAL SIGN Aquarius

DAY OF THE WEEK Wednesday

From the heavens it came, a downpour so potent it washed the leaves from the trees and caused the seas to swell. It quenched the Earth in sweetness, bringing brightness and depth to the landscape, and filled the air with a unique scent to stimulate the senses. The rain fell, and the rainmaker, for that's what they called him, watched.

In those early days he was only too happy to oblige his creator and consort, Terra the Earth. They were a partnership made in heaven: dual sides of the same coin, for she had made him to reflect all her needs. He was the father of the sky, the great provider, the air that kissed her lips, and the rainmaker who nourished her soul. His name was Uranus.

In the beginning, when she had created the Earth from her own womb, birthing the planet into existence, she had been a solitary being and that had been enough. But Terra was as wise as she was motherly, and soon realized that for there to be growth and expansion she would need the assistance of another, one as great as herself. Love flowed through her every movement, but it needed direction and a partner to share it with. With this in

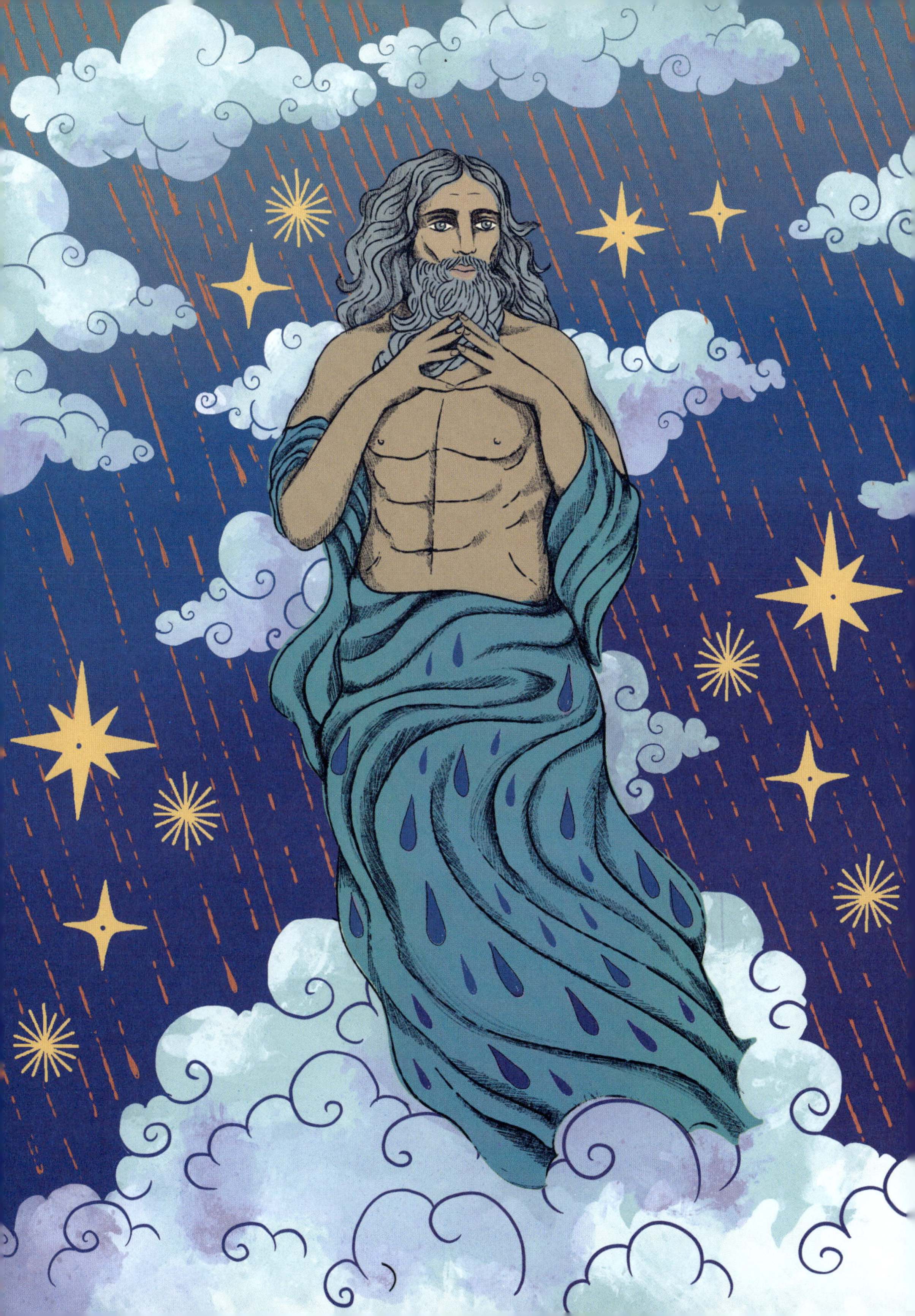

mind, she created Uranus, a god in his own right and a mighty force to match her own.

Bare chested, with rippling muscles and a long flowing beard, he was the personification of the heavens, and a man of great stature. When he sat on his throne in the sky, his blue-green robes would fall about him, casting an ethereal glow that became synonymous with the planet. He wore a cloak threaded with raindrops—enough to last the Earth's lifetime.

When their eyes met for the first time it was not as mother and son or creator and creation, but rather as two souls who could make each other complete. So the romance began, and it would last for what seemed like an eternity. While she was imbued with the qualities of the Earth, stable and grounded with a level-headedness that complemented her caring ways, he was the opposite. His mind was a whirl of activity, filled with lofty ideals and unique thinking. He could be ingenious and inventive and would often surprise his love with gifts from the sky to make her smile, like a luminous rainbow or a vibrant sunset. But being such a forward-thinker he also had a tendency to obsess, creating confusion when there was none. And when it seemed her attention was elsewhere, upon the many children they had conceived together, his emotions could get out of hand.

In truth, Uranus was jealous and tainted with paranoia. He was convinced that his children would overthrow him, in more ways than one. After all, he had always had the Earth to himself but now she spread her love among her offspring, which left little for him. And while he continued to make the rainfall to sustain her, his heart was consumed with envy and his head was a sea of suspicion.

"I must do something to make this right, to restore the balance of my love," he thought. But what to do? "I will destroy them all, I will steal them away, and then she will be mine again."

He rubbed his hands together with glee. It was a good plan, and one he could carry out quickly, for he knew exactly where he could hide his children. Gathering them to him, he summoned all of the original powers that Terra had gifted, and in an outburst filled with venom, he consigned his offspring to the lowest, loneliest pit beneath the Earth, known as Tartarus. As dark as it was grim, this hellish hole was a place of suffering, but he thought nothing of subjecting his children to this torment. As long as they were safely tucked away, hidden from their mother and unable to escape, he was happy. Nothing could challenge him, and no one could seize his crown.

What he failed to realize was that Terra was everywhere and nowhere at the same time, and nothing could be hidden from her. She was aware of her husband's failings, and of his deep-seated distrust. She knew that the fear within his soul would turn to hatred, and that this would be fatal for the family she had created, and the planet as a whole.

Fearing for her children, Terra hatched her own plan. Deftly, and with the magic in her hands, she broke away a lump of flinty stone from her body, the Earth. As steely sharp as it was solid, she crafted it into a giant sickle with jagged teeth, a weapon so enormous it would be able to make short work of any godly appendage. Then, calling on the remaining Titans who had been saved the fate of the other children, she urged them to act.

"We must stop Uranus. He is out of control and his extreme thoughts will be the end of all of us."

"But how?" they cried. "You shaped him and made him a match in power and strength. How could any of us possibly defeat him?"

"I did," she nodded, "that is true, but I have crafted this sickle for that purpose. Whoever is brave enough to wield the weapon and slice away his manhood, for that is what is needed, will defeat him. It will be enough to diminish his power and humiliate him."

A hush fell upon the gathered crowd as they considered the enormity of the task—and then out of the silence came a voice filled with passion.

"I will do it," said Saturnus. "I have no fear of him."

Lying in wait for the nighttime, when Uranus was at his most vulnerable, and asleep, Saturnus slipped between the shadows. When he was sure that his father was asleep, he hefted the sickle high into the air and brought it down with a mighty thud upon his father's manhood. As skin separated from skin, and the blood fell, he cast his father's genitals into the ocean.

Uranus cried out in anguish. His heart thundered in his chest, and his life's blood poured from the heavens, in a great and powerful shower. The light in his eyes flickered, and it seemed that he might lose himself completely, as the truth of what had happened hit him. His worst fears had come to pass, for he had always believed that one of his children would be his downfall, and yet he had underestimated the Titans, believing that they, among all of his offspring, would remain faithful.

"Saturnus!" he yelled, and his voice echoed as the wind carried it through the cosmos.

Then a deeper understanding occurred, as he realized that Terra, his love and co-creator, must have been the primary force for his demise. She had known what to do, and how to bring him down. She had urged his own son to do her bidding. His anger swelled, rising through his chest as he released a breath that scathed the Earth with a tendril of spite but did little to hurt her.

"How could you?" he whispered.

"How could you?" she replied, pushing him away. She turned her attention to her hidden children, the ones who languished in Tartarus. At last, they were free to rejoin the world and reunite with their mother.

The blood from the wound continued to fall upon the Earth in a deluge of glistening droplets that formed rivers at her feet, and the swirling pools that collected took on a new shape. They became three vengeful goddesses known as the Erinyes, or the Furies, deities who could never be controlled and who would unleash their wrath on men for generations to come. And then came the giants, another product of the bloody downpour and a race of beings whose size and stature grazed the clouds and made the Earth shudder with each footfall.

The scarlet stream was constant, and was gradually absorbed into the Earth, taken deep within the soil until it reached the roots of the trees. There, it was transformed from the blood of Uranus into the veins of the forests, and the trunks of the tallest ash trees. And the beings that came forth next were the Meliae, a race of woodland nymphs who would become the guardians of the forest, and protectors of the trees. Spritely, but made of the Earth, and mixed with the rainmaker's blood, they were fiercely gifted, but hard to find among the flora and fauna.

Finally, from the foam of the genitals cast into the ocean, there was a stirring, as the froth of sea spray charged like a herd of white stallions. It seemed that all of the gods and all of the gathered beings who lived upon the Earth held their breath, turning their attention to the great body of water that lapped against the shore. Terra, too, awaited the arrival of the last of the rainmaker's treasures. Sure enough the waves parted, and from within the rippling depths a voluptuous creature stepped forward. She was the most beautiful goddess that had ever existed, and her name was Venus. Created from the remnants of Uranus's glory, she radiated beauty from every pore.

Slowly, steadily, peace returned to the Earth, and the gods began to assemble, to make order of the cataclysmic events that had transpired. The blood eventually subsided, and stillness took over from chaos. The pantheon was once more complete, and the captive children were returned to their mother. All was well, or so it seemed, for the rainmaker had fled, humbled by the turn of events, and reduced in power. It seemed that Uranus had been tumbled from his lofty position, and in doing so the world had evolved.

"I will take my throne now, mother," Saturnus said triumphantly, "for I surely deserve to take my father's place."

And while Terra could not deny that truth, in her heart she felt an unease that grew with every breath. Had she simply swapped one tyrant for another? Was the fate of the Earth always to be at the mercy of those whose ego was greater than anything else? Would it ever end?

Somewhere in the heavens a wraithlike form skulked. Disguised by the shadows of the clouds, he could not be seen from the Earth, but that didn't mean he didn't exist. He was immortal and made that way by the one who had engineered his vanquishing. Once the greatest god of all, cohort to the Earth and her partner of choice, he had somehow lost his way, his ingenious greatness, and in doing so incurred the wrath of the one he loved. But he was still there, watching and waiting, crying for all that he had once held dear. And when those tears fell, which they did often, it would rain in cascading sheets of sorrow. Each droplet filled with remorse and swallowed by the Earth.

URANUS RITUAL TO SPARK INGENUITY AND PROMOTE NEW WAYS OF THINKING

You will need: A trash can, an apple, and a knife or potato peeler.

This ritual helps you shed restrictive layers of thinking, and open your mind by getting to the core of what's important. It allows you to tune in to the ground-breaking energy of the planet Uranus.

- Place a trash can on the floor between your feet, sit on a chair, and take the apple in both hands. Consider that this piece of fruit represents your brain, and the way you think. To open your mind, you need to shed those restrictive beliefs and those layers of thought that might limit your thinking.
- Before you begin, ask Uranus to bless you with its energy, then take the apple and begin to peel away the skin with the knife or peeler.
- Imagine that with each layer of peel, you are removing limitations and beliefs that might hold you back.
- Let the peel fall to the floor and continue to shed the skin until all of it is gone. Slice the remaining apple in half so that you can see the core and seeds.
- While holding the apple, say, "I go back to my core and uncover new and exciting opportunities and ideas."
- To finish, cast the peel into the trash. Eat the remaining apple, place it in compost, or leave it outside for the birds and other animals.

✶ **AFFIRMATION**

"I go back to my core and uncover new and exciting opportunities and ideas."

NEPTUNE
Behold the Sea

PLANETARY ASSOCIATIONS
Empathy, intuition, emotional sensitivity, calmness, turbulence.

ASTROLOGICAL SIGN Pisces

Standing on the Mediterranean shoreline, looking out to sea, it's easy to imagine the way things used to be, and how the Earth was molded and shaped by the gods, crafted by fury and passion, and then set at ease for humankind to make their own.

Did the Roman gods know what was to come, and how their creation might evolve? Perhaps they had an idea. After all, the planet was nothing more than a concept picked from the heavens and brought into being. It would take more than their magic to make it what it is today. Of course, the gods each had their part to play, and in those early days it was a battle of will and ego, of who was the greatest, the father of all.

The deities had always coveted this crown, and none more so than Saturnus, who considered himself to be the almighty, the driving force behind existence. After all, he had usurped his father from the throne, and so it was only right that he should be rewarded for his prowess. The role fit him well, and his head swelled with pride, but superiority is dangerous when coupled with conceit, and despite appearances he was weak of heart, believing that his children would do the same to him, and steal his mantle. Getting himself into a state, the king of the gods made a decision.

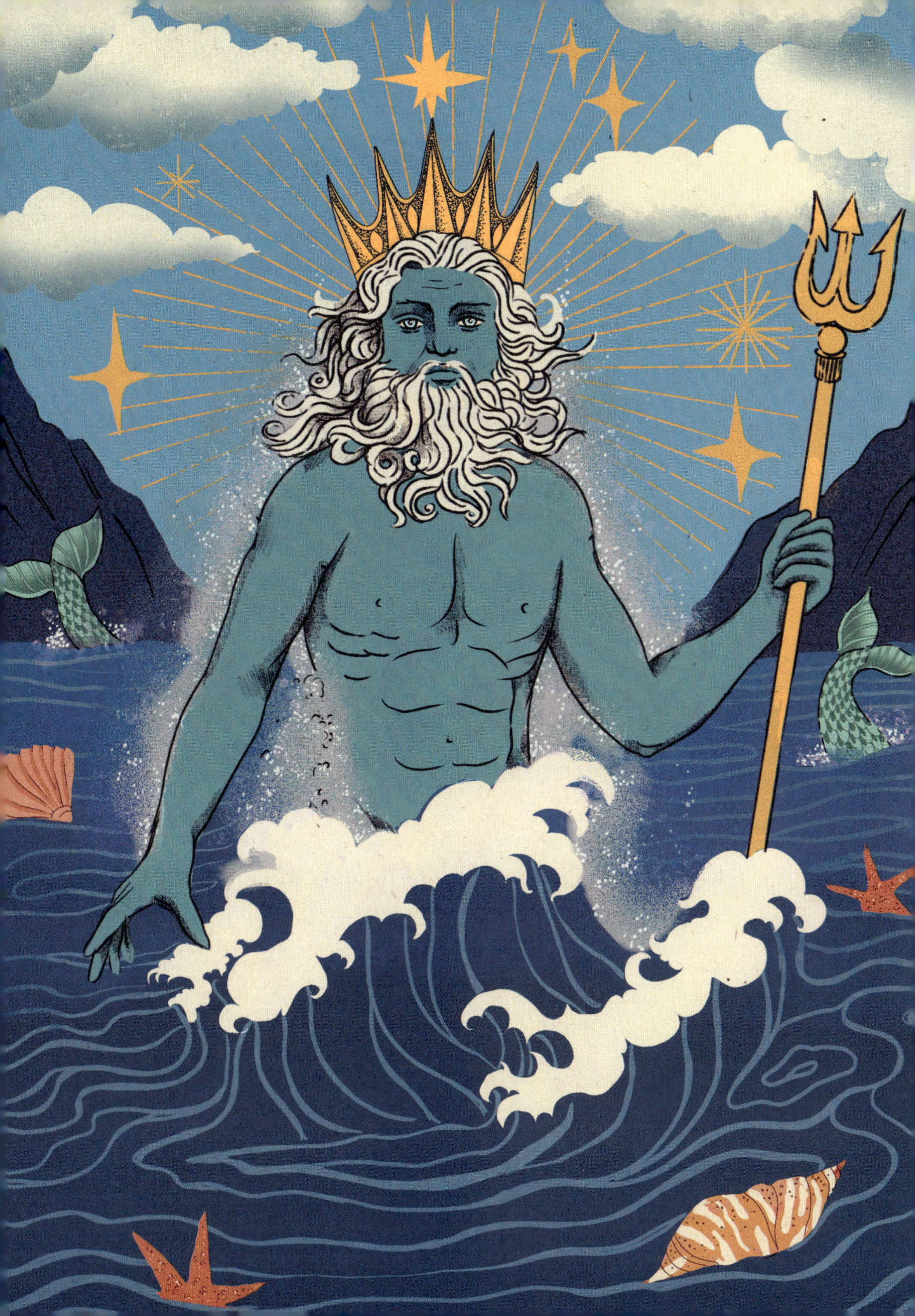

When each of his children were born, he would swallow them whole in a bid to save his throne and keep them with him. At least if they lingered in his belly they could do no harm. And so that is what he did.

Each time his beautiful wife, the goddess Ops, fell pregnant, he would clasp his hands with glee and promise to love his offspring, but when the fateful day of birth arrived he'd be there to consume the newborn before it had even taken its first breath. And so it was that Neptune, son of Saturnus, was swallowed and left to languish in his father's stomach for eternity.

But destiny cannot always be predicted, as Saturnus was about to learn, for while he could control that which he had conceived, he could not control his wife's emotions. Like any mother, Ops was beside herself with grief and enraged by her husband's actions, and so on learning she was with child once more, she hatched a plan. When the baby Jupiter was born she hid him from sight and, instead, presented a stone wrapped in swaddling to her beloved.

"Here my love," she whispered, "this is your son."

In response, Saturn took the child and swallowed it whole. As he did, his face drained of color.

"I . . . cannot . . . breathe!" He gasped and clawed at his throat.

The stone sat, an uncomfortable presence in his gullet, and he clasped his chest, rubbing furiously in a bid to loosen the load. He wretched and heaved over and over, until the entire contents of his stomach were repelled, and there before him stood all of his children fully grown, including his son Neptune.

While the rest of his brood were understandably livid with their father, Neptune stood still and appraised the situation silently. With a calm brow and a steady eye, he listened as the others planned their revenge, how they would overthrow their father, and how Jupiter, the last born and the only one not to have been consumed, would take his seat at the helm of the heavens. If anyone had cared to look and ask, they might have seen a different side to Neptune, or known that beneath the tranquil exterior, turbulent waves of emotion rumbled, but Neptune was not one to rant. He kept his anger deep within, beneath the gentle ebb and flow of his chest, and instead agreed to go along with their plans, knowing that he would never be part of the ruling gods that would govern Rome. He would be overlooked, as people often are when they speak little.

And so the tide turned, and Saturnus befell the same fate as his father. Jupiter, being the mightiest of all his children, usurped him and stepped proudly into his shoes. And each one of the deities were given a role, a dominion which they could rule over and make their own. For Neptune, it was the sea and all bodies of water, from the smallest trickle of a spring to the streams and rivers that flowed from his veins. While this seemed trivial to the other deities, who governed land and time itself, to Neptune it was the perfect pairing, for he was nothing if not fluid in his ways, and able to move freely wherever the fancy took him.

He took a wife, Salacia, a pretty young deity who governed the salt waters, and together they existed in a timeless flow, a spectral dance that rolled upon the surface of the waves. Theirs was a romance of twin souls, for they were almost one and the same in their thoughts and values, and they loved nothing more than to ride the ocean in their silver chariot, pulled by a team of glimmering seahorses. They had many children—sparkling, finned beauties who swam among the fishes.

In those days, the Earth was just a seed, a piece of a much larger puzzle, and one of many planets spinning in the Universe. It had no structure, no hills or valleys, no islands or plateaus, nothing to shape it, or help new life to grow. No forests, jungles, deserts, or shorelines, no barriers, or boundaries, to keep things in or out. Nature could not exist in its entirety without first finding its roots in something, a realization that Jupiter came to swiftly.

"We need to shape the Earth; we cannot just leave it hanging. We need to mold it, to create a place where life can exist, so that we can furnish it with people who will worship and adore us." He spoke with fervor, as he gazed at the gathered pantheon. "Who will assist me in this challenge?"

As always, the gods tumbled over themselves to speak first, to be gifted with the task in hand, but it was Neptune who eventually caught their eye, for he couldn't help but chuckle.

"What is it, brother?" Jupiter asked. "What do you find so funny?"

Neptune shrugged and tugged at his white beard. "You are all so funny," he sighed. "You shout and yell, you demand attention, believing that the louder you are, the more powerful this makes you. And yet you fail to see that real power comes from within."

The gathered clan began to jeer, their voices raised and angry like thunder, until Jupiter waved his hand to silence them. "Very well, brother, it is obvious you think that you, made only of water, are more powerful than any of us, so, I am going to give you the responsibility of shaping the Earth. Let us see what you can do." And he laughed, "I doubt you'll be able to shift a grain of sand."

Neptune nodded, "I will do what I can, brother."

The other gods parted, giving Neptune the floor to demonstrate his magnificence. They gathered in clusters, giggling and sniping, waiting for the god to fail. Even Jupiter sat back in his golden throne with a wide grin on his face, ready to be entertained.

Taking his trident in both hands, Neptune closed his eyes. Beneath heavy lids, he could feel their mockery. He knew they were waiting for him to fail, but they had always underestimated his strength and the passion with which he governed the sea. Taking a deep breath, he allowed all of that emotion, all of the anger, pain, and suffering, all of the light, love, and the loathing at the way he was so often treated, to fill him up, and then he struck. He slammed his trident into the ground with such force that it seemed to split the Earth in two. In that moment, Neptune opened his heart and mind, and let the two merge, bringing the unconscious watery world of his dreams into the conscious solid world of reality—everything was consumed, torn apart in a torrent of sea spray.

The land was swallowed, just as Saturnus had swallowed his children, buried beneath a riot of plundering waves, the surge of the ocean and all of the rivers united. Even the world of the gods became nothing more than a cascading avalanche of water. It rushed and it roared, it stripped and it carved, eating away whole chunks of the planet, slicing at rock, and creating patterns and crevices that adorned the landscape. It filled every last part of the world as it was, until all that was left was sea. The Earth was no more but a broiling cauldron of liquid, floating in mid-air.

Somewhere in the confusion, the cries of the gods could be heard. Their pleas became louder as they tried to hold on, to retain their own shape and form and not be sucked into the whirling vacuum, along with everything else. Even Jupiter shared his despair, calling out for his brother to regain control, and stop the madness. But the problem was that Neptune had kept a lid on his emotions for so long, and to finally unburden himself was such a relief. To show the other deities that he was just as powerful, if not more, and that he had a place in the world and a purpose, felt good and freeing. But it was then that he remembered why he had never lost control before, because he knew this—he had always known his own strength, and the talents and gifts with which he'd been blessed. He did not need to show off or seek their adulation. He knew who he was and did not need to stoke his own ego. Neptune was happy in himself and that was enough.

In that moment, he found his compassion and composure once more and released his grip on the mighty trident.

"Blow the conch," he called to his son Triton. "It will break the spell and take back the waters."

Pressing the enormous shell to his lips, Triton blew, and the sound that came out stopped the world from turning.

Slowly, almost in a dream-like state, the seas and rivers, the streams and lakes, and every tiny drop of water, began to subside, to retreat and merge together, to become organized and ordered upon the land. And as the liquid evaporated it revealed a new Earth, changed and weathered by the great flood. Countries emerged between separate oceans and fields, and meadows grew alongside winding rivers and streams. Lakes formed— twinkling, crater-like holes from which the trees and hills could overlook— and the planet became whole and fit for purpose, just as Jupiter had wanted.

As the dust settled, the deities fell to their feet, and Jupiter, too, bowed his head in a mark of respect that was quite out of character for the king of the gods. A hush fell upon the pantheon, in a silent understanding that true power and might did not have to be paraded ostentatiously, that even the quietest and humblest, the ones who keep their feelings to themselves, have the ability to make waves and make their mark upon the Earth.

And so it was that the contours of the world were born, and the Roman people rejoiced. "Behold the sea!" they cried joyfully, for while they recognized that Jupiter was the king of all, it was Neptune who had truly shaped their land.

NEPTUNE RITUAL TO CALM THE MIND AND BALANCE EMOTIONS

You will need: A warm bath, geranium essential oil, and a large shell.

This ritual embraces the fluid aspects of the planet Neptune and the associated god. It helps you to recognize and acknowledge your feelings and soothe the mind.

- Run yourself a warm bath and add in several drops of geranium essential oil. This lovely scent has healing and grounding properties.
- Swirl the oil into the water with your hand and inhale the fragrant steam. Breathe deeply and imagine drawing in the aroma, taking it into your belly and then releasing any stress with your outward breath.
- Immerse yourself in the bath and let the warm water soothe your body.
- Close your eyes for a moment and imagine you are floating in the sea. Enjoy the sensation as the water caresses your skin.
- Hold the shell in both hands as you soak and think about how you feel right now and what is important in your life. If something is bothering you, bring it to mind, and acknowledge it.
- Take a deep breath and, as you exhale, imagine pouring all of those feelings into the shell.
- Repeat this process for two or three breaths, then dip the shell into the water, and say, "I release my fear and worry, I embrace my emotions, and let the element of water soothe my soul."
- To finish, simply relax in the water, breathe, and enjoy the tranquil atmosphere you have created.

✳ **AFFIRMATION**

"I release fear and worry. I embrace my emotions, and let the element of water soothe my soul."

PLUTO
The Wealthy One

PLANETARY ASSOCIATIONS
Endings, transformation, rebirth, rejuvenation, intensity, acceptance.

ASTROLOGICAL SIGN Scorpio

Since the dawn of time, the god of the Underworld has worn many faces—some twisted, disfigured, and hidden by the light; others victorious and easy upon the eye. Depending on where you are in the world, he shifts and changes.

While most mortals perished in this shadowy Underworld, the Roman god ruled his domain with a degree of fairness. He was neither good nor bad, but interpreted his role as that of a gatekeeper and a caretaker of souls. His name was Pluto, son of Saturnus and Ops, brother of Jupiter, and lord of the subterranean realm.

Unlike most of his siblings, Pluto was not motivated by avarice or a need for power, and perhaps that is why he was ultimately rewarded with Earth's riches. He didn't destroy the land in his hunt for treasure, nor did he appeal for worship or a lofty position under Jupiter's rule. Pluto demanded very little, for in his heart he knew that whatever he was gifted, he would find value in. His brother Jupiter could not understand Pluto's reticence to lead and his desire to stay out of the limelight.

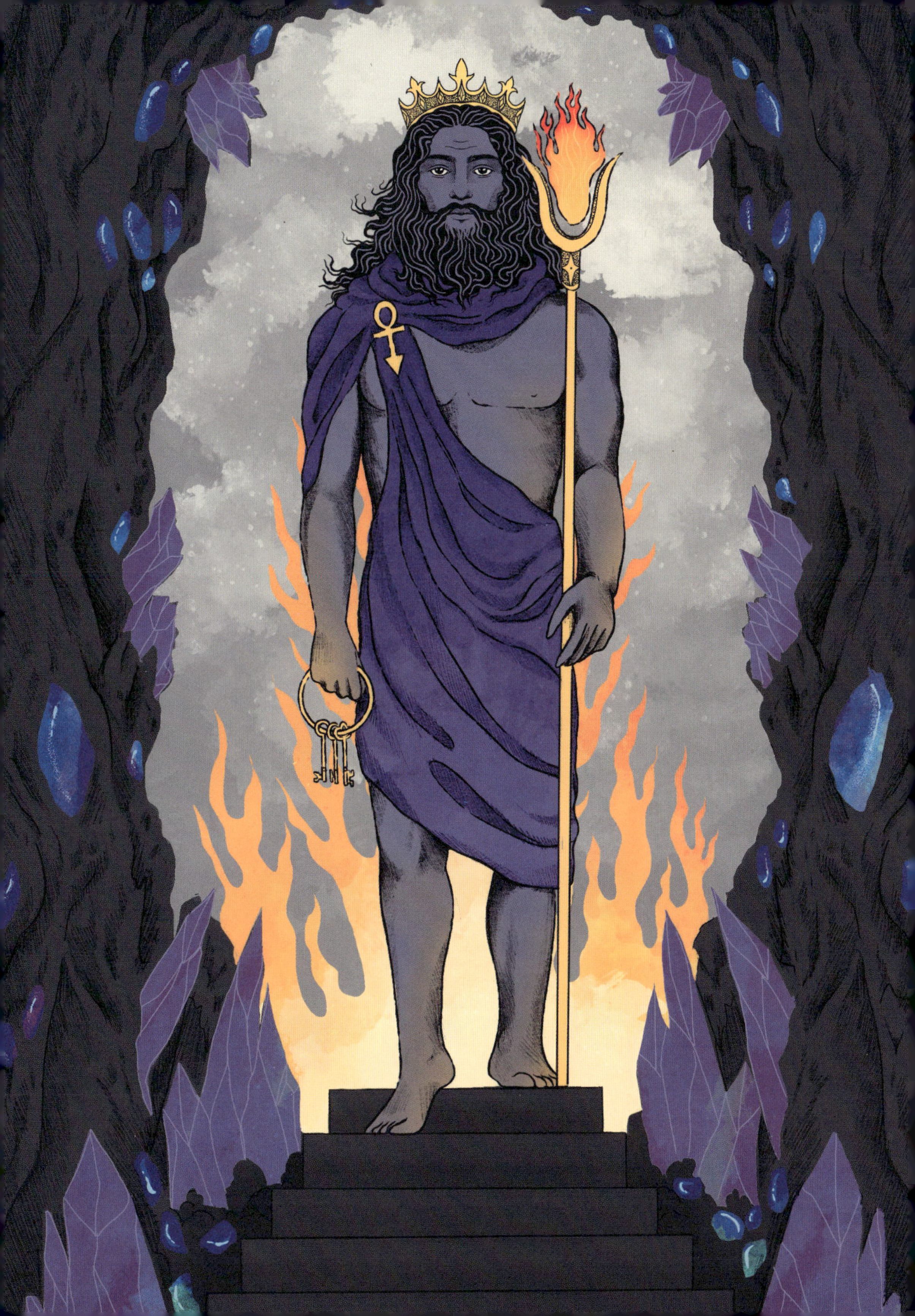

"You are a god; you should be worshipped. Do you not want to sit at my right hand and be exalted?"

Pluto furrowed his brow. "If that is your wish, then I will do your bidding, but I am happy to be wherever you place me."

Jupiter smirked. "Very well, brother, I have the perfect place for you. You will be the lord of the Underworld, the gatekeeper of lost souls. You will frequent the deepest, darkest places where only the dead can see you, and that will be your kingdom. See how much that pleases you!"

If it was meant as an insult, Pluto did not see it. In the great lottery that was the division of heavenly roles, he was happy with his prize and vowed to do his best.

The other gods and goddesses were amused by this. "Can he not see that you have given him nothing but a pile of rotting earth? What kind of a palace will he make out of that?" they scoffed.

Jupiter grinned. "He is as clueless as he is weak. He will never be rich and adored like us."

But while the other deities plotted and schemed their way to the top of the pantheon and plundered the Earth for treasure, Pluto settled into his new home.

He shifted the soil and molded cavernous chambers beneath the surface of the Earth. He created a great hall where he could sit and survey his domain and greet those who came to his world. He mined the depths with precision and care, and painstakingly chiselled a path toward the core of the planet, for it seemed to him that he had been given a vast empire to explore. And in doing so he discovered great wealth, for the Earth was rich with jewels, gold, and iron ore. There was an abundant supply that he could mine until the end of time.

"By the power of Jove!" he exclaimed. "What a blessing my brother has given me."

And Pluto, being a fair and reasonable being, decided that he would share his prosperity with the people of the Earth. Each time he rose from the Underworld on one of his many visits to the other realms, he brought with him such treasures, from nuggets of gold that he lay in the glistening rivers and streams, to jewels and stones that he etched into the landscape. It seemed that wherever he went he distributed some part of his wealth, and for that the Roman people loved him, and began to call him "the wealthy one." They were no longer afraid of death or the shadowy realm, for it seemed it was a place of good fortune, ruled by a bountiful god. And because of his capacity to distribute the Earth's gifts throughout the land so that anyone could happen upon them, Pluto soon became associated with luck. He naturally evolved into a god who could control the fates of humankind and bless them with good fortune.

"How can this be?" raved Jupiter from the heavens. "How does my brother achieve such adulation, when he is the god of the Underworld? It does not make any sense!"

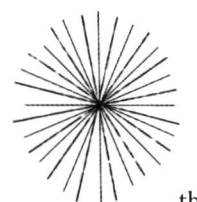

His brother's popularity was troubling, and he longed to change this, but the only thing he could do was to send more souls into the gloomy Underworld, in the hope that death would be enough to sway the living and make them hate the god.

At this time, there lived a great mystic and a gifted musician named Orpheus. Known to the Greeks as well as the Romans, he was hugely popular, and his music had a magical quality that could soothe his listeners to sleep and influence their thoughts. A master of the lyre, among other things, he could weave the most enchanting melodies, and create beauty out of nothing.

Orpheus was in love with Eurydice, and she would accompany him on his travels throughout Rome. Known for her charm and ability to dance to her husband's music, she was pursued by many, but only had eyes for Orpheus. One day while out walking, she was chased by an ardent admirer. In her haste to get away, she stepped on a viper. The snake bit her foot and she died instantly.

Whether Jupiter had a hand in her fate, it is hard to tell, but what was true was that he would do anything to besmirch the reputation of the Underworld and the goodwill that his brother had accrued. He longed to make him look a lesser god in the eyes of the people.

Orpheus was devastated at the loss of Eurydice, and tried everything to revive her, even playing his most beautiful songs to bring her back to life, but nothing worked. Her soul was lost to the Underworld, and there was only one course of action. He journeyed deep beneath the Earth to Pluto's sunken palace and begged an audience with the god.

"Let me play some music for you, let me entertain you for as long as you desire with my lyre, and if it makes you happy, if it satisfies your soul, then please let me be reunited with my love," he pleaded.

Most other gods might have dismissed Orpheus with a wave of their hand, but Pluto, being fair of heart and somewhat lonely himself, decided that there was nothing wrong in hearing the young man play. After all, he had little other entertainment, and secretly desired a diversion to lift his spirits. And so Orpheus began to play, and as he did, his heart opened and he channeled all of his emotions into this one piece of music. He closed his eyes, and let the feelings flow into each note, and the melody that this produced was soulful and sweet. Each delicately placed verse was a story in its own right, a message about the meaning of love and how two souls could be united even in death. The music rang through the hollows, echoing against the cold stone. Pluto sighed and let the lullaby carry him away, and for a moment he forgot who he was, but a pause in the music made him come to his senses and he motioned for the playing to stop.

"Orpheus, I will grant you your wish, for it seems to me that you know the true value of love, but I cannot have other gods thinking me foolish or weak. And so for this reason I would ask that you follow my one rule." He paused. "You may lead Eurydice back to the land of the living, and she will follow you all the way, but you must not look back at her until you reach the other side. If you do, she will be lost to you forever."

Orpheus nodded. "I understand, Lord of the Underworld, and I thank you. I promise to heed your words."

"Be sure you do," said Pluto. "I have been fair and just, have I not?"

"Yes, great one, you have. It is true what they say, you are 'the wealthy one.'"

Pluto smiled. "Then be on your way, and know that she is walking behind you."

With that, Orpheus left, taking the long and treacherous trail back up through the Earth, through the jagged rocky landscape, and the twisting crevices. He took each step slowly, so that his love would be able to keep up, but despite this, he could not hear her. If she followed then it was silently, and he began to wonder if the god had been true to his word.

A glint of daylight could be seen through a chink of rock, and they were almost at the surface, ready to cross over into the land of the living, but Orpheus couldn't wait any longer. He had to know if Eurydice was with him, and so in that final moment, he turned to look at her.

What he saw ripped his heart in two, for she was indeed one step behind, but being still in the Underworld she was wraith-like in form and engulfed in shadowy tendrils. Her eyes were empty, and as her mouth opened to scream, her entire body quivered and curled in on itself until she was no more than dust.

Orpheus cried out in horror, but there was nothing he could do. The god had set a rule, and he had broken it, and this was his punishment. And perhaps in that moment, in the tale of Orpheus's sorrow, Pluto darkened his reputation, for he had acted with vengeance and terror—like the god of the Underworld. And perhaps that is what Jupiter had wanted all along. Or maybe it was merely a part of the picture, for in truth, Pluto had not lied and, like any king, had set the rules for a reason. The Underworld was not a place for the living, and its secrets were to remain hidden until the time came to cross over. Pluto knew this and was simply protecting Orpheus from the truth.

And so he became neither good nor bad. He simply was the god of the Underworld, a gatekeeper to the next life, and "the wealthy one," for he had accepted his place in the world with grace and embraced the positives of this existence. Despite Jupiter's best efforts to undermine him, Pluto had made the transformation from one world to another and learned the secrets of life and death. And that made him the richest being of them all.

PLUTO RITUAL TO EMBRACE CHANGE AND PROMOTE TRANSFORMATION

You will need: Space where you won't be disturbed, soft cushions, and some relaxing music.

This ritual harnesses the progressive energy of this unique planet, by helping you accept the ebb and flow of situations. It combines a breathing exercise with visualization to promote change.

- Arrange the cushions so that you can sit comfortably, with your back straight, and your lower back supported.
- Play the soothing music.
- Close your eyes, and let the music carry you away to your happy place.
- Position both hands on the area just above your naval. Take a long deep breath in, and count for four slow beats. As you exhale, feel your body relax, and count out for four slow beats as you release the breath. Continue to breathe in this way for at least a minute.
- Notice the warmth in your fingers, and how this gentle energy begins to whirl beneath your hands.
- As you breathe in, visualize the ocean lapping against the shore.
- For every inhale, picture a wave rolling in, and for every exhale, picture the water retreating from the coastline.
- Continue to see the ocean and feel the ebb and flow of the water.
- Engage your other senses and imagine what else you can hear, smell, and feel.
- To finish, say, "I am like the sea, I ebb, I flow, I embrace change within me."

✳ **AFFIRMATION**

"I ebb, I flow, and I embrace change within me."

THE SUN
The Unconquered

PLANETARY ASSOCIATIONS
Joy, confidence, courage, brightness, vitality, boldness, leadership.

ASTROLOGICAL SIGN Leo

DAY OF THE WEEK Sunday

Where would we be without the Sun? It's a question that the Ancients pondered daily, as they watched this scorching ball of fire rise into the sky upon heavenly wings: a dial of light so potent it could change the shape of the landscape, bathing it in brightness.

Its warmth, while soft upon the skin, could burn with ferocity, causing fever and pain, and yet it was soothing, too, and much needed after the biting chill of winter. With the power to make things grow, to raise tiny flowerheads from their Earthly beds and encourage the trees to blossom, it was a nurturing, encouraging force and the primal source of all life. But should the heat become too much, then the land would dry out. The soil would crack, and the leaves would turn brittle and fall from the stem. The Sun was tempestuous, reliable in its travels but unpredictable in its moods, and so the Ancients made up stories to explain this. They created a deity that, depending on where you were in the world, took on many different forms.

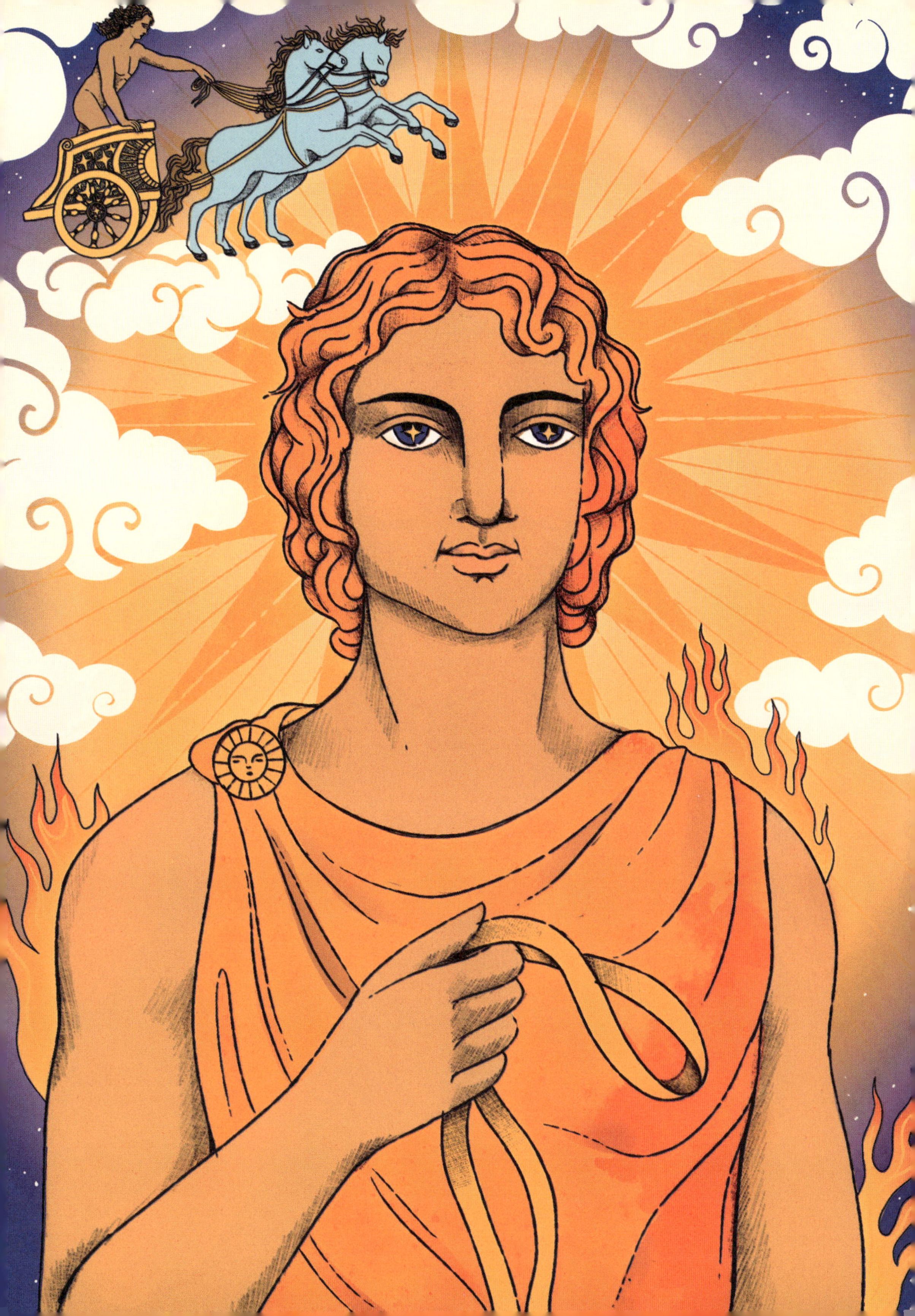

To the Romans, who attributed the planets with their godly status, the Sun was Sol Invictus, otherwise known as the "Unconquered Sun." A mighty flame-haired being, he bore the many faces of his counterparts, being always present in the sky wherever you were in the world. And since he was much revered, this made him proud and self-assured. He loved nothing more than to boast of his success and would beam with joy at his achievements.

"Am I not the most powerful of all the gods?" he would say. "I rise every day and I vanquish the darkness. My smile lights up the Earth as I soar through the sky. There is no other like me."

It was true he was victorious each morning, banishing the night with his fiery halo, and then to be sure he had eliminated the shadows, he would ride his golden chariot through the sky, casting rays of warmth in every direction. Pulled by four impressive steeds, the chariot known as a *quadriga* moved at such speed that it would sear a path through the clouds, sometimes slicing them in two as it charged forward. The people would stare at Sol's magnificence and shield their eyes, for his power was too mighty for them to behold with the naked eye. The emperor Aurelian, who had first introduced the god to the people of Rome, knew this and, being a sworn follower and the founder of the Cult of Sol, declared that he should be considered the most powerful of all the pantheon. He built a stunning temple in honor of Sol in Rome and urged his people to worship there every day.

"We must keep him happy for he serves us well," he advised, and the people did exactly what he said.

In return, the Sun god lapped up the attention and shone even more brightly in the sky, and so the cycle of day and night continued, much to everyone's delight.

The gods, however, were less enamored with Sol's confidence. His cheerful disposition was often mistaken for arrogance, and his continual brightness served as a reminder of the immense, life-giving power he had at his fingertips. Each deity had their own cross to bear. They wanted to be top of the tree, and the one most worshiped by the Romans. It seemed unfair to them that Sol only had to rise from his bed and shine his light to gain their favor.

"What makes him so special?" they would cry. "We all have our gifts, but we do not boast about them like he does!"

In truth, they were all as bad as each other, and being deities, longed to be deified. Power struggles had always existed amidst the pantheon and would continue as long as humans continued to idolize them.

"We should put him to the test, challenge him!" the deities suggested.

And so, after much discussion, the pantheon decided upon a chariot race. After all, Sol was a gifted horseman and claimed that nothing and no one could stop him. But while the idea of a race was a popular one, finding a challenger was not so easy. Each of the gods had a reason why they shouldn't be picked for the job. The gods of the sea were adamant that if they left their domain, the ocean would rise up and swallow the Earth. Those concerned with the Underworld said it would be chaos if they left their post, for who would control the lost souls? The war gods claimed that their strength and presence was needed to instill courage upon the battlefield and that they had little time to spare for such trivial pursuits. While those who meddled in Earthly concerns felt their presence was needed with the people to imbue them with calm and advise them. And so it fell to Luna, the goddess of the Moon, to take up the challenge. She would be the one to chase her brother through the sky, and this seemed to make sense, for she already had her own chariot, known as a *biga*, and two powerful horses.

Sol, for his part, was amused by the suggestion of a contest, but also thrilled to be able to show off his skill and speed. "Let the festivities commence upon my birthday!" he declared gleefully. "It will be the perfect culmination to my celebrations."

And so the great race was set for December 25, the day that Sol had first unleashed his light upon the world, also known as the "*dies natalis invicti*" and the celebration of the Winter Solstice.

The gods gathered together, taking their pews among the stars in anticipation of a great race, and there was much speculation and chatter. But as the morning came and the Sun began to rise, the Moon was nowhere to be seen. This didn't deter Sol, he was already leaping into action, determined to take advantage of his sister's absence. Harnessing his four stealthy horses, he took his seat in the glowing chariot. With a flick of his hands upon the reins, they were off and lifting into the sky.

It seemed that Luna was lagging behind, that her silvery steeds were not yet fixed in place, and her chariot was far from ready, but even so, she tried with all her might to rise from the ground. She drew a deep breath and cast her gentle light in the sky, but it paled beneath the burning rays of her brother, and from the Earth no one could see her. Once again she tried to push forward, to take her place in the cosmic stadium and catch up with Sol, but her graceful movements and shifting shape were no match for the Sun's speed and vitality and her luminescence was a faint glimmer in the blue sky.

The wheels of Sol's chariot rattled and shook, and the horses' legs made short work of the heavens. Emerging from behind clusters of cloud he took center stage and gathered even more pace, until it was clear that he couldn't possibly be caught.

From the ground, the people stared. They were in awe of the blazing performance in the sky, while the gods were also speechless. It seemed there was no stopping Sol. Luna, though she had tried, could not catch her brother. She knew that it was not her time or place to shine, and that she was a goddess of the night sky—that was where she felt most at home, and so, admitting defeat, she faded into the background.

"No one races a chariot like Sol Invictus!" the emperor Aurelian exclaimed as he watched the commotion. "He is an example to us all to do what we do best, and to do it with confidence."

Following the lead of the Sun, the emperor made a pact that chariot races should be a key part of any festivity, and a main attraction within the Roman Circus.

"Let us honor the talents of our Sun god and build a temple to Sol Invictus within the Circus Maximus in Rome. It will be a great place where we can go and experience the thrill of a chariot ride through the sky."

Then he decreed that the same honor should be given to Luna, for she, too, was a chariot racer. "We will build a temple to the Moon goddess at the Circus Maximus. Let brother and sister stand side by side and be worshipped in the same way."

Within each temple he placed a stone statue to represent the god and goddess, and the eternal ride they embarked upon daily for the benefit of everyone on Earth.

And so it was that chariot races for both *quadrigae* and *bigae*, became commonplace in the circus and a popular form of entertainment for the Roman people.

As for Sol Invictus, he remained victorious and unconquered, as his name suggests. His eternal passage through the sky remains continual, an unstoppable cycle and a key part of life upon Earth.

Honored by people around the world, whatever their culture or religion, the Sun has become a symbol of joy and brightness, synonymous with new life and vitality. An ever-present ball of warmth, encouraging growth and movement, it is a reminder from the heavens that once we have found our place and purpose, we should embrace it and never be afraid to let our light shine.

SUN RITUAL TO BOOST POSITIVE ENERGY AND PROMOTE JOY

You will need: A mat and some space, preferably in front of a window where you can see the sunrise.

This exercise is best performed first thing in the morning. It's a good way to harness the power of the Sun, and help you feel energized for the day ahead.

- To begin, throw open the curtains and greet the Sun. Even on a gray day, the fiery ball is still present in the sky, so if you can't see it, imagine it beaming down on you.
- Next, stand with your feet hip-width apart on the mat. Roll forward from the waist and let your arms and hands hang toward the floor. You might want to clasp your calves, or touch your toes, if you can.
- Take a couple of deep breaths in this position and, when you're ready, draw a long, slow breath in, and slowly unfurl.
- Continue to raise your body and your arms upward in a sweeping motion, until your arms are pointing to the sky.
- Hold this position for a few seconds and continue to breathe deeply.
- Gently bring your arms out to the side, at shoulder level, so that you create a cross shape.
- Continue to take slow, deep breaths as you stand in this position.
- Finally, inhale deeply through your nose and, as you do, bring your arms forward in a hugging motion. Imagine that with this one motion you are embracing the Sun and drawing its light and energy into your body.
- Bring this breath into your chest and hold it there, before exhaling a steady stream of air from your lips.
- Repeat the exercise at least two more times and continue to draw the Sun's warmth and energy into your body.
- To finish, relax in a standing position, look out at the world, and say, "The Sun imbues me with light, love, and positivity!"

✷ **AFFIRMATION**

"The Sun imbues me with light, love, and positivity!"

THE MOON
The Light Within

PLANETARY ASSOCIATIONS
Hidden emotions, intuition, psychic perception, imagination, feminine power.

ASTROLOGICAL SIGN Cancer

DAY OF THE WEEK Monday

In the first days of existence, there was the primordial darkness: an inky soup that spread like a dark whirring ocean and covered the vast expanse of the heavens. It was a rippling river that looked almost velvet to the touch, but was made of nothing but air, for while it seemed to have strength and substance, it could not be captured in any form. This was the sky, but it was not as we know it today.

In those earliest moments at the dawn of time, the sky was a blank canvas, waiting for creation's paintbrush to bring it to life. And while there were no people to see it, to give voice to what it could possibly be, or to make sense of the vista, there were the gods and goddesses, the deities who were responsible for shaping all things.

As each new god or goddess was born, they were gifted a purpose and a reason for being, and it was this that colored the Earth, and eventually gave it structure. Among those first deities were the Titans,

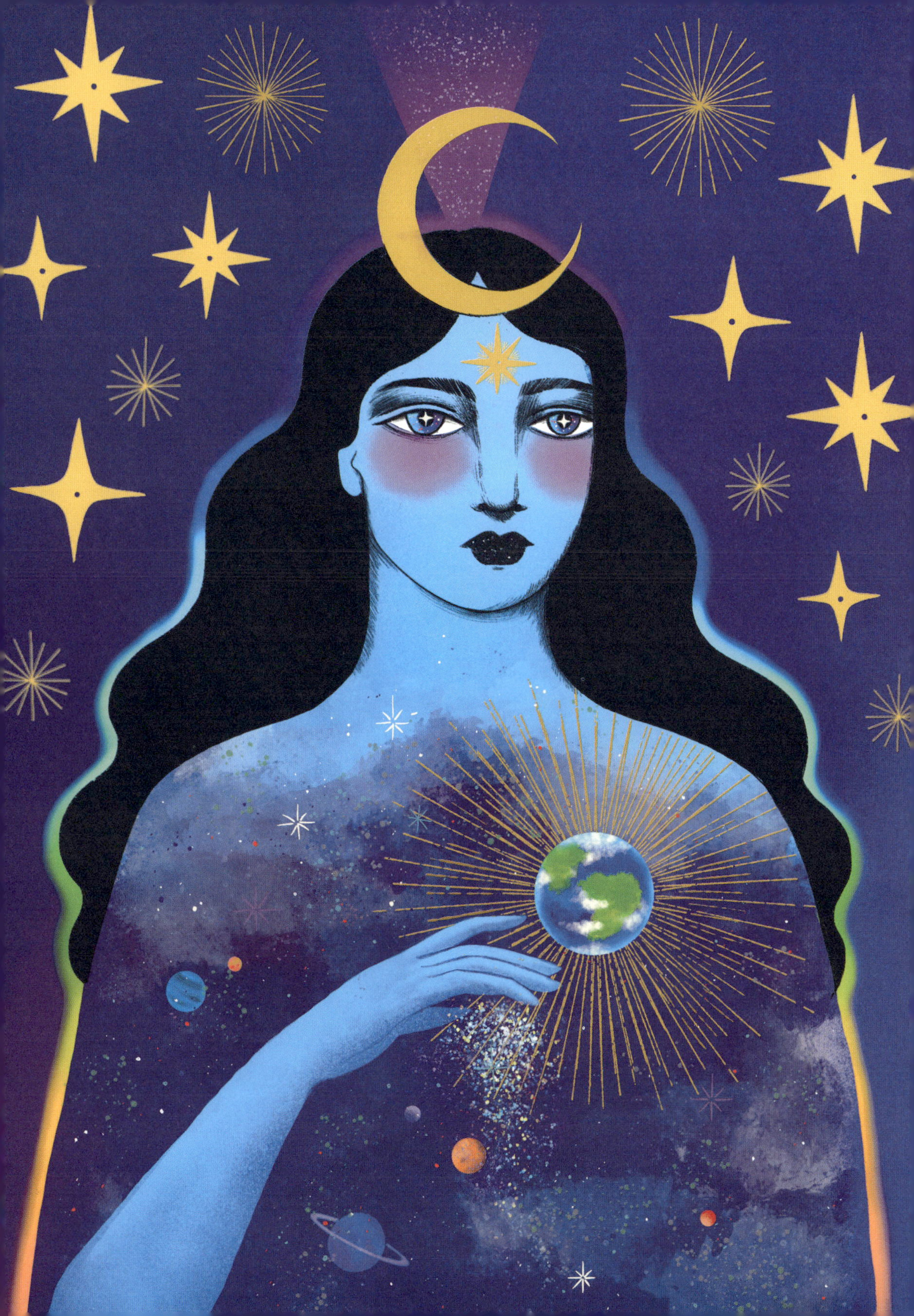

an impressive race of beings filled with immense power. When they moved, the planet moved with them, and the light that spread from their aura was so bright and all-encompassing, it could blind even the mightiest of gods. Their offspring were equally as potent, having harnessed the energy of their parents, but also having a new understanding of the world, and so the pantheon grew and with it came new life and vision.

And so it was that the great Titan god Hyperion, giver of heavenly light and wisdom, and his consort Theia, a radiant beauty and goddess who reflected the brilliance of his light, gave birth to their brood of magical children. Their son Sol was renowned even before he emerged from the womb. It seemed that he would grow in significance to become one of the most prominent within the heavenly clan. There were whispers of his greatness among the other deities, who were surely jealous of the newborn's strength, for when he entered the world he brought a light so bright that it burned a path and scorched the land beneath. Soon, he became recognized in his own right as the Sun.

Then there was Aurora, the goddess of the dawn, a gentle, compassionate being whose fair face was to be the first that anyone would see when they began their day. Her warmth could light up the sky and would always herald the coming of her brother. She was welcomed with open arms wherever she roamed.

Finally, there was Luna, a solitary, soulful being, who upon first glace appeared sombre in comparison to her siblings. Her light was dim and her face milky pale, and it seemed to the other gods that perhaps Luna might never really amount to much. She certainly didn't have the strength to stand out like the rest of her family.

She would watch her brother and sister quietly, studying their every move. The way they danced across the sky, and the joy they scattered with spectral fingers seemed to come easy to them, but for Luna it was more complicated. She didn't fit within the waking hours. Her light, though otherworldly, was not bright enough to make a difference. Her glow was understated, beneath the glare of her brother's charms. And soon, she began to fade into the background, an outsider in the world of the gods. She flowed through the days, never really achieving anything, or at least that's how it felt to her.

"Can you not shine like me?" her brother would ask. "Have you *really* tried?"

But Luna would shake her dark curls, scattering tiny shards of moondust about his feet, and cry, "I am not like you. I cannot burn a path through the sky, no matter how hard I try."

"Perhaps you could join me each morning and ride in my chariot at dawn?" suggested Aurora. "You would be praised by the people for your rare beauty, and they would be happy to see you."

"But I am not you," Luna said softly, "I do not herald the coming of the day, that is not my place."

"Then what is?" asked Aurora. "You must have a purpose. We all do."

And it was true, every god and goddess since the beginning of time had a reason for being, a role that they took to heart and a domain that became their realm, whether it was the mountains and the woods, the dark, feral wild places where all manner of creatures lurked, or beneath the briny deep of the sea, in one of the many watery kingdoms that covered the land.

Luna sighed and looked down at the dusty Earth.

"My heavenly light barely touches the ground, and I cannot maintain it. It ebbs and flows with each breath I take, swelling to the whole, and then diminishing to nothing. I do not control my power. It controls me."

Her father, Hyperion, had been watching for some while and decided to step forward at that moment, to try and shed some light on the situation.

"Luna, only you have the answer. Look within. Trust your feelings, and you will know what to do, and where you belong."

That night, as her brother and sister slipped into slumber, plunging the Earth into darkness once more, Luna stepped barefoot from her bed. She was restless, unable to drift into dream, her mind filled with thoughts that tumbled behind her eyes. Her translucent skin cast a glimmer of light upon the fields and valleys, as she stepped into the shadows. Her white robes billowed about her ankles as she weaved gracefully over rocks, grass, sand, and pebbles. She longed to know the answer to her plight, and with each stride her anticipation grew, along with her emotions, which streamed like tendrils of light from her eyes. She looked up to the heavens with a question in her heart and felt a sudden weightlessness beneath her pallid flesh. The heaviness of not knowing her true purpose was gone, replaced by an intuitive understanding, a perceptiveness that surged through her body, and she realized that she was actually enjoying herself. Her journey had taken her far, and she had covered almost all of the planet in what seemed like a few short moments. Her steps, though weary at first, were now like feathers twisting upon a breeze. They carried her far and wide so that she covered every contour with ease.

Luna took a breath and placed her hands upon her chest. A well of excitement bubbled beneath; she felt alive amidst the cloak of night. Her eyes sparkled, casting diamond-like rays in every direction, and her aura illuminated the blanket of the sky. She stretched her arms into the air, flicking her slender fingers, and the residue that fell from her fingertips became a scattering of stars. She gasped with delight, and the breath that poured from her lips cast an ethereal glow upon the Earth below.

"This is what I am meant to do, and this is where I'm meant to be!" she exclaimed.

Slowly, an understanding formed in her mind, and the shifts in her appearance, her changing body each month, all became clear and necessary. She didn't need to control it, this was her power. She was forever evolving, and the transitions she experienced would become a part of nature, and a way to navigate the world for those who were lost in the dark. She would

THE MOON

be the clock they would look to, the all-encompassing, divine feminine power, for she encapsulated every woman who lived and breathed. As she changed from new, to crescent, then full, before waning into the dark of the Moon, she was the three aspects of womanhood, the maiden, the mother, and the crone, making her one of the mightiest of all the deities.

"I am the Moon!" she called, lifting her face upward so that the light within could caress the entire Earth as it was meant to do, and she remained that way until morning came.

Aurora was the first to notice her absence, as she harnessed the white and pink horses to her chariot and began the steady rise into the sky to mark the dawn of the day. It seemed that her sister had disappeared into thin air, or perhaps she was hiding. And later, as she passed her brother, handing over the baton of light into his fiery grip, she whispered, "Where is Luna? Have you seen her this morning?"

Sol shook his head, scattering vibrant sunlight in every direction. Making his way through the sky, he scoured the Earth in search of his missing sibling, but it seemed she had vanished from sight. It didn't matter how brightly he shone; he could not pinpoint her whereabouts. It was only when the dim light of dusk set in and Sol began his gradual descent, that he saw his sister emerge from the clouds.

"Luna, where have you been?"

The goddess simply smiled beatifically, and in that one expression everything became suddenly clear. As the night huddled snugly to the craggy landscape, clinging tightly to the rocks and mountains, and vanquishing every last drop of Sol's sunshine, Luna took center stage. She rose, at first shrouded in mist, and then she unveiled her shining beauty for all to see. Wearing her crescent Moon crown with a veil of stars to cover her womanly curves, she looked every inch a Moon goddess, and her energy could be felt far and wide. From the pull of tides to the awakening of tiny saplings, she cast her ghostly light and those who saw it were either soothed and emotional, or driven half-mad with inspiration.

The people of Rome were taken aback by the glory of the Moon and the way she made them feel. They began to follow her patterns, to chart her journey throughout the month, and they gave thanks for her loveliness. They called her a goddess and embraced the gifts that she bestowed. They instinctively petitioned her and worked with her magic during every phase. And Luna became hallowed and revered among the other deities. She found love in the arms of the shepherd prince Endymion and gave birth to an array of dazzling stars. She had a dalliance with the king of the gods Jupiter and secured her place in the history of ancient Rome, and eventually within every mythology and culture throughout the world.

Luna had finally found her purpose and her seat in the heavens, but despite her magnificence she never forgot what it felt like to be an outsider—to hold a different kind of light within.

MOON RITUAL TO BOOST YOUR INTUITION AND CREATIVITY

You will need: A good view of the Moon in any of its phases, and a piece of moonstone.

This ritual will help you embrace the Moon's gentle light, and use this energy to spark your imagination, and allow your intuition to flow.

- If you can, stand outside beneath the light of the Moon, or in front of a window where you have a clear view of this dazzling orb.
- Spend a few minutes clearing your mind with some deep breathing.
- Hold the moonstone in your cupped hands, and gaze at the Moon. Moonstone has a loving energy, which helps to sharpen intuition and increase your psychic perception.
- Let your chest soften, and draw a long breath in. As you do, imagine you're drawing down the light of the Moon, taking it deep into your chest.
- As you exhale, extend the breath, and imagine the light seeping into every part of your body. Feel its cool, calming energy refreshing you. As you do this, you might notice that your body begins to tingle as your psychic senses open up.
- Continue to breath in this way and picture the soft glow of the Moon covering you from head to toe. Imagine it's a cloak of light encasing you, and keeping you safe, while also allowing you to tap in to your intuition.
- Bring the moonstone up to your heart chakra, which is situated in the center of your chest, and imagine absorbing the energy of this stone, taking it deep into your heart.
- Hold the stone here for a minute and close your eyes. Use this time to let any thoughts, feelings, or psychic insights arise. Don't force anything. Simply relax, and let images and emotions flow through your mind.
- When you're ready, open your eyes, give your body a gentle shake, and make a note of how you feel and anything you can remember.

✳ **AFFIRMATION**

"Like the Moon, my inner glow illuminates the darkness."

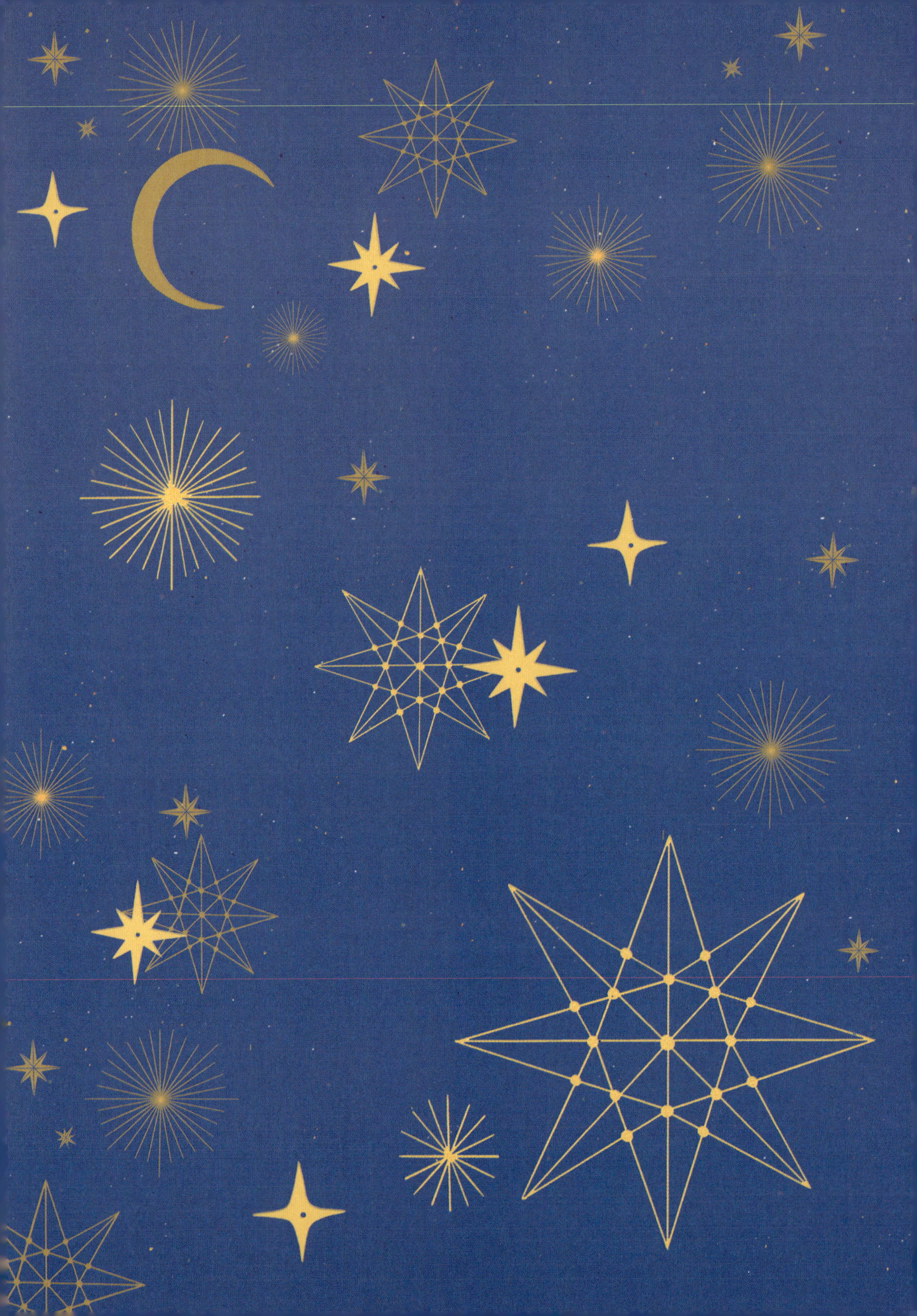

"I reach for the stars every day."

A FINAL WORD

There is nothing more otherworldly than standing beneath the night sky and gazing at its magnificence. The enormity of the vista is a reminder that anything is possible and your potential is unlimited. All you have to do is believe.

Look to the constellations for inspiration and you will see a million stories threaded in their pretty patterns. Be encouraged by the epic tales of each Zodiac sign and take their lessons to heart. Absorb the beauty of each planet, including the one that is your home, and find an even deeper enjoyment by knowing the myth that created the name and the associated deity. Stand in your power as you stare upward, and let these narratives weave their magic, and you will realize that everything is connected.

    The tales in this book can help you discover where you came from and find a common link with the Ancients, and their hopes and dreams. You'll hopefully begin to see how the Earth was shaped, and how we, as a race, moved forward and evolved. Most importantly, this will help you find your place within the world, and understand who you are, and how to make your mark. But this is only the beginning of your journey. Embrace celestial energy and let the narratives in this book be a springboard from which you can explore the fascinating realm of astrology, and its powerful influence upon your life.

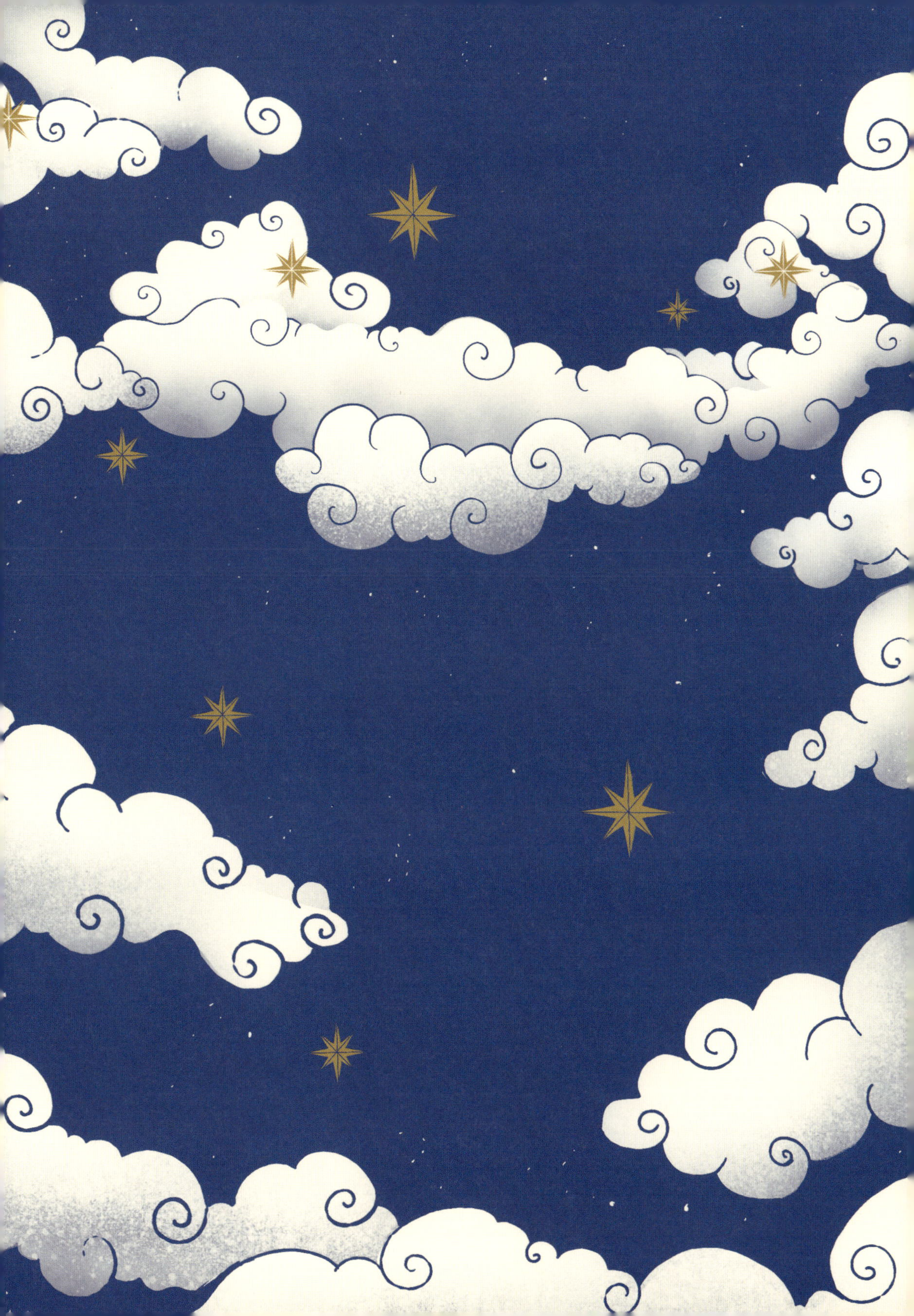

AFFIRMATIONS

ASTROLOGICAL SIGN AFFIRMATIONS

ARIES
"I reach for the stars every day."

TAURUS
"I am loved. I am loving. I love myself."

GEMINI
"I embrace both sides to make me whole, and let true harmony take control."

CANCER
"My inner light ignites my imagination."

LEO
"My light shines brighter with every breath I take."

VIRGO
"I am in tune with the natural world, and move with each transition."

LIBRA
"I am centered and happy."

SCORPIO
"I live with passion and follow my heart in all things."

SAGITTARIUS
"I allow my spontaneity to flow and embrace new adventures!"

CAPRICORN
"Every breath I take imbues me with clarity."

AQUARIUS
"My heart guides me toward my true purpose."

PISCES
"I release these emotions and open myself up to the flow of love."

PLANET AFFIRMATIONS

MERCURY
"I express myself with creativity and flair."

VENUS
"I see beauty. I am beauty."

MARS
"My personal power grows with every breath."

JUPITER
"I strive for success in everything I do."

SATURN
"Each moment of the day offers me the chance to reflect and recharge."

URANUS
"I go back to my core and uncover new and exciting opportunities and ideas."

NEPTUNE
"I release fear and worry. I embrace my emotions, and let the element of water soothe my soul."

PLUTO
"I ebb, I flow, and I embrace change within me."

THE SUN
"The Sun imbues me with light, love, and positivity!"

THE MOON
"Like the Moon, my inner glow illuminates the darkness."

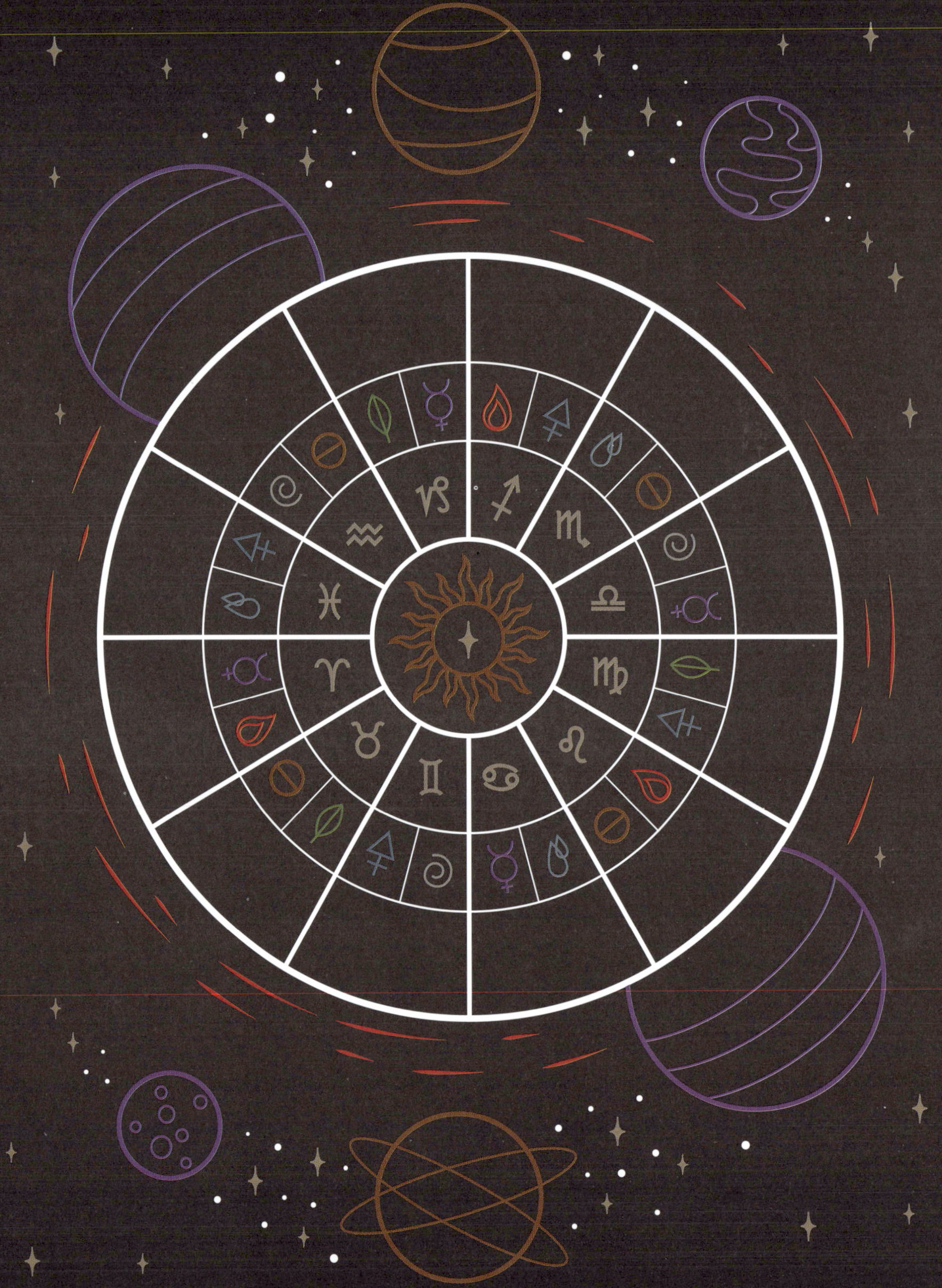

YOUR BIG THREE

While your Star sign (also known as your Sun sign) is the astrological sign most people tend to be familiar with, it doesn't stop there. Your astrological 'big three' is made up of your Sun sign, Moon sign, and Rising sign, which, together, characterize your entire personality, inside and out. You may wish to explore in depth the stories behind all of yours. Below is an explanation of what each of these signs represent, how you can work them out, and what they reveal about you.

SUN SIGN (ALSO KNOWN AS STAR OR ZODIAC SIGN)

REPRESENTS: The sign the Sun was in when you were born.

BASED ON: Your date of birth, and so is usually the same sign your birthday falls in each year. But it is worth double checking what sign the Sun was in, in the year you were born, as precise dates for each Zodiac sign can change by a few days each year.

REVEALS: Your outer personality and energy. This is the sign that predominantly influences you, including your motivations, and is consequently core to your identity and sense of self.

MOON SIGN

REPRESENTS: The constellation the Moon was in when you were born.

BASED ON: Your time of birth, since the Moon sign changes every two to two-and-a-half days. If you know your time of birth, there are many online calculators to help you work out your Moon sign. If you don't, it is still worth checking, since the Moon doesn't change signs every day. If the Moon did change signs on your birthday and you don't know your exact time of birth, read about both signs and choose the one you relate to the most.

REVEALS: Your inner personality and emotions. While your Sun sign is about how others see you, your Moon sign is more about how you see yourself, in private. Understanding it can lead to greater self-knowledge, and, in particular, what you need to feel safe and secure.

RISING SIGN (ALSO KNOWN AS ASCENDING SIGN)

REPRESENTS: The constellation that was on the eastern horizon when you were born.

BASED ON: Your date, time, and place of birth. Rising signs change every two hours and require the most information, which can be inserted into online calculators to work your own out, but if you don't know your time of birth you can use the time the Sun rose on the day in the place you were born instead. If this doesn't feel right, you can also read about each sign and choose the one you relate to the most.

REVEALS: The first impression you make on other people. This sign is all about the mask you wear in public, and how you present yourself to the world.

CREATING YOUR OWN RITUAL

If you want to experiment and create your own rituals and practices to tap in to each astrological sign or planet, you can use the associated materials below as a starting point. Simply select one or a few, and see what feels right!

ASTROLOGICAL SIGNS

ARIES
Crystal—Red Jasper
Birthstone—Diamond
Herb—Rosemary
Flower—Honeysuckle
Color—Red

CANCER
Crystal—Moonstone
Birthstone—Ruby
Herb—Rosemary
Flower—White Rose
Color—White

TAURUS
Crystal—Aventurine
Birthstone—Emerald
Herb—Mint
Flower—Poppy
Color—Green

LEO
Crystal—Tiger's Eye
Birthstone—Peridot
Herb—St John's Wort
Flower—Sunflower
Color—Orange

GEMINI
Crystal—Agate
Birthstone—Pearl
Herb—Lemongrass
Flower—Lavender
Color—Yellow

VIRGO
Crystal—Sodalite
Birthstone—Blue Sapphire
Herb—Fennel
Flower—Chrysanthemum
Color—Brown

LIBRA
Crystal—Rose Quartz
Birthstone—Opal
Herb—Ginger
Flower—Rose
Color—Blue

CAPRICORN
Crystal—Lapis Lazuli
Birthstone—Garnet
Herb—Caraway
Flower—Pansy
Color—Gray

SCORPIO
Crystal—Citrine
Birthstone—Topaz
Herb—Basil
Flower—Geranium
Color—Black

AQUARIUS
Crystal—Onyx
Birthstone—Amethyst
Herb—Valerian
Flower—Orchid
Color—Turquoise

SAGITTARIUS
Crystal—Turquoise
Birthstone—Blue Topaz
Herb—Sage
Flower—Carnation
Color—Purple

PISCES
Crystal—Calcite
Birthstone—Aquamarine
Herb—Seaweed
Flower—Water Lily
Color—Aquamarine

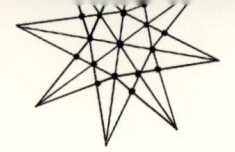

PLANETS

MERCURY
Element—Air
Crystals—Blue Lace Agate, Agate
Colors—Brown, Yellow, Green

MARS
Element—Fire
Crystals—Ruby, Garnet, Red Jasper
Color—Red

VENUS
Elements—Earth, Water
Crystals—Rose Quartz, Emerald, Amazonite
Colors—Pink, Magenta, Green

JUPITER
Elements—Air, Fire
Crystals—Lapiz Lazuli, Azurite
Colors—Purple, Mauve

SATURN
Element—Earth
Crystals—Jet, Onyx
Colors—Gray, Charcoal

URANUS
Element—Air
Crystals—Clear Quartz, Diamond
Colors—Silver, White

NEPTUNE
Element—Water
Crystals—Sapphire, Amethyst
Colors—Blue, Aquamarine, Violet

PLUTO
Element—Fire
Crystals—Obsidian, Smoky Quartz
Colors—Black, Dark Brown

SUN
Element—Fire
Crystals—Citrine, Golden Topaz, Helidor
Colors—Orange, Yellow, Gold

MOON
Element—Water
Crystals—Moonstone, Selenite
Colors—Silver, White

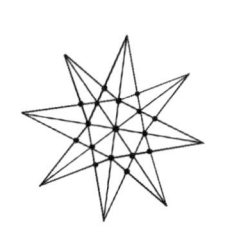

GLOSSARY OF GODS AND GODDESSES

GREEK DEITIES

Aphrodite: Goddess of love and beauty. Mother of Eros. She rode the fish with her son to escape the Titan Typhon.
Find her in: Pisces
Roman equivalent: Venus, born from the cast-off genitals of the god Uranus. She is the wife of the god Vulcan, lover of Anchises and mother of Aeneas.
Find Venus in: Venus, Uranus

Apollo: God of archery, prophecy, music, and medicine. Son of Zeus and twin brother of Artemis. He took over control of the Oracle of Delphi after Themis.
Find him in: Libra
Roman equivalent: Apollo, who gifted Mercury the Caduceus.

Artemis: Goddess of chastity, hunting, and childbirth. Daughter of Zeus, twin sister of Apollo, and friend and hunting partner of Orion.
Find her in: Scorpio
Roman equivalent: Diana

Demeter: Goddess of the grain and harvest. Mother of Persephone and sister of Zeus and Hades. The constellation Virgo was created in her honor, and marks the re-emergence of her daughter from the Underworld, and the beginning of spring.
Find her in: Virgo
Roman equivalent: Ceres

Eros: God of love and sex. Son of Aphrodite. He rode with his mother on the fish to escape the Titan Typhon.
Find him in: Pisces
Roman equivalent: Cupid

Gaia: Goddess of the Earth. She created the scorpion to kill Orion and stop him killing all her creatures. Mother of the Titan Typhon.
Find her in: Scorpio, Pisces
Roman equivalent: Terra, consort of Uranus and mother of Saturnus. She gave her son the sickle to kill Uranus after he became a threat to her family and the whole Earth.
Find Terra in: Uranus

Hades: God of the dead and king of the Underworld. Brother of Zeus and Demeter. He became the husband of Persephone after seizing her from the Earth and forcing her to live with him in the Underworld for six months of the year.
Find him in: Virgo
Roman equivalent: Pluto, god of the Underworld, gatekeeper and caretaker of souls. Son of Saturnus and Ops, brother of Jupiter and Neptune. He was moved to return Eurydice to Orpheus on hearing his music, but Orpheus broke the deal and Eurydice returned to the Underworld.
Find Pluto in: Pluto

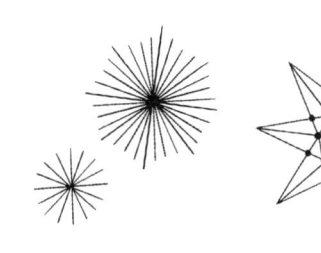

Hera: Queen of the gods, goddess of women and marriage. Second wife of Zeus. She was guardian of Karkinos the crab and the Nemean Lion, and made them both into constellations after their demise.
Find her in: Cancer, Leo
Roman equivalent: Juno, queen of the gods and wife of Jupiter. Mother of Mars.
Find Juno in: Mars

Hermes: Messenger of the gods, god of travelers, traders, and thieves. He delivered gifts to Tros of Dardania after Zeus took his son as his lover.
Find him in: Aquarius
Roman equivalent: Mercury, the master of mayhem, who loved to spend time on Earth among mortals. He tricked Battus into going back on his word to prove humans and gods were not so different.
Find Mercury in: Mercury

Nephele: Goddess of the clouds, mother of Phrixus and Helle. She appealed to Zeus to save her children when they were threatened by their stepmother Ino.
Find her in: Aries
Roman equivalent: Nebula

Pan: God of the wild, shepherds, and flocks. Father of Crotus.
Find him in: Sagittarius
Roman equivalent: Faunus

Persephone: Queen of the Underworld. Daughter of Demeter, wife of Hades after being stolen away. She spends half of the year on Earth nurturing the land with her mother, and the other half ruling the Underworld with her husband.
Find her in: Virgo
Roman equivalent: Proserpina

Themis: Goddess of justice and reason, first wife of Zeus. Mother of the Horai and Morai. She offered guidance and dispensed justice to humankind, and the constellation Libra was mapped in her honor in the shape of the Scales of Justice.
Find her in: Libra
Roman equivalent: Justitia

Zeus: King of the gods, lord of the skies. Brother of Hades and Demeter, husband of Themis (1), and Hera (2). Lover of Europa and Ganymede, and father of Polydeuces and Heracles. He mapped many constellations in honor of those he loved and to thank those who had served him and his family.
Find him in: Aries, Taurus, Gemini, Cancer, Leo, Virgo, Libra, Scorpio, Sagittarius, Capricorn, Aquarius, Pisces
Roman equivalent: Jupiter, king of the gods. Son of Saturnus and Ops and brother of Neptune and Pluto. He cast his father out of the heavens to take the throne, and made Numa Pompilius king of Rome. As ruler of the deities, he plays a role in many of his family's stories.
Find Jupiter in: Venus, Jupiter, Saturn, Neptune, Pluto

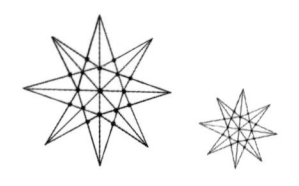

ROMAN DEITIES

Anna Perenna: Goddess of time and the new year. She tricked Mars into marrying her by taking on the form of Minerva.
Find her in: Mars
Greek equivalent: n/a

Aurora: Goddess of the dawn. Daughter of Hyperion and Theia, sister of Sol and Luna.
Find her in: The Moon
Greek equivalent: Eos

Flora: Goddess of flowers and spring, who helped Juno conceive Mars.
Find her in: Mars
Greek equivalent: Chloris

Hyperion: God of heavenly light and wisdom. Consort of Theia and father of Sol, Aurora, and Luna.
Find him in: The Moon
Greek equivalent: Hyperion

Janus: God of beginnings, transitions, time, and endings. He has two faces, which enable him to look into the past and the future. He helped Saturnus after he was cast out of the heavens.
Find him in: Saturn
Greek equivalent: n/a

Luna: Goddess of the Moon. Daughter of Hyperion and Theia and sister of Sol and Aurora. One-time lover of Jupiter. Wife of Endymion. The Roman emperor Aurelian built her a temple at the Circus Maximus so she would be worshipped alongside her brother.
Find her in: The Sun, the Moon
Greek equivalent: Selene, lover of Zeus and possibly mother of the Nemean Lion.
Find Selene in: Leo

Mars: God of war. Son of Juno. Admirer of Minerva but married Anna Perenna after she appeared as Minerva to teach him the importance of containing passion.
Find him in: Mars
Greek equivalent: Ares, lover of Aphrodite and father of Eros.

Minerva: Goddess of wisdom and commerce. Daughter of Jupiter.
Find her in: Mars
Greek equivalent: Athena

Neptune: God of the seas and all bodies of water on Earth. Used them to shape the Earth. Son of Ops and Saturnus, brother of Jupiter and Neptune, husband of Salacia and father of Triton.
Find him in: Neptune
Greek equivalent: Poseidon

Ops: Goddess of the Earth and fertility. Wife of Saturnus and mother of Jupiter, Neptune, and Pluto. She tricked her husband into swallowing a stone instead of Jupiter in order to save all her children.
Find her in: Saturn
Greek equivalent: Rhea

Salacia: Goddess of the salt waters. Wife of Neptune.
Find her in: Neptune
Greek equivalent: Amphitrite

Saturnus: God of time, agriculture, and the harvest. Son of Uranus and Terra, husband of Ops and father of Jupiter, Neptune, and Pluto. He swallowed all his children bar Jupiter to prevent them from taking his throne. He was cast out of the heavens but made amends on Earth. Founder of Saturnalia.
Find him in: Saturn, Neptune
Greek equivalent: Cronus

Sol Invictus: God of the Sun. Son of Hyperion and Theia, brother of Luna and Aurora. The Roman emperor Aurelian introduced his worship to Rome and began chariot races in his honor.
Find him in: The Sun, the Moon
Greek equivalent: Helios

Theia: Consort of Hyperion, mother of Sol, Aurora, and Luna.
Find her in: The Moon
Greek equivalent: Theia

Triton: Son of Neptune, father of mermen. He blew the conch shell to bring back the waters after Neptune released them on Earth.
Find him in: Neptune
Greek equivalent: Triton

Uranus: Former god of the skies and ruler of all. Consort of Terra, father of Saturnus. Creator of Meliae. He was overthrown by his son and had his genitals cut off, from which Venus was born. (Uranus is the Latinized version of the Greek Ouranus; he is also known as Caelus.)
Find him in: Uranus
Greek equivalent: Ouranus

Vulcan: God of fire, volcanoes, and blacksmiths. Son of Jupiter and Juno and husband of Venus.
Find him in: Venus
Greek equivalent: Hephaestus

INDEX

A

abundance
  Jupiter and 110–15
  Saturn and 116–21
acceptance, Pluto and 134–9
action
  Mars and 104–9
  ritual to promote 21
adventurous characteristics, Sagittarius and 64–9
Aeetes, King 19–20
Aeneas 101, 102
affirmations 156–7
aggression, Mars and 104–9
air element
  Aquarius and 76–81
  Gemini and 28–33
  Libra and 52–7
Alban Hills 118
Alcmene 36
ambitious characteristics
  Leo and 40–5
  Scorpio and 58–63
Anchises 100–2
Ancilia 114
Anna Perenna 107–8, 166
anxiety
  Pisces and anxious characteristics 82–7
  ritual to release 87
Aphrodite 85–6, 164
Apollo 164
  Mercury's Caduceus 92
  and Themis 55
applause 67–8
Aquarius 76–81
  affirmations 81, 156
  creating your own ritual 161
  ritual to find your true voice and follow your heart 81
  Uranus and 122–7
Argonauts 30
Aries 16–21
  affirmations 21, 156
  creating your own ritual 160
  Mars and 104–9
  ritual to promote action and motivation 21
Artemis 60–2, 164
artistic characteristics, Pisces and 82–7
Ascending sign 159
assertive characteristics
  Aquarius 76–81
  ritual to help you assert yourself 109
Asterius, King 26
the astrological signs 12–87
  affirmations 156
  astrological 'big three' 159
  creating your own rituals 160–1
Athamas 16–19, 20
attention
  Aquarius and attentive characteristics 76–81
  Leo and attention-seeking characteristics 40–5
Aurelian 142, 143–4
Aurora 148–9, 150, 166
Aventine Hill 113, 114

B

Babylonians 14
balance
  Libra and balanced characteristics 52–7
  rituals to promote 33, 57
Battus 94, 95–6
beauty
  ritual to help you see the beauty in the world around you 103
  Vsenus and 98–103
Biga 143, 144
body, ritual to recharge the 121
Boeotia, ancient Greece 16, 19
bold characteristics
  Aries and 16–21
  Leo and 40–5
  the Sun and 140–5
brightness, the Sun and 140–5
the Bull 22–7

C

Caduceus 92, 96
calmness, Neptune and 128–33
Cancer 34–9
  affirmations 39, 156
  creating your own ritual 160
  the Moon and 146–51
  ritual to develop empathy and psychic perception 39
Capitoline Hill 114
Capricorn 70–7
  affirmations 77, 156
  creating your own ritual 161
  ritual to promote clarity and focus 75
  Saturn and 116–21
Castor 28–32
change
  Gemini and changeable characteristics 28–33
  ritual to embrace change 139
charming characteristics, Libra and 52–7
Circus Maximus, Rome 144
clarity, ritual to promote 75
Colchis 19–20
communication, Mercury and 92–7
competitive characteristics, Aries and 16–21
confidence
  Leo and confident characteristics 40–5
  ritual to boost confidence 6, 45, 109
  ritual to help you express yourself with 97

the Sun and 140–5
courage, the Sun and 140–5
crab, Cancer the 34–9
creativity
   ritual to boost 151
   Taurus and creative characteristics 22–7
   Venus and creativity 98–103
Crete 24–5, 26, 72
critical characteristics, Virgo and 46–51
Crotus 64–8
Cult of Sol 142
the Cup Bearer 76–81
Cures 112
curiosity, Mercury and 92–7

D
Dardania 78, 79–80, 101
dedicated characteristics, Virgo and 46–51
Delphi, temple of 54, 56
Demeter 46, 48–9, 50, 164
determined characteristics, Aries and 16–21
diligent characteristics, Virgo and 46–51
the Dioscuri 28–33
divine feminine energy, Venus and 98–103
driven characteristics, Aries and 16–21
dynamic characteristics, Aries and 16–21

E
the Earth 58–62, 128, 131, 146
   Capricorn and 70–7
   formation of 90
   Pluto and 134, 136
   ritual to connect with the Earth 51
   Taurus and 22–7
   Terra the Earth 122, 124–6
   and Typhon 82, 84, 85

and Venus 100
and Virgo 46–51
easy-going characteristics, Libra and 52–7
eccentricity, Uranus and 122–7
emotions
   Cancer and emotional characteristics 34–9
   the Moon and hidden emotions 146–51
   Neptune and emotional sensitivity 128–33
   ritual to balance the emotions 133
   and your Moon sign 159
empathy
   Cancer and empathetic characteristics 34–9
   Neptune and 128–33
   ritual to develop 39
endings, Pluto and 134–9
Endymion 150
energy
   Mars and 104–9
   ritual to boost positive energy 145
   and your Star sign 159
engaging characteristics, Gemini and 28–33
enigmatic characteristics, Scorpio and 58–63
equality, Saturn and 116–21
the Erinyes 125
Eros 85–6, 164
Eupheme 64
Europa 22–6
Eurydice 137–8
expression
   Cancer and expressive characteristics 34–9
   ritual to help you express yourself easily 97

F
fair-minded characteristics,

Libra and 52–7
Father of Souls 70–7
feminine power, the Moon and 146–51
fertility, Venus and 98–103
fickleness
   Mercury and 92–7
   Sagittarius and 64–9
fire element
   Aries and 16–21
   Leo and 40–5
   Sagittarius and 64–9
fish 82–7
Flora 106, 166
focus
   Capricorn and focused characteristics 70–7
   ritual to promote 75
forceful characteristics, Aries and 16–21
freedom-loving characteristics, Sagittarius and 64–9
Friday, Venus 98–103
friendly characteristics, Aquarius and 76–81
the Furies 125

G
Gaia 58, 61, 62, 82, 164
Ganymede 78–80
Gate of Men 34–9
Gemini 28–33
   affirmations 33, 156
   creating your own ritual 160
   Mercury and 92–7
   ritual to create a sense of harmony and balance 33
generous characteristics
   Leo 40–5
   Pisces 82–7
goals, rituals to help you achieve your 21, 115
goddess of the grain 46–51
gods and goddesses

169

glossary of 164–7
see also individual gods and goddesses
Golden Age 120
Golden Fleece 30
the Golden One 116–21
the Golden Ram 16–21
grace, Venus and 98–103
Greeks, ancient 14–15, 34
  Greek deities 164–5
Grove of Ares 20

H
Hades 48, 49–50, 164
hardworking characteristics, Virgo and 46–51
harmony
  rituals to promote 33, 57
  Saturn and 116–21
heart, rituals to follow your 63, 81
Helicon, Mount 66
Helle 16, 18–19
Hera 36–7, 165
  Nemean Lion 37, 40–2, 43–4
  and Zeus 36–7, 40–2, 43, 44, 55
Heracles 36–8
  and the Nemean Lion 37, 43, 44
Hermes 79, 165
hidden emotions, the Moon and 146–51
Hillaera 30
honest characteristics, Capricorn and 70–7
Horai 55
horizons, ritual to help broaden your 69
humble characteristics, Virgo and 46–51
the hunter and the hunted 58–63
Hydra 37–8
Hyperion 148, 149, 166

I
Ida, Mount 101
Idas 30, 31
ideas, Mercury and 92–7
Ides of March 114
imagination
  the Moon and 146–51
  Pisces and imaginative characteristics 82–7
  Uranus and 122–7
impressions, Rising sign and first 159
indecisive characteristics, Libra and 52–7
independent characteristics, Aquarius and 76–81
ingenuity, ritual to spark 127
innovative characteristics, Aries and 16–21
Ino 18–19, 20
inquisitive characteristics, Gemini and 28–33
intelligent characteristics, Aquarius and 76–81
intensity
  Pisces and intense characteristics 82–7
  Pluto and intensity 134–9
intuition
  Cancer and intuitive characteristics 34–9
  the Moon and 146–51
  Neptune and 128–33
  Pisces and intuitive characteristics 82–7
  ritual to boost 151
inventiveness
  Aquarius and inventive characteristics 76–81
  Uranus and 122–7

J
Janus 118–20, 166
Jason 30
joy

ritual to promote 145
the Sun and 140–5
Julian calendar 113
Juno 104–6, 107, 108
Jupiter 91, 101–2, 104–6, 110–15, 118
  affirmations 115, 157
  creating your own ritual 162
  and Eurydice 137
  and Luna 150
  and Neptune 131, 132
  and Numa 112, 113–14
  and Pluto 134–7, 138
  ritual to tap in to your inner wisdom and help you achieve your goals 115
  Sagittarius 64–9
  and Saturnus 130

K
Karkinos the crab 36, 37–8
Khrysomallos, Krios 19–20
King of the World 40–5

L
Lady of Good Counsel 52–7
Laelaps 25
Latini 119
Latium 118–19, 120
leadership, the Sun and 140–5
Leo 40–5
  affirmations 45, 156
  creating your own ritual 160
  rituals to boost confidence and self-esteem 6, 45
  the Sun and 140–5
Libra 52–7
  affirmations 57, 156
  creating your own ritual 161
  ritual to promote harmony and balance 57
  Venus and 98–103
the light within 146–51
logical characteristics, Capricorn and 70–7

love
  ritual to boost the flow of love in your life 87
  Taurus and loving characteristics 22–7
  Venus and 98–103
loyal characteristics, Taurus and 22–7
Luna 143, 144, 148–50, 166
Lynceus 30, 31

M
Mars 91, 104–9, 166
  affirmations 109, 157
  Aries and 16–21
  creating your own ritual 162
  ritual to boost confidence and help you assert yourself 109
the Meliae 126
Mercury 91, 92–7
  affirmations 97, 157
  creating your own ritual 162
  Gemini and 28–33
  ritual to help you express yourself easily, with confidence 97
  Virgo and 46–51
mind
  ritual to calm the mind 133
  ritual to recharge the mind 121
Minerva 106, 107–8, 166
modest characteristics, Cancer and 34–9
Monday, the Moon 146–51
the Moon 18, 24, 25, 146–51
  affirmations 51, 157
  Cancer and 34–9
  creating your own ritual 163
  cycles of the 113
  Luna 143, 144
  ritual to boost your intuition and creativity 151
  and Selene 42

Moon sign 159
Morai 55
the Morning Star 98–103
motivation
  Aries and motivated characteristics 16–21
  rituals for 21, 51, 63
Mount Helicon 66
Mount Ida 101
Mount Olympus 31, 42, 48, 56, 67, 70
  Ganymede and 78, 79, 80
  and Typhon 84–5, 86
movement, Mars and 104–9
the Muses 64, 66–8

N
Naiad 64
negotiation, Mercury and 92–7
Nemea 40, 43
Nemean Lion 37, 40–5
Nemesis 55
Nephele 16–18, 19–20, 165
Neptune 128–33, 166
  affirmations 133, 157
  creating your own ritual 163
  Pisces and 82–7
  ritual to calm the mind and balance the emotions 133
Northern Hemisphere 44
Numa Pompilius 112–14

O
Olympus, Mount 31, 42, 48, 56, 67, 70
  Ganymede and 78, 79, 80
  Typhon and 84–5, 86
Ops 118, 130, 134, 167
Oracle 18–19
Oracle of Delphi 54–5
order, Jupiter and 110–15
Orion 60–2
Orpheus 137–8

P
Pan 64, 66, 165
passion
  Mars and 104–9
  Scorpio and passionate characteristics 58–63
peace, Saturn and 116–21
Persephone 46–50, 165
personality, and your astrological 'big three' 159
persuasive characteristics, Libra and 52–7
pessimistic characteristics, Capricorn and 70–7
Phoebe 30
Phrixus 16, 18–20
Pisces 82–7
  affirmations 87, 156
  creating your own ritual 161
  Neptune and 128–33
  ritual to release anxiety and boost the flow of love in your life 87
the planets 88–151
  affirmations 157
  creating your own ritual 162–3
  formation of 90
  see also individual planets
playful characteristics, Sagittarius and 64–9
Pluto 134–9
  affirmations 139, 157
  creating your own ritual 163
  ritual to embrace change and promote transformation 139
  Scorpio and 58–63
Polydeuces 28–32
power, Jupiter and 110–15
practical characteristics, Virgo and 46–51
Pricus 72–4
the Princess and the Bull 22–7
progressiveness, Uranus and 122–7

INDEX 171

psychic perception
  the Moon and 146–51
  ritual to develop 39

Q
Quadriga 142, 144

R
the Rainmaker 122–7
rebellion, Uranus and 122–7
rebirth, Pluto and 134–9
recharging, ritual to recharge body, mind, and spirit 121
recklessness, Uranus and 122–7
rejuvenation, Pluto and 134–9
resilience, Mars and 104–9
responsible characteristics, Capricorn and 70–7
rising sign 159
rituals
  creating your own 160–3
  see also individual astrological signs; planets
Romans
  movement of the constellations 90–1
  Roman deities 91, 166–7
  Roman Empire 114
  the Sun 142
romantic characteristics, Pisces and 82–7
Rome 92–4, 98, 102, 107, 110, 112–13, 114, 119, 120, 130
  the Moon and 150
  Roman Circus 144
  Roman forum 120
Romulus 110
rules, Saturn and 116–21

S
Sagittarius 64–9
  affirmations 69, 156
  creating your own ritual 161
  Jupiter and 110–15

ritual to promote spontaneity and help you broaden your horizons 69
Salacia 130–1, 167
Saturday, Saturn 116–21
Saturn 116–21
  affirmations 121, 157
  Capricorn and 70–7
  creating your own ritual 162
  ritual to recharge body, mind, and spirit 121
Saturnalia 120
Saturnus 116–20, 128–30, 167
  children 130, 132
  and Neptune 130
  and Pluto 134
  and Uranus 125, 126
satyrs 66–8
Scales of Justice 52, 54, 56
Scorpio 58–63
  affirmations 63, 156
  creating your own ritual 161
  Pluto and 134–9
  ritual to motivate and inspire you to follow your heart 63
sea goats 72–4
secretive characteristics, Scorpio and 58–63
Selene 42
self-esteem, rituals to boost 27, 45
self-expression, Mercury and 92–7
self-sufficient characteristics, Virgo and 46–51
sensitive characteristics, Cancer and 34–9
sensual characteristics, Taurus and 22–7
sociable characteristics, Gemini and 28–33
Sol Invictus 142–4, 148, 167
  and Luna 143, 144, 148, 149, 150

Southern Hemisphere 44
Sparta 28, 31
spirit, ritual to recharge the 121
spirituality, Jupiter and 110–15
spontaneous characteristics
  Gemini and 28–33
  ritual to promote spontaneity 69
  Sagittarius and 64–9
Star sign 14, 159
the Starry Steed 64–9
steadfast characteristics, Taurus and 22–7
strength, ritual for 51
structure, Saturn and 116–21
success
  Jupiter and 110–15
  Mars and 104–9
the Sun 19, 22, 25, 140–5, 148
  affirmations 145, 157
  creating your own ritual 163
  formation of 90
  Leo and 40–5
  and Luna 143, 144, 148, 149, 150
  Persephone and 49, 50
  ritual to boost positive energy and promote joy 145
Sun sign 14, 159
Sunday, the Sun 140–5
Sword of Truth 55

T
talkative characteristics, Gemini and 28–33
Talos 25
Tartarus 82, 84, 86, 124, 125
Taurus 22–7
  affirmations 27, 156
  creating your own ritual 160
  ritual to promote well-being and boost self-esteem 27
Venus 98–103

172   THE STORIES BEHIND ASTROLOGY

tenacious characteristics,
    Taurus and 22–7
Terra the Earth 122, 124–6
Theia 148, 167
Themis 52, 54–6, 165
thought, rituals to promote
    new ways of thinking 127
Thursday, Jupiter 110–15
Titans 125, 146–8
transformation
    Pluto and 134–9
    ritual to promote 139
trickery and tricksters,
    Mercury and 92–7
Triton 132, 167
Tros of Dardania 78, 79–80
truthful characteristics,
    Aquarius and 76–81
Tuesday, Mars 104–9
turbulence, Neptune and
    128–33
the Twelve Shields 110–15
Tyndareus, King 28
Typhon 42, 82–6

U

the Unconquered Sun 140–5
Underworld 25, 48, 84, 143
    Eurydice and 137–8
    Pluto and 134, 136–8
Uranus 116, 122–7, 167
    affirmations 127, 157
    Aquarius and 76–81
    creating your own ritual 163
    ritual to spark ingenuity
    and promote new ways of
    thinking 127

V

Venus 91, 98–103, 126
    affirmations 103, 157
    creating your own ritual 162
    Libra and 52–7
    ritual to help you see the
    beauty in the world around
    you 103
    Taurus and 22–7
Virgo 46–51
    affirmations 51, 156
    creating your own ritual 160
    Mercury and 92–7
    ritual for strength,
    motivation, and to connect
    with the Earth 51
vitality, the Sun and 140–5
voice, ritual to find your true
    81
Vulcan 100, 167

W

war and peace 104–9
water element
    Cancer and 34–9
    Pisces and 82–7
    Scorpio and 58–63
the wealthy one 134–9
Wednesday
    Mercury 92–7
    Uranus 122–7
wellbeing, ritual to promote
    27
Winter Solstice 120
wisdom
    ritual to tap in your inner
    wisdom 115
    Venus and 98–103

Z

Zeus 19, 20, 76–8, 165
    and Crotus 67–8
    and Demeter 49
    Europa and 22–6
    and Ganymede 78–80
    and Hera 36–7, 40–2, 43,
    44, 55
    and the Nemean Lion 40–2,
    43, 44
    and Orion 62
    and Persephone 49–50
    and Polydeuces 28, 30, 31–2
    and Pricus 73, 74
    and Selene 42
    and Themis 52, 54, 55–6
    and Typhon 82, 84–5, 86
Zodiac signs 15, 159

ACKNOWLEDGMENTS

Like the mapping of a constellation, this book has been a universal endeavor, with many gifted contributions. I'd like to thank the brilliant team at Leaping Hare, including Monica Perdoni, Sophie Lazar, and Katerina Menhennet, for their help in shaping and creating this tome. I'd also like to thank the talented Chloe Murphy for knowing just how to nip and tuck my words and bring out the sparkle. Huge thanks and gratitude to the wonderful illustrator, Jennifer Parks for taking my stories and bringing them to life in the most magical of ways.

I have always been fascinated by the celestial realm, and the myths and legends that bring the Zodiac signs and planets to life. From the astrological influence of the signs to the otherworldly beauty of the planets, it's no wonder the heavens are a constant source of fascination here on Earth.

NOTE:

Please take care when practicing the rituals in this book. Some of the rituals in this book use essential oils. Used properly, in the ways recommended here, these oils are safe for most people, but anyone can have a sensitivity to them as to any other product. If that is the case for you, do the ritual without the essential oil, since there are many effective parts to each ritual. You will find particular contraindications with each individual oil recommendation. It is generally wise to err on the side of caution and avoid essential oils and herbs in pregnancy, except when properly prescribed by a qualified professional. Ylang ylang in particular should not be used by those who are pregnant because its safety is not known, nor should geranium oil be used in early pregnancy. Rosemary essential oil should be avoided by people with epilepsy. Bergamot is poisonous for dogs to ingest, so keep the bottle well away from them.

ABOUT THE AUTHOR

ALISON DAVIES is a storyteller and writer who runs workshops at universities throughout the UK on how stories and narratives can be used as holistic tools for teaching, healing, and learning. She has a keen interest in folklore, wellbeing, and nature and is the author of *Tales Behind the Tarot*, and *Goddess Stories* (Leaping Hare Press). Alison has written a host of in-depth features on astrology, planetary associations in magic, and the myths and legends of the constellations over the years for a variety of magazines including *Take a Break*: *Fate & Fortune* and *Kindred Spirit*. She is also the author of *Written in the Stars* and *Cosmic Rituals*, both published by Quadrille. Her Star sign is Taurus and in her spare time she can be found gazing at the Moon.

ABOUT THE ILLUSTRATOR

JENNIFER PARKS is an illustrator, ceramicist, and tattoo artist living in the US. She is a mystic, a mother, and an animist. She loves nature and is surrounded by the lush greenery of the PNW and has many animal friends, including cats, a dog, squirrels, raccoons, birds, and a possum. She believes in magic and spirits and everything in between. Her website is www.spectralgardens.com and her Instagram handle is @spectralgardens.

OTHER TITLES IN THE SERIES

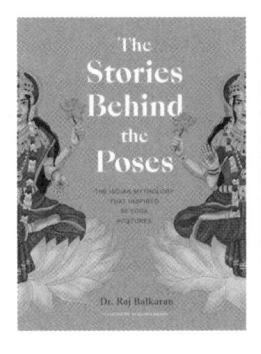

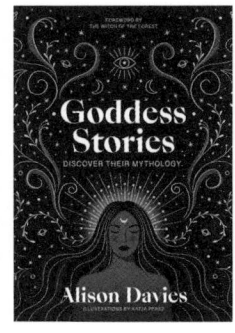

Quarto

First published in 2024 by Leaping Hare Press,
an imprint of The Quarto Group.
One Triptych Place
London, SE1 9SH,
United Kingdom
T (0)20 7700 6700
www.Quarto.com

Design and illustrations copyright © 2024 Quarto
Text Copyright © 2024 Alison Davies

Alison Davies has asserted her moral right to be identified as the Author of this Work in accordance with the Copyright Designs and Patents Act 1988.

All rights reserved. No part of this book may be reproduced or utilised in any form or by any means, electronic or mechanical, including photocopying, recording or by any information storage and retrieval system, without permission in writing from Leaping Hare Press.

Every effort has been made to trace the copyright holders of material quoted in this book. If application is made in writing to the publisher, any omissions will be included in future editions.

A catalogue record for this book is available from the British Library.

ISBN 978-0-7112-9074-7
Ebook ISBN 978-0-7112-9075-4

10 9 8 7 6 5 4 3 2 1

Illustrations by Jennifer Parks
Illustration on p158 by Viki Lester
Design by Nicki Davis
Editorial: Chloe Murphy and Monica Perdoni
Senior Designer: Renata Latipova
Editor: Katerina Menhennet
Production Controller: Rohana Yusof

Printed in China